"Talking about any aspect of the case endangers myself and my contact. It endangers you," Teagan said

"I'm sure I'm capable of watching out for myself."

"Of course you are, but the way you can help the most is by steering clear of the compound and keeping everyone else as far away as possible."

Zach nodded, unable to keep the irony out of his voice. "Steer clear of you. I wonder why that has such a familiar ring to it?"

"You're making this more personal than it has to be, Zach."

"Probably because it is personal. Have you forgotten what you meant to me at one time?"

"What we felt for each other was a long time ago." Teagan reached out and placed the palm of her hand against his chest. "I never meant to hurt you, Zach. At the time I thought leaving was the right thing to do." She paused and then delivered the final blow. "And even now, I know it was."

Zach leaned in, the weight of his body resting against her hand. "Well, you thought wrong."

Dear Harlequin Intrigue Reader,

At Harlequin Intrigue we have much to look forward to as we ring in a brand-new year. Case in point—all of our romantic suspense selections this month are fraught with edge-of-your-seat danger, electrifying romance and thrilling excitement. So hang on!

Reader favorite Debra Webb spins the next installment in her popular series COLBY AGENCY. *Cries in the Night* spotlights a mother so desperate to track down her missing child that she joins forces with the unforgettable man from her past.

Unsanctioned Memories by Julie Miller—the next offering in THE TAYLOR CLAN—packs a powerful punch as a vengeance-seeking FBI agent opens his heart to the achingly vulnerable lone witness who can lead him to a cold-blooded killer…. Looking for a provocative mystery with a royal twist? Then expect to be seduced by Jacqueline Diamond in *Sheikh Surrender*.

We welcome two talented debut authors to Harlequin Intrigue this month. Tracy Montoya weaves a chilling mystery in *Maximum Security,* and the gripping *Concealed Weapon* by Susan Peterson is part of our BACHELORS AT LARGE promotion.

Finally this month, Kasi Blake returns to Harlequin Intrigue with *Borrowed Identity.* This gothic mystery will keep you guessing when a groggy bride stumbles upon a grisly murder on her wedding night. But are her eyes deceiving her when her "slain" groom appears alive and well in a flash of lightning?

It promises to be quite a year at Harlequin Intrigue….

Enjoy!

Denise O'Sullivan
Senior Editor
Harlequin Intrigue

CONCEALED WEAPON

SUSAN PETERSON

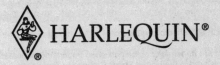

TORONTO • NEW YORK • LONDON
AMSTERDAM • PARIS • SYDNEY • HAMBURG
STOCKHOLM • ATHENS • TOKYO • MILAN • MADRID
PRAGUE • WARSAW • BUDAPEST • AUCKLAND

ISBN 0-373-22751-5

CONCEALED WEAPON

ABOUT THE AUTHOR

A devoted *Star Trek* fan, Susan Peterson wrote her first science fiction novel at the age of thirteen. But unlike other *Star Trek* fan writers, in Susan's novel she made sure that Mr. Spock fell in love. Unfortunately, what she didn't take into consideration was the fact that falling in love and pursuing a life of total logic didn't exactly go hand in hand. In any case, it was then that she realized that she was a hopeless romantic, a person who needed the happily-ever-after ending. But it wasn't until later in life, after pursuing careers in intensive care nursing and school psychology, that Susan finally found the time to pursue a career in writing. An ardent fan of psychological thrillers and suspense, Susan combined her love of romance and suspense into several manuscripts targeted to the Harlequin Intrigue line. Getting the go-ahead to write for this line was a dream come true for her.

Susan lives in a small town in northern New York with her son, Kevin, her nutball dog, Ozzie, Phoenix the cat and Lex the six-toed menace (a new kitten). Susan loves to hear from readers. E-mail her at SusanPetersonHI@aol.com or visit her Web site at susanpeterson.net.

Books by Susan Peterson

HARLEQUIN INTRIGUE
751—CONCEALED WEAPON

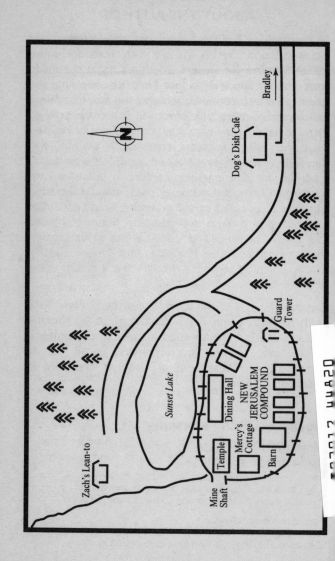

N

Bradley

Dog's Dish Café

Sunset Lake

Zach's Lean-to

Mine Shaft

Temple

Mercy's Cottage

Dining Hall

NEW JERUSALEM COMPOUND

Barn

Guard Tower

CAST OF CHARACTERS

Sheriff Zachary McCoy—Zach McCoy must revisit the pain of the past when he finds his ex-love Teagan in deep cover inside a dangerous doomsday cult just a few miles outside his hometown.

Teagan Kennedy—Tough, dedicated ATF special agent Teagan Kennedy knew she'd have to take the chance she'd run into her former lover, Zach McCoy, when she took the undercover assignment inside the Disciples' Temple. But someone had to bring the fanatical Reverend Daniel Mercy to justice.

Reverend Daniel Mercy—Charismatic and controlling, Daniel Mercy runs his breakaway religious cult with a deadly mix of charm and intimidation. His warped plan for bringing about the end starts the clock ticking for both Zach and Teagan.

Cyrus Mackie and Eddie Zelser—Ruthless henchmen totally dedicated to Reverend Mercy, they'll do whatever it takes to keep the perks and privileges coming their way.

ATF Special Agent Miguel Lopez—A well-seasoned senior ATF agent who believes in taking calculated risks and covering his partner's back.

Jenna Parker and Helen Wade, M.D.—Zach's sisters are devoted to their brother and determined to see that he isn't hurt again by the same woman.

Birdie—A lovable bluetick hound who has never forgotten the person who raised and nurtured her as a pup.

To Chris
who believes in my writing as much as I believe in hers

Chapter One

The explosion's shock waves hit Sheriff Zachary McCoy's lean-to on Sunset Lake around 10:00 p.m. They rocked the uneven plank floor so hard that Zach rolled off the side of his cot and hit the floor with an elbow crunching thud.

By the time he scrambled out of his sleeping bag and stumbled to the edge of the lean-to, the familiar darkness overhanging the small Adirondack lake was lit up like a Fourth of July celebration gone wild.

Birdie, Zach's bluetick hound, nudged him and whined softly. Her wet nose pushed against the palm of his hand, telling him that she didn't like the looks of the yellow flames and black smoke rising up over the lush treetops.

Zach gave Birdie's left ear a reassuring scratch.

No need to guess the location of the explosion. The only other inhabitants of the lake were Zach's reclusive neighbors, a religious group who had bought up almost half the lakefront property nearly two years ago. Calling themselves The Disciples' Temple, the group had set up camp about nine months ago, arriving in a caravan of beat-up old school buses repainted green.

As soon as the camp was built and people started to arrive, Zach had gotten curious. Although he was used to people buying property high in the Adirondack Mountains as a means of "getting away," this particular group's intense need for privacy bordered on the paranoid.

But in spite of all this, Zach considered any neighbor a friend, and he wasn't about to let the group handle this or any crisis alone.

Not to mention the fact that he was the county sheriff and obligated to help.

He grabbed the cell phone out of the pocket of his Carhart jacket and then checked his watch. 10:02 p.m. It would take the trucks from town at least twenty minutes to make it up the winding mountain road leading to the lake. By then, whatever structure had caught fire would probably be gone. He could only hope the fire stayed confined to one building and didn't spread.

He punched in 911.

"Nine-one-one. How may I help you?" the voice on the other end asked.

"This is Sheriff Zachary McCoy. There's been an explosion out at The Disciples' Temple property—Sunset Lake south side. We're going to need trucks and an ambulance."

"This is Ellie Stanton, Sheriff. I got a call from the place about five minutes ago. It was the guy who runs the place—a David or Daniel Mercy. He told me *not* to send anyone. Said that they had things under control."

"I don't care what Daniel Mercy said. I want the trucks up here pronto, Ellie."

"He told me he wouldn't let anyone on the property, Sheriff."

Zach ran a exasperated hand through his hair. Reverend Mercy had to be off his rocker.

"Look, Ellie, I don't care what this guy said. I want to hear sirens wailing up this mountain in two minutes flat. Make sure the ambulance comes, too." His hand tightened on the cell phone. "I have a feeling this guy doesn't realize how bad things are."

"On their way, Sheriff. I'm dispatching the fire department right now. Should I tell them you'll be there to give them a hand with Reverend Mercy?"

"Yeah, I'm headed over right now. Tell the boys to look for me. Maybe I can convince this paranoid fool to let us help."

Zach tucked his phone back in his jacket pocket and quickly dressed, grabbing his hat before strapping on his gun.

Birdie had already taken off across the rough terrain, headed for Zach's battered '88 Dodge pickup. When she reached the truck, she put her front paws on the running board and waited. She didn't glance in Zach's direction but instead kept her eyes focused on the passenger's side door. Zach knew she was letting him know that there was no way he was getting out of the campsite without her riding shotgun.

Zach glanced in the direction of the lake again. The blaze had settled into a steady crackle of orange flames. It looked as if some type of building stood at the center of the explosion, but it was hard to tell due to the high wooden fence encircling the entire compound.

Zach shook his head. He didn't know too many people who bought waterfront property and then fenced everything off, including their view of the lake. Didn't make a lot of sense to him, but then nothing about the inhabitants of The Disciples' Temple did.

As he ran around the front of the truck, Birdie's tail hit the side with a resounding thud. She was reminding him not to try and get out of the driveway without her.

Zach climbed into the cab and reached across to open the passenger side door. Birdie piled in.

"Okay, girl, you can come along. But plan on staying in the truck once we get there."

Birdie turned her soulful brown eyes on him, her expression seeming to indicate she'd comply. But Zach wasn't fooled. She was only placating him. Birdie liked action, and the crackling flames across the lake fit that description just fine.

A FEW SHORT, body-jarring moments later, Zach pulled his pickup outside the gates where the name The Disciples' Temple—New Jerusalem stretched across in large, crudely painted red letters. No Trespassers Allowed took up the bottom portion of the sign.

As always, the front gates to the compound were tightly secured. The fence was made of planks of dark hard pine, the bark still on. Each plank was nudged in so close to the next that nothing could squeeze between them. The only light came from a string of security lamps strung along the top. Zach couldn't help but wonder if the fence had been built to keep the inhabitants in rather than intruders out.

The fence stretched in both directions, completely enclosing the compound. Zach had walked the fence line when it was first installed, before the camp was inhabited by the group. He had a thing for knowing what went on in his county.

The fence itself must have cost a small fortune to build. The wood alone must have set the group back more than a few thousand. The word in town was that the group purchased the wood from the local sawmill. The mill owner, Ted Sterling, had been more than happy to comply with the order, especially since the demand for lumber had been down lately. Like the rest of the country, Bradley, New York, was suffering an economic downturn.

Zach pulled his truck up next to the small guardhouse squatting to the left of the gate opening. He glanced inside. Empty.

A simple wooden bench and countertop were the only

things inside. No phone. No intercom system. No amenities. Pretty basic.

Definitely rustic.

A small door, built into one of the main gates was where people got in and out when there wasn't any need to open the huge double gates. But there was no bell or knocker there, either. A pretty good indication that the Temple members weren't interested in guests.

Zach pounded his fist on the gate, the rough wood scraping against his knuckles. If people were in there fighting the fire, there wasn't much of a chance that they'd hear him over the roar of the flames.

Stepping back to his truck, he reached in the front window and laid on the horn. Birdie threw back her head and howled along.

He kept his hand on the horn until the door built into the gate swung open and two scruffy-looking men stepped out. Heavily bearded and dressed in well-worn jeans and green T-shirts with Staff embroidered over the pocket, they both looked less than pleased about being summoned.

Zach stepped closer. "I saw the flames. Is everyone okay?"

"Everything's fine, Sheriff," the taller of the two said, shouldering his way in front of the smaller man.

Zach had seen both men in town a few times, shepherding a group of silent members into Enno's Big M grocery store or Trainor's Hardware Store. The heftier one drove the beat-up, oversize van, filling it with groceries and other supplies.

No one in town seemed to mind the group's reserved, almost unfriendly attitude. Not when they paid in cold, hard cash.

"How'd the fire start?" Zach pressed.

"Just a small explosion in one of the bunkhouse's kerosene stoves. But we've got everything under control."

"I've got a fire truck on its way up. Ambulance, too."

"No need for that, Sheriff. Reverend Mercy has already called down and told people that we won't be needing their help." The man's roughly lined face settled into softer, more conversational lines. It wasn't hard for Zach to figure out the two had been sent out to placate him. To soothe his worries and to get him to move on.

In spite of his softer expression, the posture of the man's heavily muscled shoulders told Zach the guy wasn't planning on budging an inch.

In other words, no one was getting past him.

"Just thought we could offer a hand," Zach said. "Neighbors are big on that around these parts."

"And we appreciate that neighborliness, Sheriff. But we have our own fire department, and the blaze will be out before your trucks get halfway up the mountain."

Zach smiled and shrugged. "Maybe. But you never know—someone might end up needing medical attention."

The spokesman scowled. "We have our own medical people to take care of things."

Then, as if realizing he didn't come off sounding too neighborly, the guy smiled again. But for some reason, the smile didn't seem to convey any real degree of warmth or friendliness. In fact, Zach thought he looked like someone reading from a script—a script that instructed him to "Insert smile here."

"I'm glad to hear you're so well equipped," Zach said. "But I'm sure you won't mind if I come in and take a look around. We get kind of concerned about fires in these parts. We don't like to take the chance of them getting out of hand and destroying half the Adirondack Park."

The smile disappeared again as quickly as it had appeared. "Like I said, Sheriff, we've got everything under control. No need for you to bother anyone."

"No bother." Zach took another step closer, leaning a bit

to the right to see around the two men. They closed ranks and cut off any view of the camp beyond. "I really think I need to check things out, gentlemen. It's my job as the local sheriff."

"And this is private property, Sheriff."

The smaller guy behind the spokesman shifted uneasily and glanced over his shoulder. Zach was fairly certain someone with authority was standing right behind the door, just out of his sight.

"And I'm responsible for the citizens of this county, so I'm going to have to insist."

"What seems to be the problem, Cyrus?"

Daniel Mercy stepped out into the open. It was Zach's first face-to-face meeting with the man, but there was no doubt in his mind that he was the famous but reclusive Reverend Daniel Mercy.

Zach figured he was about forty-five, give or take two years on either end. He was tall, almost as tall as Zach's own six-three and dressed all in black. His hair, a thick chestnut-brown and streaked with fine shots of silver, was worn long and pulled back away from his even-featured face, secured in a ponytail at the back of his head. A neatly trimmed goatee completed his saintly persona.

He was physically fit, his arms well muscled beneath the cloth of his simple black T-shirt. But it was his eyes that captured Zach's attention. Overly large in a narrow face, they were the color of liquid coal. Bottomless.

"The sheriff here doesn't believe me when I say that everything is under control, Reverend," Cyrus said.

Mercy glanced in Zach's direction, one dark eyebrow raised in mild inquiry. "You have reason to distrust our word, Sheriff?"

Zach stepped closer, offering a hand. "Evenin', Reverend.

I'm Sheriff Zach McCoy. We've spoken on the phone a few times."

Mercy grasped his hand, his fingers wrapping around Zach's with a power that was unquestionably firm. Zach applied a little pressure of his own, watching a touch of amusement light the corner of the reverend's dark eyes.

"Ah, yes, I remember, Sheriff. You helped me with that little problem of the teenage boys trying to use our lakefront property for an impromptu drinking party." He smiled, his lips moving effortlessly to showcase a set of dazzling white teeth. "It's a pleasure to finally meet you in person."

Zach didn't imagine for a moment that Mercy felt any degree of warmth in finding him standing on his doorstep. But he could imagine that the man's smile made more than a few women swoon with appreciation. This man was a born salesman. A skilled manipulator.

"He's insisting that we let him in, Reverend," Abel pressed, obviously not happy with Mercy's gentle treatment of Zach's demands.

The reverend's smile widened. "But of course. He's the lawman in these parts, and he's just doing his job." Mercy stepped back and made a sweeping motion with one slender, well-manicured hand. "Please, Sheriff, come right in. Welcome to my humble home."

Zach found it hard to believe that after all these months he was actually getting through the front door. Nodding his thanks, he stepped over the threshold into the camp.

The compound was a scene of orderly confusion. A long narrow building engulfed in flames was the center of attention. A brilliant orange line of fire ran along the peak of the disintegrating roof.

The building was wood, and the fire was eating it so fast there didn't seem time to save even a small portion of the building. Black smoke and soot stained everyone's face, telling Zach that they'd all climbed out of their beds and hit the well as soon as the fire was discovered. Apparently there were no slackers in Mercy's organization.

"Was anyone trapped inside the building? Anyone hurt?" Zach asked.

"Actually, we were quite lucky. The building isn't in use yet. No one was inside," Mercy assured him.

In spite of the building being a total loss, the inhabitants of the compound appeared in no mood to turn it over to the relentless hunger of the flames. Three lines of people stretched out from a large, centrally located well.

Two of the lines of women and teenagers were passing bucket after bucket of water down the line. A bigger line of heavily muscled men manned two fire hoses. Off to one side, a small group of youngsters huddled together, their eyes wide with excitement and fear.

Zach couldn't help but be impressed with the grim determination on the adults' faces. Their equipment was a bit antiquated, but their dedication was as fierce and deep as any volunteer fireman Zach had ever come across.

"The fire trucks from town should be here any minute. They'll give you a hand."

Mercy smiled indulgently and shook his head. "You misunderstand, Sheriff. I only allowed you inside the gates because I wanted you to see that we're perfectly capable of handling anything the Good Lord throws our way."

"But we can help. Your people look exhausted."

Mercy shook his head. "We're fine, Sheriff. This is God's work, and they will do God's work until they drop." He clasped his hands together. "With me at their side to support them, of course."

Before Zach could respond, he heard a shout and turned to see Birdie streak past, charging the closest line of people manning the buckets. A few children squealed in panic and ran to hide behind their mothers. Their small hands twisted in the cloth of their mothers' baggy overalls and they peeked out. Birdie barked and yelped as she bounded her way down the line.

"Birdie!" Zach yelled, and then glanced apologetically in Mercy's direction. "Sorry, she usually doesn't take off like this. Birdie! Come!"

Birdie ignored him, running down the line, sniffing and nosing the people as if she were on a mission.

Concerned, Zach stepped forward, worried she'd get in someone's way and ruin the fragile alliance he had somehow managed to strike up with the Temple's leader. But as he moved, the crowd parted, and he suddenly found himself staring directly down the twin barrels of a double-gauge shotgun.

Chapter Two

At this close range, Zach figured he'd be blasted clear down to the lake if the gun actually went off. So he froze in place, careful to keep both hands well clear of his holster.

A shocked silence settled over the crowd, and Zach forced himself not to touch the butt of his own revolver. The only sound in the huge compound was the sharp crack of the flames consuming what remained of the empty bunkhouse.

"Okay, let's all take a deep breath here." Zach raised his hands above his waist. "I don't know about you, but I'm definitely not looking for trouble."

Mercy stepped forward and laid a hand on the barrel of the rifle. He gently forced the weapon down. "Relax, Jacob," he said, his tone soft and soothing, almost hypnotic. "The man only wants to get his dog."

A collective sigh of relief settled over the crowd, and after a few moments, they began passing buckets again. The rifleman stepped back, his expression wary and suspicious, as if he still didn't trust that Zach wasn't planning something subversive.

Birdie, unaware of the averted disaster, weaved in and out of the bucket brigade, sniffing excitedly until she reached one of the women at the back of the line. At least Zach thought the person was a woman. It was hard to tell as she seemed swallowed up by a pair of oversize painter's overalls and well-worn green canvas jacket.

Birdie jumped up, placing her paws on the woman's narro shoulders and let out a howl. The sound was pure, unadulte ated hound-dog joy.

Birdie's pink tongue whipped out and swiped wildly acro the woman's face. Zach sighed. Not too many people appr ciated getting slimed by an overly excited hound. Especial when said dog was trying to stick her tongue down yo throat.

But instead of screaming or running, the woman simp pried Birdie's paws off her shoulders and gently set her bac down. She pressed the palm of her hand to the top of tl hound's head, keeping her from reasserting her dominanc Birdie whined, openly expressing her distress.

But then, the woman looked up and her eyes met his acro the wide expanse. Zach sucked hot air. Hot, bitter-tasting a that burned his mouth and lungs. It was like breathing h ash.

Teagan Kennedy.

Where the hell had she come from? And what the hell wa she doing inside a religious fanatic's camp trying to put o a damn fire?

From beneath the brim of her cap, Zach saw Teagan's ey widen. It was too dark to see their color, but Zach didn't nee to see them to know exactly what they looked like.

Their shade was a memory locked away deep inside hir They were the color of a rare emerald mined from the deepe mine in Africa. A color so clear and heartbreakingly shar that he often thought he saw them in his dreams. Uncomfor able dreams that reminded him of times past, ones he tried forget as soon as he woke.

There was no doubt in his mind that she recognized hir too. The sharp flash of surprise told him all he needed know. She'd recognized him as easily as if they'd just see

ach other an hour ago, instead of one cold winter morning
even years earlier.

"Someone you know?" Curiosity flooded the deep timbre
f Mercy's voice. He turned and allowed his gaze to skim the
ength of the line, finally settling on Teagan. His movements
aused the hair on the back of Zach's neck to stand on end.

Teagan stiffened, her hand sliding off Birdie's head and
nto the pocket of her jacket. Zach could tell she didn't want
im to acknowledge her. In fact, he was pretty sure she
vished she could disappear into the crush of people behind
er.

"No, Birdie just gets a little rambunctious sometimes,"
,ach said. "Hope she didn't scare anyone."

"You at the back of the line, bring that dog up here,"
Mercy ordered.

Teagan paused only for the briefest second. Zach was pretty
ure no one else noticed the slight pause, but then he knew
er too well. Her movements were typically quick and self-
ssured. She wasn't one to hesitate or struggle with a decision.
Iell, that had always been Teagan's gift. Her ability to make
ecisions quickly and commit to them without question. Un-
ortunately, committing to *him* hadn't been one of those de-
isions she'd made.

She slipped her fingers through Birdie's collar and led her
orward. Birdie followed without complaint, her hound face
lmost smiling in lopsided relief as she gazed up into a face
he loved more than anyone else on earth, including Zach.

A bluetick hound never forgets her master, and Birdie knew
hat Teagan had been the one to cradle her against her stom-
ch and feed her during those first few months of life. True
ove never died when it came to a bluetick.

The fire had almost entirely consumed the bunkhouse and
he glow of the flames backlit Teagan as she made her way
over. Not even the baggy overalls and shapeless jacket could
ide the smooth glide of her long limbs.

She was a natural athlete, had been for as long as Zach had

known her. If she wasn't out playing rugby, she was runnir track or riding a mountain bike pell-mell down some mou tain trail. A woman of rare and beautiful grace. A woma who, seven years ago, had turned away from him and nev looked back.

Startled at his loss of concentration, Zach glanced at Merc The man was watching Teagan with the same intensity ar focus Zach imagined he'd given her himself a moment ag But Zach couldn't shake the feeling that something unpleasa oozed through the man's pores as he watched Teagan.

Something dark and predatory.

The lines of his elegant face seemed curious, as if he wa seeing Teagan for the first time. A smile of appreciation a peared.

"Here's your dog," Teagan said in an achingly famili voice. A voice with just a touch of raspiness to it. A dee throaty sound that sent tiny shivers down Zach's spine.

He slipped his fingers beneath Birdie's collar and savore the feel of Teagan's fingers sliding over his. It was like th touch of sweet heaven returning. A touch of paradise after a eternity of crawling across a desert.

"Sorry she jumped you," he said. "She's usually muc more well behaved."

"It's probably just the excitement of the fire. Maybe it sta tled her." She stepped back, keeping her head low enoug that it was hard for him to see beneath the brim of her hat.

He wondered if her hair was as long and luxurious as had been the year she'd left. She'd had a thick fall of blac lazy curls.

He had loved touching them, wrapping them around h fingers and sliding them across his face as he lay beside h in bed.

"What's your name, Sister?" Mercy asked, the syrup smoothness of his voice breaking into Zach's thoughts.

"Teagan. Teagan Benson."

"Ah yes, Teagan. Unusual name, Sister." Mercy glance

Zach. "Teagan is new to the Temple. She joined us nearly
week ago from our Temple in the Boston area."

Teagan nodded, her hands loosely folded in front of her
nd her head bowed. It was as if she was listening to her
master. Her expression compliant, her eyes downcast. Zach
ould only hope it was an act.

"Teagan, meet Sheriff McCoy. He keeps the peace around
hese parts. Keeps the hordes at bay, so to speak."

Zach offered a hand, a part of him dying to touch her again,
f only for a moment. But she didn't respond, both hands
lasped tightly together. Instead, she nodded and waited si-
ently.

"Please don't be offended by what may seem like rudeness
n the part of Sister Teagan, Sheriff." Mercy's eyes seemed
o search out Zach's.

It was a disturbingly penetrating look, one that made Zach
tch all over. He stared calmly back, resisting the urge to break
ye contact. "No offense taken."

"In our faith, it isn't seemly for an unmarried woman to
ouch a man not of her family," the Reverend said. "We are
ery conscious here of avoiding the ways of the flesh."

Zach dropped his hand to his side and nodded politely at
Teagan. "I'm sorry, I didn't know. I meant no disrespect."

"Of course you didn't. And I'm sure Teagan didn't take
our action as a form of disrespect." He turned those intense
yes back to Teagan. "You weren't offended, were you, Tea-
an?"

The sharp tone of Mercy's voice sawed at the edge of
Zach's nerves. It was as if the man wanted Zach to witness
he control he held over one of his followers. He had no trou-
le admitting to himself that he didn't like the power this man
eemed to have over anyone, Teagan included.

"I wasn't offended, Father," she said obediently.

Without pulling his gaze off Teagan, Mercy asked, "I noiced you got here rather quickly, Sheriff. Were you already
n the area patrolling?"

Zach didn't miss the edge of suspiciousness underlyin
Mercy's voice. Apparently Mercy didn't like the possibl
ramifications of Zach getting to the compound so quickly. N
doubt he suspected that Zach had been out snooping aroun
the perimeter of his compound. As much as Zach didn't min
making the man a little uncomfortable, he didn't want to mak
the tension between the cult and the townspeople any worse

"I own a small piece of property up here. I enjoy a fe
days of camping every once in a while."

"Oh, so you're the McCoy who owns the land on the othe
side of the lake—the property with the lean-to on it. Quite
nice little spread."

Again, Zach got the impression that the man was givin
him a message, letting him know that he'd investigated th
property. He wasn't about to let the comment pass unnotice
"I guess that means you've been over to check out my sid
of the lake, huh?"

"I like to know who my neighbors are."

An answer but not a true admission of guilt.

"Stop over anytime. I make a mean pot of coffee."

"I don't drink coffee, Sheriff. It is a stimulant." Merc
smiled indulgently. "But it's nice of you to offer."

Zach shrugged. "Now that I know, I'll try to have a ther
mos of lemonade handy."

"No need. I have a feeling that we're going to be too bus
around here to do much visiting."

"Sounds like you're under a time crunch."

"Yes, we are. The Lord is coming and we need to be pre
pared."

Before Zach could ask Mercy if he might be interested i
elaborating on that comment, the fire trucks and ambulanc
barreled up the last part of the mountain road and turned int
the encampment's driveway.

WITH THE SUDDEN appearance of the firemen from town, Tea
gan stepped back, determined to blend into the crowd of peo

ble watching the final licks of fire consume the bunkhouse.
She could hear the overly polite verbal sparring between Reverend Mercy and the sheriff just fine from the back of the
line.

In the short time she'd been behind the walls of the Temple's compound, Teagan had learned that no one wanted to
look like they were too curious about anything that was going
on. As usual, Daniel Mercy's comment about the Lord's time-
line sent a twinge of concern through her.

Her attention was diverted when the trucks from town
rolled up to the gate. The crowd around her shifted uneasily.
Something told Teagan that Daniel Mercy wasn't about to
swing the gates open to the crew from town, and the possibility of a angry confrontation made her tense.

She was pretty sure Zach knew Daniel Mercy's frame of
mind as well as she did, and she had to trust that he'd defuse
the situation. Ruining her cover was not an option at this
point. She had too much to do before that was even a consideration—if it was an option at all.

But Teagan had also seen a sharp glint of determination
lurking deep within Zach's startling blue eyes. Something she
knew all too well. A look that could mean he wasn't about
to back down.

The women in line parted and Teagan slipped in between
them, murmuring her thanks as she disappeared behind them.
Several of the women nodded wearily. None spoke.

Everyone in The Disciples' Temple seemed to understand
only too well the concept of conforming. No one wanted to
be singled out or marked as a troublemaker.

Teagan hadn't seen any outright cruelty, but the hollow
eyes and drawn faces of the sleep- and food-deprived members told her all she needed to know. These people were
beaten down. Drained. No dissenters were allowed in this
camp.

Most had given up trying to throw water on the structure,
recognizing that the bunkhouse was a total loss. Luckily the

fire hadn't jumped to any of the other buildings, kept confined to the one structure by a crew who had wetted down the roof of the four closest bunkhouses. The Temple members might be weary, but they had shown they knew how to work as a well-oiled unit.

Teagan glanced in Zach's direction. He was focused on Daniel Mercy, a calm, reasonable expression cutting across the clean lines of his face. He lifted one hand and took off his Stetson, running his fingers through his wheat-colored hair and wiping the sweat off his forehead before putting the hat back on.

She sucked in her lower lip, and for the briefest moment she remembered how it used to feel to run her fingers through those magnificent strands of hair, marveling in the thick, silky texture.

Teagan shook herself. Obviously she was more tired than she'd originally thought. For the past seven years, she had successfully managed to keep those traitorous thoughts from slipping in, and now, the simple act of seeing Zach had opened what she thought was a securely locked door. She slammed it shut again.

"Why don't you let us soak down what's left of the structure?" Zach asked. "Both the trucks from town are full. We can use our water and you can keep from running your well dry."

Mercy shook his head. "Our well is fine, Sheriff."

Teagan watched the knot of muscles tighten in Zach's right cheek. She almost smiled. No doubt he was clenching his teeth, a habit he used to resort to whenever he argued with her, whenever he felt she was being unreasonable.

"Okay, let's compromise. My men stay outside the walls of the compound, but you let them hand the hose in to your men. That way, your men can wet the structure down thoroughly."

Teagan smiled. Damn, she'd forgotten how good he was at creating a compromise. The man had a gift. He knew how to et his way without forcing anything down anyone's throat. He was hard-nosed but willing to bend.

Mercy paused, considering Zach's offer. After a moment, he nodded in agreement. "I accept your terms, Sheriff." He nodded his head toward Abel. "Open the main gates."

Abel started to protest, "But, Reverend—"

Mercy cut him off with a quick slash of his hand. "Do as I ask." He glanced back at Zach. "We welcome the help. Have your men hand the hoses through the gates to my men."

Within twenty minutes, the fire was completely out, the final few embers smothered beneath an onslaught of high-powered water. Teagan studied what was left of the bunkhouse. A soggy pile of charred boards outlined the former structure. Water dripped from the few pieces left standing.

Ashes and soot filled the air. The bitter taste of smoke flooded the back of her throat, and the stench of burning wood and hot metal permeated the night air.

In one corner of the bunkhouse stood the suspected culprit—the darkened remains of a kerosene heater. The metal had melted halfway down to the base, and the entire thing tisted sadly to one side.

There'd been a malfunction of some sort. It made Teagan leery of sleeping in any of the other bunkhouses for another night. But then, she didn't have much choice.

She glanced in the direction of Reverend Mercy's humble abode—a neat cottage with real electric lights and hot running water. No faulty kerosene heater for the reverend.

From what she'd seen up to this point, the good father didn't want for much. Only the best for the leader of The Disciples' Temple. This was in sharp contrast with what his loyal flock had to put up with.

A quick glance toward the main gates made Teagan realize that the men from town were already beginning to roll their hoses back on their trucks for storage. Zach had been right, the fire truck's hoses were far superior to anything Reverend Mercy had on site.

The Temple women stood in small clusters, watching i silence. Mercy motioned for several male members to assi the townspeople, and within a few minutes, the hoses wer stored neatly back on the trucks.

The firemen climbed aboard, a few leaning out the window to wave as the trucks rumbled over the stone-strewn roadwa and headed back down the mountain. The reverend and som of the men immediately bent to the task of rolling and storin their own gear. The women herded the children back towar the other bunkhouses.

Teagan searched the milling crowd for a glimpse of Zac Somehow during the collaborative effort to put out the fir Daniel Mercy had forgotten about his uninvited guest.

Teagan smiled. Zach obviously hadn't changed much ove the years. He was still the charming chameleon she'd know in college, a quality she'd always admired in him.

She might know how to silently blend in, but Zach kne how to assimilate through the use of his abundant charm an skillful ability to talk his way into any situation. The man wa a born communicator. Sometimes she had felt as though h could overwhelm her with that ability to talk.

A few seconds later, she spied him hunkered down next t the burnt bunkhouse ruins. He had a long stick in his han and he was using it to sift through the soggy mess surroundin the destroyed heating unit.

Teagan edged over to him.

"Good thing no one was sleeping in here," he said withou looking up.

"One more night and it would have been filled with ne members," she admitted softly.

He pointed to the darkened marks around the base of th stove. "Some kind of malfunction, I'd say. Mercy should tak it back to the manufacturer."

"Do you really think they'd own up to their responsibi ity?" a voice interrupted.

Startled, Teagan glanced over her shoulder to see Reveren

Mercy standing directly behind her. Damn, the man was like a cat, he moved around so quietly.

He smiled, the coolness of the smile putting a freeze along the edges of Teagan's already-exposed nerves. She bowed her head and stayed silent.

"You look tired, Sister." Reverend Mercy reached up and brushed her hair back from her face, his fingers trailing lazily along the side of her neck. The touch was intimate and totally unexpected. Teagan kept her body still, willing him to stop.

"Perhaps I should have you come back to my house for a bit of herbal tea. A chance for you to relax after such an exciting night."

Teagan suppressed a shiver, and out of the corner of her eye, she saw Zach unfold his long frame from his cramped position. The tightness around the corners of his mouth told her he didn't like the reverend's proprietary manner.

She tried to warn him with a quick glance. She needed him to know that Reverend Mercy was only acting this way for his benefit—the pasture bull asserting his dominance in the presence of the intruding male.

"I'm fine, Father, just a little tired." She stepped back, hoping he didn't take her retreat for what it was—an attempt to get away from him. She infused her smile with a touch of innocence, a blatant attempt to disarm him. "If you don't mind, I think I'll just head off to bed."

Reverend Mercy studied her with his penetrating eyes, the darkness of their color seeming to shift and change with the flickering light from the torches illuminating the courtyard.

His look chilled her. It was as if he could reach inside her, twist around inside her brain and read her actual thoughts. A tiny thread of dread wrapped around her already-frayed nerves. This man was more than dangerous.

He was evil.

Finally, he nodded and motioned for her to leave.

As she walked away, she heard him say to Zach, "I'm

going to have to ask you to leave now, Sheriff. My floc
needs their sleep after such an exhilarating evening.''

She was too far away to hear Zach's response, but the low
deep tones of his voice comforted her as she walked acros
the courtyard. What she wouldn't give to leave with him now
She had a strange, uncomfortable premonition that thing
were not going as smoothly as she'd hoped.

She climbed the porch steps and then glanced back, he
hand on the doorknob. Zach's eyes met hers across the ex
panse, his body still and expectant. She nodded silently an
disappeared into the darkened bunkhouse.

Chapter Three

ach watched Teagan melt out of the forest like a whisper of
moke drifting on a night breeze. She was hatless, with her
air falling down around her shoulders, the length and color
ke a curtain of black satin. The ends shimmered like silver
the moonlight.

"I was wondering when you'd show up," he said, pushing
e end of his stick farther into the hot coals of the campfire.
fire he'd built as soon as he returned to the lean-to, knowing
e'd show up.

"Want a cup of coffee?" He paused and then laughed bit-
rly. "Oh, wait, you aren't allowed to drink stimulants, are
ou?"

Teagan laughed, a soft sound that sent a flood of memories
sweet and painful coursing through Zach that, for a brief
oment, he thought he might die from the sensations.

"Go ahead and pour me a cup. I miss the caffeine so much
think I could gnaw on a handful of espresso beans and still
t get my fill." Birdie trotted over and nuzzled her hand,
ading her back to the fire, her brown eyes soft with adora-
n.

Teagan threw a leg over the opposite log and sat down,
retching her long legs out in front of her. One tanned ankle
eked out from beneath the cuff of her baggy pants, and

Zach tried unsuccessfully to shake off a sudden and une[x]
pected pang of longing.

The sight of her ankle brought back a forgotten memory[,]
a memory of that same tanned, slender ankle slipping out fro[m]
beneath the handmade quilt his mother had given him wh[en]
he'd left for college. He and Teagan had started living t[o]
gether at some point during their junior year at Plattsbur[g]
State, cramming all their belongings into his tiny studio apa[rt]
ment on Court Street.

He remembered getting ready for calculus class while Te[a]
gan slept, her face pushed fiercely into her pillow and h[er]
body wrapped around the warm spot he'd left behind. She['d]
always been a restless sleeper, thrashing about until her ha[ir]
tangled and her feet were left sticking out from beneath t[he]
covers. The sight of her slender ankle struck Zach hard, cau[s]
ing a sharp wave of protectiveness to wash over him.

He hadn't wanted to leave the warmth and safety of the[ir]
small apartment, and the thought of immersing himself in [a]
cold, jumbled world of numbers irritated him to no end. A[ll]
he wanted was to lie back down, wrap himself against Te[a]
gan's warm curves and rock them both into sweet oblivio[n.]

In the end that's exactly what he did. And what did it g[et]
him? A failing grade on his calculus final, that's what.

Sighing, Zach reached down and pulled the stick out of t[he]
coals, blowing on the tip until it glowed bright orange-red[.]

"You okay?" she asked.

"I'm fine. Nice of you to ask, though." He stomped t[he]
heavy lug sole of his boot down on the tip of the stick, grin[d]
ing out the burning embers. As he picked up the metal co[f]
feepot to pour her a cup, he asked, "You sure no one sa[w]
you leave the compound? Any chance they followed y[ou]
here?"

She accepted the cup, her cool fingers brushing against t[he]
back of his hand and nudging his heart rate up another not[ch.]
"No one saw me. And even if someone spied me leaving t[he]
camp, they'd never be able to keep up."

She glanced across at him, the brilliant green of her eyes sparkling with confidence, a lopsided smile curving a gentle dent in her left cheek. Zach's heart tightened. The tiny dimple that was so familiar, so well remembered, that Zach was sure he saw that in his dreams, too.

"You taught me well, Zach. I can still remember my Woodsmanship 101 classes way back when. I've never forgotten a single lesson."

She was placating him. "That was a long time ago," he said gruffly.

Teagan shrugged and sipped the coffee. Her lashes, thick and dark, swept the upper curve of her cheek as she savored the brew. "You have no idea how good this tastes." She glanced around. "Any chance you've got anything to eat? They keep our rations pretty low down there. No doubt, they figure that the hungrier we are, the less inclined we are to ask questions."

Zach nodded and got up. He grabbed a bag of homemade turkey jerky out of the truck and threw it to her. She caught it with one hand, her face lighting up at the sight of the thick strips of dried meat.

Nearby, Birdie collected her rope tuggie toy and brought it to Teagan, her eyes hopeful. Instead, Teagan unzipped the bag and dug in, tearing off a huge chunk and chewing ravenously. "Heavenly. Your mom make it?"

Zach nodded again and then tried not to stare at her as she swallowed and tore off another hunk. Birdie dropped the rope and nudged her arm. She whined until Teagan tossed her some.

"Why didn't anyone inform me that you were going into the camp undercover?"

A slight smile tugged at one corner of her mouth and she threw Birdie another half strip. "Why do you assume I was dropped in? Maybe I simply quit the Bureau and joined The Disciples' Temple."

Zach snorted and picked up his mug, blowing on the steaming liquid before answering. "Somehow I don't see that a fitting in with your profile, Agent Kennedy. You aren't th cult-joining type."

"I joined ATF, didn't I?"

Zach sipped his coffee, the feeling of bitterness returning Yeah, she joined the ATF and left him in her wake.

In fact, she hadn't looked back even once. She had simpl packed her belongings in a single suitcase and left town choosing to do it while he was tied up taking a final exam No doubt she'd thought he'd make a fool of himself beggin her to stay. Sadly, Zach wasn't too sure he wouldn't hav done just that given half a chance.

Teagan was never one to favor dramatic scenes. She like things pretty cut-and-dried. Not that Zach liked creating scene. But he was from a family that thrived on communi cation, and sometimes their communication got lively an loud.

Hell, if a person didn't speak up in Zach's family, they go drowned out. With six sisters ganging up on him, he'd learne early in life to speak up and keep speaking until he was heard But Teagan was different. She preferred things done quiet quick and clean. Quiet talks, quick decisions and clean part ings.

During their two years together, Zach had tried to figur her out, to find the delicate balance between their differen personalities. But as hard as he'd tried, he'd never seeme able to dig under her carefully constructed wall of protection He'd figured out fairly early that her father didn't approve o him—hated him actually. Zach had been confident he coul win the old man over if given half a chance. But Teagan neve gave him that chance.

He had understood that family pressures weighted heavy on Teagan. Her parents divorced when she was nine, and he mother spent years in and out of hospitals. So naturally, a lo had fallen on Teagan's shoulders, but she rarely shared any of this with him.

No matter how hard he cajoled, pried and outright asked, the real Teagan had hovered just out of his reach. Oh, the sex had been good. Damn good, in fact. But Teagan had always kept a little part of herself protected. Shrouded. No doubt her reserve made her an outstanding ATF agent, but reserve was a lousy trait in a lover.

"Are you going to tell me what's going on?" he asked.

"I hadn't planned on it." She grinned good-naturedly, an apparent attempt to take the sting out of her words. "I can't say that I ever expected to run into you."

"Yet you knew that my family owned the fifty-six acres right across from the place you were sent to investigate. Strange." Zach didn't plan on giving an inch.

Teagan shrugged, the cloth of her shirt stretching across her shoulder blades. She looked leaner than Zach remembered. He struggled to suppress the strong pull even that small movement caused. The slenderness of her frame was deceiving. He knew from experience that she was tough, capable of running effortlessly and elegantly for miles, leaving most grown men weeping in her dust.

"I remembered." She glanced around. "Not much chance I'd forget this place."

"I guess not. You and I camped out here enough times."

He watched, but there was no flicker of sadness or regret on her face when he mentioned the good times. It was as if she'd wiped them completely from her memory.

"To be honest, I thought I'd be in and out of Mercy's camp fast. His reputation as being totally paranoid on the topic of outsiders convinced me that he wouldn't be inclined to invite the local sheriff in for chitchat."

Zach waited. He knew from experience that the less he talked the more he left things in her court. Teagan was an expert at playing this game, but Zach was pretty sure he'd learned a few things over the past few years. He planned on holding his own.

"It was for your own safety, Zach. If I let you know I was

going to be here, you could have slipped and endangered us both.''

Zach gritted his back teeth. Wonderful. Now Teagan figured she needed to protect him. He ignored the comment and waited her out.

''I thought any contact with you after all these years would only confuse the issue more.''

Zach didn't even bother to touch that one. If that's what she thought then there wasn't going to be any sudden meeting of the minds. She had no idea how he felt about her, and he wasn't about to try and tell her. Or better yet, let her know that his family thought he was a total loon for not moving on with his life.

Teagan started again. ''They sent me in because it's in my records that I spent a lot of time hiking this area during my college years. They figured if anyone could find out what was going on it would be me.''

''So what's going on? Are you looking for firearms? Explosives? Drugs? What?''

She stared across the fire at him, her expression blank. There wasn't any doubt in Zach's mind that the look signaled her unwillingness to discuss the specifics of her mission. Typical Fed behavior.

Zach jerked his wrist, flinging the contents of his cup into the thick brush ringing the campsite. ''From the look on your face I'm guessing that you're shutting me out.''

She shrugged.

''What do you think I'm going to do? Tell Mercy that the ATF is sitting on his doorstep?''

''You know that isn't the issue, Zach. I'm not permitted to discuss any aspect of my mission with anyone outside the Bureau.'' Teagan sighed. ''Let's just say that the Bureau is interested in what Daniel Mercy is up to.''

''That's a cop-out and you know it. Are you working alone or are my woods crawling with ATF agents?''

''I have a contact inside the cult. We're trying to keep this operation small. No leaks.'' She stood up and moved a short distance away. ''Talking about any aspect of the case endangers myself and my contact. Hell, it endangers you.''

''I'm sure I'm capable of watching out for myself.''

''Of course you are, but the way you can help the most is by steering clear of the compound and keeping everyone else as far away as possible.''

Zach nodded his head, unable to keep the irony out of his voice. ''Steer clear of you. I wonder why that has such a familiar ring to it?''

''You're making this more personal than it has to be, Zach.''

''Probably because it *is* personal. Have you forgotten what you meant to me at one time? Or are you still too busy running away from anything that smacks of intimacy that you can't even consider the possibility that I care about what happens to you?''

''What we felt for each other was a long time ago.'' There was a small catch in her voice, but she didn't look away. The line of her jaw tightened in denial.

Zach stood up and closed the distance between them. He didn't regret seeing the dark shadow of pain shooting through the depths of her exquisite eyes at his verbal attack. A part of him wanted to hurt her, to make her feel something.

Anything.

Sure he was being petty, but damn it, he wasn't the kind of man who didn't talk about what he felt. Growing up in a family of women taught him that emotions weren't the enemy. Silence was.

But before he could step closer, Teagan reached out and placed the palm of her hand against his chest, stopping him cold.

''I never meant to hurt you, Zach. You have to believe me when I say that.'' The warmth of her hand seemed to soak down through the cloth of his shirt, scorching his skin.

''At the time, I thought leaving was the right thing to do.''

She paused and then delivered the final blow. "And even now I know it was."

Zach leaned in, the weight of his body rested against her hand. "Well, you thought wrong."

The air between them crackled.

Next to the fire, Birdie sat up, her brown eyes darting back and forth between the two of them. She had always had the ability to sense when there was tension between them. She whined softly in protest.

"Stop it, Zach. You're scaring Birdie."

"Birdie's fine. You're just dodging the issue." He tried to ignore the burn of her fingertips through the heavy weave of his shirt. "The way you left was wrong."

Teagan dropped her hand and turned away. "I've been wrong before, and I'm sure I'll be wrong again. But there isn't much I can do about it now except apologize." She lifted her chin, using one hand to jam her hair back away from her face. "My only excuse is that I was young and unequipped to deal with all the emotional stuff that went along with our relationship."

"And what about now?" Zach pressed.

Teagan glanced away, the dark strands of her silken hair swinging forward to brush her cheek. "What do you mean?"

Zach touched her chin, pulling her gaze back toward him. "Now are you able to handle the emotions that go into a relationship?"

"We—we're different people now, Zach. I have my career. You have yours." She stepped back away from his touch, her need to escape obvious. "I'm sorry, I have to get back to the compound. If they discover me missing, I'll have blown everything."

Zach nodded, stuffing his hands into the pockets of his jeans. He forced his voice to sound casual. Nonchalant. "Sure. No problem. If you need anything, you know where to find me."

He walked back to the fire, bending down to slip his hand

rough Birdie's collar. "Go ahead. Go quick. I'll hold Birdie
o she won't follow you."

Her gaze met his, and it comforted him a little to see his
wn sadness reflected in her eyes.

"Zach, I—"

"Just go, Teagan. I never thought I'd say this, but I'm
eginning to think that you leaving without an explanation
was actually a favor."

Teagan nodded, accepting the rejection. "I knew you'd
ome around to my way of thinking. Goodbye, Zach."

She slipped into the velvety darkness of the surrounding
orest without another word.

A single branch snapped and then silence descended over
is camp. She'd disappeared as quietly as she'd arrived.

Birdie whined and Zach tightened his fingers around the
oft weave of her collar. A harsh burning sensation invaded
he back of his throat.

Damn fool.

He was a damn, sentimental fool. Why had he even alluded
o the possibility that there might still be something between
hem?

Because he had no shame. No pride.

Birdie whined again, and Zach reached up and clamped his
and over her warm muzzle. Birdie's brown eyes blinked in
urprise. He'd never shut her up before. Her eyes begged an
xplanation.

"Get used to it, Birdie. She doesn't have time for us while
he's out saving the world." He glanced toward the spot
where she'd melted back into the thick blackness of the
woods. Nothing. Just darkness and leaves whispering of the
pproaching dawn. "We'll just watch her back, girl. Make
ure no one tries to hurt her."

Birdie leaned her head against his chest; her wet nose nuz-
led his neck, speaking her agreement.

A SHORT TIME LATER, Teagan climbed over the porch railing
f her assigned bunkhouse and landed lightly on her toes. She
aused, listening.

Nothing—just the deep-throated croaks of the frogs occupying the thick brush surrounding the compound. For a moment, she found the chorus soothing. She leaned back again the cool wood of the bunkhouse and breathed deep.

The meeting with Zach had taken more out of her tha she'd anticipated. All those stored memories had come flooding back like an unleashed herd of wild mustangs. It had take all her control not to react. Not to grab his hand and pull hi to her.

She sighed and straightened, pushing away the errant emotions connected to thoughts of Zach. There was no time dwell on treasures lost. She needed to pay attention to he mission. Her life and the life of Miguel, her contact, depende on it.

A tiny twinge of satisfaction rippled through her when sh realized she'd gotten back within the confines of the compound without any of the sentries seeing her. Apparently sh hadn't lost her touch.

She glanced out over the vast encampment. Hard to believ that New Jerusalem had built the place in such a short perio of time. The biggest building was the gathering house—th Temple. Yellow light from the windows spilled out on th grass. The lamp of eternity was always lit, mainly because n one knew when Reverend Mercy was going to call them t worship. Teagan had learned early that there was no set schedule within the camp. Like many cults, Daniel Mercy and hi crew kept all the followers off balance.

The compound was empty, but Teagan could see the sentries posted along the outer perimeter. She pressed her bac against the wall of the bunkhouse and crept toward the doo No sense in tempting fate and risking getting caught now.

As she put her hand on the knob to ease it open, a floo of yellow light soaked the front porch, pinning Teagan in i center. She froze.

"Out for a little early-morning stroll, Sister?"

Teagan bit her bottom lip, forcing her heart back down out of her throat. She should have known she'd be caught. There wasn't much this group missed, and something told her that Reverend Mercy wouldn't have been able to resist having someone check her bed.

Bracing herself, Teagan turned around.

Cyrus Mackie and Eddie Zelser, Daniel Mercy's two closest personal assistants, stood at the bottom step. There was no missing the smarmy smirk of triumph on Cyrus's face. No doubt he'd been waiting all evening for just this opportunity to confront her.

She had little doubt he had alerted Daniel Mercy about her unsanctioned trip outside the camp's perimeter. The guy had been on her since she stepped on the camp's rattletrap bus six days ago in Boston. She had successfully rebuffed his pitiful overtures, reminding him of the Father's rules against the sexes mingling outside the sanctity of marriage.

Of course, Cyrus hadn't appreciated her pious lecture, telling her that he was part of the inner circle and the Father didn't begrudge him anything. Teagan had moved to sit with one of the older women who had two children, shifting one of the wiggling toddlers onto her lap and focusing on playing Itsy-Bitsy Spider with the little girl.

Her rebuff had earned her more than one reprimand over the past few days, but Teagan had initially figured she'd wait him out. But now she wondered if she'd maybe underestimated Cyrus's staying power. Apparently he wasn't done pursuing her.

"The air in the cabin was a little stuffy," she said, coming to stand at the edge of the porch. "I couldn't sleep so I took a short walk down by the water."

"You should know by now that the Father doesn't want anyone outside the gates without his permission. You seem to have a problem obeying the Father," Cyrus said. "You need to come with us and answer to him."

Teagan didn't panic. She never panicked, and she was good when backed into a corner. She'd handle this situation like she always did—with calm, rational thinking.

Nonetheless, her heart pounded as the two men closed in on either side of her and hustled her across the compound.

She stumbled a bit on the steps of the Temple, and Cyrus jerked at her impatiently. Teagan's mind raced. She needed to come up with a plan. A reason to explain her trek outside the walls of the compound.

Failure to finish this operation was *not* an option. She had a job to do and she planned on succeeding—no matter what it cost. She settled on her story, confident she'd win the battle of wills she knew was to come.

Chapter Four

The Disciples' Temple was a huge cavernous room built into the opening of an old mine shaft. As far as Teagan had been able to tell since arriving at the camp, the architects of the Temple had simply constructed the chapel as an extension to the huge mine entrance.

Someone—Teagan couldn't remember who—had told her that the old cave had been sealed off years before when the mining company left the area. But some clever builder had designated the outer opening of the cave as the front of the church. It gave the front a grotto-like feel. Large slabs of stone had been blasted out of the rock and used to build the altar.

As she stepped inside, her eyes struggled to adjust to the dimness. The only light came from hundreds of flickering candles lining the outer edge of the floor and leading up to the carved stone altar.

To the right of the altar sat Reverend Mercy's chair, a microphone attached to one armrest. Perhaps a word more appropriate than *chair* was *throne*. It was a magnificent stone structure with a high back and a three-step dais leading up to it.

The room was cool, a light breeze flowing from back to front. If she listened carefully, she could hear the soft whisper of the wind coming from the back of the cave, most likely through the cracks in the wall. She couldn't tell, though, because thick velvet drapes covered the entire back wall.

There were no windows, only the outer wood of the enclosed structure and then the stark stone walls of the cave. No big surprise. The reverend didn't want anyone's attention focused on anything other than him when he was preaching.

There were no pews or chairs of any type. Just hard bare floor. From previous prayer services, sessions that seemed to drag on endlessly, Teagan knew that no one was permitted to sit on anything while in Daniel Mercy's presence. One either knelt or sat cross-legged on the hard-packed earth, an act guaranteed to make a person's knees ache and body cramp. No doubt he thought it kept them all humble.

The truly devoted, those handful of indoctrinated souls who had demonstrated their zeal and willingness to conform, were given the privilege of wearing the brilliant red vest of the "Chosen Elite" and allowed to kneel on small, narrow prayer rugs.

Of course, it was the few nonconformists who worried Teagan the most. Over the past week, she'd witnessed more than a few tearful confessions of unworthiness. Confused, exhausted individuals were dragged in front of the group to confess their sins—usually women. They'd launch into rambling, tearful dissertations on past mistakes and their current failures to grasp or live by the Temple's ideology.

Cyrus propelled her forward, his meaty hand clamped around her upper arm. Even his partner struggled to keep up with him as he marched her up the center of the Temple. Their feet kicked up tiny puffs of dirt and dust as they moved.

In the dim light, Teagan could make out Daniel Mercy, sprawled in his chair, one leg hooked over the chair's arm and his eyes half closed. A Bible lay open in his lap, his lips moving silently as if in prayer.

For several moments no one spoke. Time stretched out between them like the silken thread of a spider's web, and Teagan couldn't help but wonder what kind of sinister plan the man was weaving to entrap her.

Just when she thought she couldn't wait one more second he looked up and stared down at her, his gaze intense and penetrating. She gazed back, careful to keep any and all defiance out of her eyes.

"I've been told that you have sinned," he said softly, the *s* seeming to slither through the cool chamber and wrap around her throat.

"No, Father." Teagan tried jerking her arm out of Cyrus's grasp, but he simply tightened his grip. He was so close, she could smell the garlic he'd consumed at dinner.

"Let her go." Daniel Mercy raised one elegant hand and motioned for her to approach. "Come closer, child. You deny acting outside the prescribed laws set down by me, your benevolent father? Laws designed to nurture and protect you."

Teagan didn't bother answering. Better to wait and see how he was going to come at her. She stood in front of him, studying him from beneath lowered lashes. The man was so unpredictable it was hard to guess what he'd do next.

"Kneel, Sister."

Before she could ask where, one of the men jammed his foot against the back of her knees. She dropped, her knees hitting the hard-packed earth with a thud.

"I only went outside the gates to clear my head, Father," she said.

He stared down at her, the darkness of his eyes making them seem like fathomless pits of sorrow. So much for her attempt at confessing; he didn't believe her.

"You took a walk to clear your head." His head dropped back to rest against the red velvet of his chair. "Yet not an hour earlier, you told me how exhausted you were. Too exhausted in fact to join me in a cup of herbal tea."

Teagan smiled apologetically. "I was overtired. I went to bed, but when I lay down, I found I couldn't sleep."

The lines of his face hardened a bit more. He wasn't buying

any of this. Why? What had she done to touch off this degree of suspicion? Other members had walked off, gotten tired of the confinement and left the compound for a few hours of solitude. Sure they'd had to face the consequences when they returned, usually a few extra rotations on kitchen duty. But as far as she could tell, none of them ever talked of getting this kind of grilling.

"Perhaps you should have spent your time on your knees, praying and asking for release from your lies, rather than walking around outside the compound."

"I prayed while I walked, Father."

He laughed. The sound didn't convey any degree of humor. He steepled his hands and leaned forward. "Tell me the truth—how do you know the lawman McCoy?"

The question came out of nowhere, hitting Teagan hard. But to her credit, she kept her cool. "I don't know him."

The reverend waved his hand and a man behind her grabbed a chunk of her hair. His fingers tangled in the long strands and tightened until his fist fit snug against the back of her skull.

When she tried to slip out from beneath his grip, he pulled her backward, jamming his knee into the small of her back and yanking her head and upper torso up over his hard-muscled thigh.

Through a shimmer of hot tears, Teagan saw Cyrus standing over her, his face twisted into a cold mask of delight. She willed the tears to disappear, telling herself they were a simple physiological reaction to the pain. She would not allow this man to gain one iota of control over her.

She bit the soft skin on the inside of her cheek, working it hard. *Concentrate, dammit. Focus on the words and ignore the haze of white pain engulfing the back of your head.*

"Answer me truthfully. How do you know Sheriff Mc-Coy?" Daniel Mercy pressed.

"I don'—"

Cyrus yanked her head back farther, and she felt several

strands of hair rip from the back of her skull. A tiny cry of protest escaped from between her lips.

God, she hated showing any weakness to these men. As much as she wanted to twist out of Cyrus's grasp, swing around and drive his smug smile up into the general direction of his nose, she knew she had to stay in her assigned role— that of the meek little nobody waitress from some greasy-spoon diner in South Boston.

"Relax, Cyrus, there's no need to scare our sister. She wants to cooperate. Don't you, Teagan?"

The fist tangled in her hair didn't loosen, and the knee remained firmly planted in her back. So much for Cyrus not wanting to scare her, Teagan thought. The guy was definitely getting off on hurting her. What's a bit of sadomasochism among cult members? From what she'd learned of this cult, that kind of behavior was pretty much a given.

"How do you know the sheriff?" Mercy's voice changed, signaling that he'd moved closer.

A few seconds later, his face hovered over hers. He smiled, his expression a classic picture of compassion and forgiveness. She hated him at that moment, resented his need to demonstrate his power and control over her. Nothing would have allowed her to give him the satisfaction of crying or asking for mercy.

Her tongue pushed against the back of her teeth, begging to rip loose a stream of sarcasm. But Teagan knew herself well enough to know that reacting to control freaks was one of her own personal major triggers, and she had worked hard over the years to not overreact. She drew on that self-control now.

Mercy reached out and gently ran the tip of his finger down the center of her neck, the nail tracing the line of her throat and coming to rest against the band of her T-shirt. "You're sweating, Sister. I predict that if you tell the truth, you will feel so much better."

His finger hooked around the band of her shirt and lightly

stroked the skin beneath. Goose bumps pebbled her flesh, and she wet her lips with the tip of her tongue. If his hand went any farther, Teagan knew she wouldn't be able to vouch for her reaction. Something told her that she just might lose it totally.

"Sheriff McCoy and I went to college together, Father. I recognized him when he entered the compound. I—I was afraid to tell you because I knew how much you distrust outsiders." She tried adding a bit of pleading into her voice. "I admit to being weak. I feared your anger."

Mercy released the band of her shirt and gently patted her cheek. "See, that wasn't too horrible, now was it?"

Before she could respond, he walked away. A few moments later, he said, "Release her."

Cyrus's released her hair and shoved her hard. She fell forward, the dirt floor scraping the palms of her hands. Pushing her hair out of her eyes, she sat up. Her scalp stung and throbbed.

When she looked up, Mercy was sitting back in his chair. He stared down at her, his eyes hooded, the gears of his brain no doubt clicking along merrily. Teagan knew she could only hope he was considering how he could use the information she had just fed him.

"Did you have an illicit affair with the man?"

Teagan shook her head. She wasn't lying. What she'd shared with Zach all those years ago could never be described as illicit. It had been something beautiful. Something wonderful, and as much as she might have looked to find those same feelings again in other relationships, she had never found them again.

"Tell me with words," Mercy ordered.

Teagan met his eyes, infusing her gaze with as much sincerity as she was able to muster. "No, Father. We only knew each other from a few classes. Nothing more."

"Well, if my intuition is right—and it's rarely wrong—our

sheriff would like to get to know you a whole lot better than as a former classmate.''

Eddie snickered, and Teagan dug her nails into the palm of her hand. They were *not* going to get to her. She was in control.

Mercy smiled, and the quality of that smile spoke of something secretive and oddly frightening. ''But it doesn't matter because we're going to use Sheriff McCoy's lust for our personal gain.''

Teagan sat back on her heels. ''How, Father? You know that you only have to tell me what you want me to do and I'll do as you ask.''

''All in good time. Until then, I want you to be nice to Sheriff McCoy. Make him feel at home. And in the end, he'll help us accomplish our mission.'' He stood up, clutching his Bible to his chest. ''Now I want you to go back to bed.''

He waved his hand dismissively and then reopened his Bible. The fiery intensity of his gaze fell away, and he focused on the page in front of him. He had dismissed her as easily as he had abused her a few moments ago.

Frustrated but aware she had to tread lightly, Teagan stood. As she walked to the back of the Temple, her sneakers hit the earth with barely audible thuds, but in the silence, they seemed to echo in the cavernous room. Behind her, she heard the soft murmur of the reverend's voice as he read aloud a passage from the Bible in his deep, hypnotic voice. '''I am the First and the Last. I am the Living One; I was dead, and behold I am alive for ever and ever! And I hold the keys of death and Hades.'''

Closing the door of the Temple behind her, Teagan leaned against it and allowed her head to drop back against the thick wood. Her hands trembled slightly, and she let out a shaky breath. She'd survived Daniel Mercy's interrogation.

She might be minus a few hairs at the back of her head, but she'd gotten out intact and without really telling him anything. Next time she might not be so lucky. But then, Teagan didn't plan on there being a next time. She planned to finish her mission and get out of this hellhole as fast as she could.

"YOU'RE MAKING a big mistake, Father. You should have never let her walk away," Cyrus said as soon as the heavy door of the Temple slammed shut on Teagan's lithe form.

Mercy settled himself deeper into his chair. He reached out and carefully hooked a finger around the smooth satin ribbon marker. Caressing it between his thumb and forefinger, he slid it between the pages and shut the book.

He lifted his head and sighed. He loved sitting in the Temple late at night, the cool air from the cave caressing his cheek and the light from the candles dancing and weaving with the rush of air. What he didn't appreciate was anyone telling him how he should conduct his business.

He leveled his gaze onto Cyrus, ignoring Eddie—for the moment anyway. He had no illusions as to why both men had remained loyal to him. Like anything, loyalty had its price, and in this case, the price was the opportunity to share in his power.

He wasn't stupid. He knew both men lived to bask in his limelight, and they knew that if they wanted to collect their fair share, they needed to stay close.

Of course, he also knew that his power brought the two men their ultimate desire—the pick of any woman in the group. And both knew this was fine with him as long as they didn't poach from his group of women.

Mercy sighed. All great men suffered the incompetence and ignorance of those who surrounded them. He was no exception. But sometimes he wished that he didn't have to deal with the results of their stupidity. Such as now.

"Tell me exactly why you think I'm making a mistake, Cyrus. Tell me so I can be awed by your all magnificent intellect."

From the frozen look on Cyrus's face, Mercy knew that the stupidity of his remark had finally sunk in. The man shifted his weight. "I didn't mean to say *you* made a mistake, Father…I—I meant that *we* made a mistake. We shouldn't trust her. Shouldn't have let her walk off like that."

"Funny, but that doesn't sound at all close to what you were trying to say a minute ago."

"She's been nothing but trouble since she came," Cyrus rushed to explain. "She doesn't fit in and she makes me nervous." He glanced at his sidekick, Eddie. "And not just me either, right, Eddie?"

Eddie just stared at him as if frozen. His mouth worked like that of a drowning fish, but no sound came out.

"The only reason she's been troublesome to you is because she turned you down flat every time you tried to seduce her."

Cyrus's lips tightened in anger. He was a man who didn't like being reminded of his failures. "Did she tell you that? Has she been telling lies about me? I demand to know what she said about me."

Mercy stood up, no longer pretending he was even slightly amused by the man's impertinence. "You *demand?*" He walked across the space between them. "Do you really think you've attained the right to demand anything from me?"

Cyrus held up his hands, his face immediately contrite. His tongue nervously wet his thick lips. "No, that's not what I meant. I—I simply asked because I only wanted to know what kind of lies she told you. You know how women lie."

Mercy stood in front of him, allowing his silence to turn up the tension another notch or two. He tilted his head back and breathed in the heady smell of fear, savoring it.

"Perhaps you don't feel that you can trust my judgment any more. Is that the problem, Cyrus? Is that why you're questioning me?"

Eddie edged sideways, putting as much distance as possible between himself and his buddy Cyrus. He was smart enough to know that he didn't want to be perceived as having anything to do with Cyrus's current blunder.

"Forgive me from questioning you, Father. I meant no disrespect.'' Cyrus kept his head down, his voice low. Mercy knew how much it took for the man to submit himself like this. ''But how can you be sure she isn't out to betray you?''

He smiled thinly and walked back to his chair. Leaning down, he picked up his Bible and set it on his lap as he sat back down. ''Do as I do, Cyrus—watch our little Teagan. In fact, watch everyone. Because the only person you should trust is me. I'm the only one who knows our Lord's true plan. Do you understand?''

Cyrus nodded, letting out a soft sigh. He knew that the crisis was over for the time being.

''Now leave me. I have some readings to complete,'' Mercy ordered, waving the two men off.

They readily complied, leaving their master to read aloud from his Bible for another two hours, neither man fully aware that Mercy was preparing himself for the final battle.

EARLY THE NEXT MORNING, Zach loaded his camping gear and Birdie into the truck and headed for town. As much as it grated on him to drive down the steep, rutted road toward town, knowing he was leaving Teagan behind, Zach also knew he didn't have much choice. Teagan had been pretty clear last night that she wasn't open to any help from him.

Her single-mindedness—her damned determination to demonstrate her ability to accomplish things all on her own—hadn't changed much over the years. She was even more driven than he remembered. He just wished he knew the name and location of her contact.

As he turned left onto Route 22, passing the Welcome to Bradley: Population 12,500 sign, Zach hit the gas. If he hurried, he'd have just enough time to catch a quick breakfast at The Dog's Dish Café before heading over to his office in Elizabethtown.

Turning into Dog's tiny parking lot, he swore softly. Not one parking slot left out front. That meant that the diner would be crowded, and he'd have to wait for a table. He drove around back, parking in the only slot open. Rolling down both windows, he patted Birdie's head.

"If you take off, there won't be any of Cade's sausage links for you."

Birdie blinked her brown eyes innocently, as if to say, "Whatever would make you think I'd do something like that?" Zach pocketed his keys and climbed the steps to the back entrance.

As he stepped through the swinging screen door, a tiny bell tinkled and the smell of fried potatoes, onions and green peppers hit him hard. His stomach rumbled.

He surveyed the cramped, elbow-to-elbow dining area, nodding to a few folks who looked up long enough to wave a quick howdy before ducking their heads back down to their chow. Not one table available. Reluctantly, he headed for one of the red vinyl stools that lined the long Formica countertop.

"Zach! Over here."

He glanced around, trying to locate the direction of his sister Jenna's voice. The oldest by fifteen years, Jenna owned The Dog's Dish Café. If health laws would have permitted, she would have willingly allowed four legged customers as well as her typical two-legged ones to dine in the place. To say she was a pet enthusiast was an understatement.

He spied her sitting in a small booth in the farthest corner of the diner. Sheets of paper were spread out on the checkered tablecloth in front of her. She lifted an arm and waved him over.

Nodding to Sally, the Dog's most senior waitress, Zach made a pouring motion. He knew Sally would deliver the prescribed cup of black coffee. He then weaved his way through the sea of folks to get to Jenna's table, slipping into the seat across from her.

"Morning," he said, taking off his Stetson and setting it on the bench beside him.

Jenna smiled, the tiny lines at the corner of her eyes settling into a familiar pattern that showcased the unusual Robin's-

egg blue of her eyes. All the McCoy offspring were recog
nizable by the color of their eyes. At least that's what thei
mother claimed anyway.

"I called you last night, but you weren't home," Jenna said
with a slight accusatory note in her voice.

"I stayed up at the lean-to."

"Heard there was a fire up at that religious place."

Zach nodded. "A faulty stove exploded."

"Anyone hurt?"

"Nope."

"So what do you think?"

Zach glanced away, accepting a mug from Sally. She
slapped down a basket of warm, homemade biscuits and
waited, pen poised over her pad to take his order.

"I'll have the French toast with bacon," he said. "And ask
Cade to fry up a few sausage links for Birdie, okay?" Sally
smiled and nodded, then headed off for the kitchen with her
wide-hipped swagger.

Jenna rapped her spoon on the table and stared at him impatiently.

"What?" he asked, laying both arms along the back of the
booth and stretching his feet out in front of him.

"I asked you what you thought. And get your big ol' feet
back on your side of the table," she said, kicking at him.

Zach lazily shifted his feet off to the left. "What do I think
about what?"

"That New Jerusalem place. A few of the boys from the
fire department were in here this morning and said you were
actually inside the place when they arrived last night."

"I was. I saw the blaze from all the way across the lake."

Zach flipped back the checkered napkin covering the biscuits and grabbed one, shifting if from hand to hand because
it was so hot. Breaking it open, he watched the steam curl
upward in a white wisp before he set it on his plate. He
reached for the small crock on the table and slathered both

ides of the steaming biscuit with sweet, golden honey before aking a quick bite.

"Damn, that's good," he said around a mouthful.

Jenna glared.

"What?" he asked.

"What do you mean *what?* I want to know what you think about that place. Everyone—and I mean everyone—has been talking about how strange the people seem." Jenna leaned forward and whispered. "And you saw that special on *Hard Exposure* last year—you know the one that talked about it being a cult. Winston Chandler came right out and said it was a dangerous doomsday cult."

Zach nodded. He remembered the nationally-known anchorman's entire exposé on the cult. It was what had made Zach wary of the group from the start.

Jenna sat back. "Helen said that a few of the women brought their kids in for checkups when they first arrived. She says that not one of them has been back since. It's like they've all disappeared behind that wooden barrier and aren't ever seen again."

"They come in and grocery shop at the Big M all the time. Besides, according to Reverend Mercy they have their own medical people." He grinned. "What's Helen crabbing about, anyway? Just last week she was complaining that she never has any time off. I'd think she'd be glad she didn't have to deal with a ton of new patients."

Someone hit the back of his head with a stinging slap. "Hey, lughead, I happen to worry when my patients don't come back for a follow-up visit."

Zach looked up, surprised to see his second oldest sister, Helen, standing directly behind him.

"Howdy, Uncle Zach," two sweet voices chorused.

His twin nine-year-old nieces, Krista and Emily, popped out from behind their mother and scooted up onto the bench next to him. They elbowed each other in their eagerness to be the first one to hug him.

"Where did you two squirts come from?" he asked gruffly, bussing them both on their sun-kissed cheeks. They giggled and squirmed away from him.

"Go bug Cade in the kitchen, you two," their mother ordered, swatting them on their denim-clad behinds. "But tell him no fried dough."

"Okay!" Krista said, grabbing her sister's hand.

"Bye, Uncle Zach." Emily flashed him a dimpled smile as her sister tugged her in the direction of the kitchen.

Zach figured both their mouths would be filled with fried dough five seconds after entering the kitchen. Poor Cade couldn't resist their charm any more than he could.

Helen motioned for him to shove over, and then slid into the seat next to him. She snagged half of his biscuit off the plate and took a huge bite out of it.

"When people don't come back, it makes me worry," she said around a mouthful of hot biscuit. "I like to think that people believe I'm a good doctor."

"Hel, if you quit hounding everyone about getting more exercise and stop eating fried dough, maple syrup and powdered sugar on their French toast, people might actually like you more," Zach teased.

Helen glanced across the table at her sister. "He ordered French toast again, didn't he?"

Jenna nodded.

"Look, little brother, I believe in preventative medicine, but if you want to clog your arteries, go right ahead. Now quit dodging my questions and tell me what it's *really* like inside that place." She glanced toward the kitchen. "Before the two monsters get tired of torturing Cade and come back for me."

Zach grabbed another biscuit out of the basket, put it on his plate and pushed it out of Helen's reach. "Where did this sudden interest in New Jerusalem come from?"

"It isn't sudden. No one in town can talk about anything

else,'' Jenna said. "And since we don't like secrets, we're going to grill you until you give us all the good goop.''

"What's to tell? It's a religious commune. People live there, work there and pray a lot.'' He shrugged. "Not much more than that to talk about.'' He certainly wasn't about to tell the two of them about Teagan and her undercover mission. Knowing his sisters, such information would be all over town two seconds after he left.

"What's their leader like? Is he as whacked-out as every-one is saying?'' Jenna's eyes twinkled mischievously as she twisted her face into her own personal interpretation of a crazed preacher.

"Uh, no. He's actually a pretty articulate guy—good-looking, too.'' He took a sip of coffee. "It's my guess that if either of you saw him, you'd be talking about jumping his bones.''

Jenna giggled and slapped his hand. "Careful. You'll ruin my reputation if someone tells Billy I'm cheatin' on him.''

"Fat chance. Everyone knows you're a lost cause when it comes to that man of yours.'' Zach smiled. He loved making his sisters laugh. As the youngest, he considered it his family duty to keep the family infused with a bit of humor.

"Any chance this religious leader is drugging those peo-ple?'' Helen asked, turning the conversation to a more serious note.

Zach set his mug down and turned his attention onto her. "What makes you say that? Did you notice anything medi-cally that would indicate that?''

"I don't know.'' Frustration shot two perfect frown lines between Helen's pale blond eyebrows. "It's just a weird feel-ing I got every time one of those women showed up at my office. They all seemed so distant. Vague, almost. Like they couldn't put two thoughts together on their own.''

"Is there a drug that's capable of having that kind of effect on them?'' Zach asked.

"Could be a drug. Or it could just be heavy-handed brainwashing techniques. Take your own best guess," Helen said.

"Why would anyone subject themselves to something like that?" Jenna asked. "Not to mention putting their kids through it."

"Because they believe in the man. History has shown that some people have the ability to make people do things they normally wouldn't even think of doing. Case in point—Jim Jones. Hell, that man was so charismatic that he convinced people to go along with their own personal suicide pacts."

Jenna leaned forward, propping her elbows on the table. "Are you saying that you think things are as serious as that out there at New Jerusalem?"

"I'm not saying anything of the sort. I was just commenting on the fact that people can be influenced to do things they normally wouldn't do. I have no real feeling for what's going on out there at the lake." But he intended to. No matter what Teagan said about staying away.

Zach waited for Sally to set his French toast down in front of him and then covered it with a good dusting of powdered sugar and a healthy dose of pure maple syrup. He dug in, hoping his sisters wouldn't question him any further on the subject. He should have known better.

"But you're going to find out what's going on out there, right?" Helen pressed.

"They have a right to their privacy, Helen." He sliced off a hunk of Cade's award-winning French toast and popped it in his mouth. As he chewed and swallowed, he motioned toward the condiments on the opposite table. "Grab me that other jar of syrup, will you?"

Jenna grunted and scooped the jar off the neighboring table. "Privacy is fine if you're following the rules of society. But if we have a group of nuts living up there, we need to know."

"Believe me, big sister, if anyone is breaking the law, I'll find out about it." He pointed his fork at his plate. "Now, would either of you mind if I ate in peace? I prefer to arrive

t work without feeling as though my stomach is going to
growl the entire morning.''

Helen stood up. "Okay, little brother, we'll leave you
alone." She glanced at Jenna. "But you better keep us
posted.''

Zach speared another hunk of French toast. "Oh, yeah, I'll
put the two of you at the top of my list of people to keep
informed.''

Helen hit his shoulder playfully. "Don't be so cocky. If
you don't watch out, Jenna and I will head up there and do
some of our own investigating.''

She and Jenna laughed.

Zach reached out and grabbed Helen's hand. "Don't even
joke about that." He allowed his gaze to capture the attention
of both sisters. "I think this man is dangerous. Don't ask me
why. Don't ask me to explain. Just take my word for it. Stay
clear of New Jerusalem and let me do my job. Okay?''

Both sisters nodded in unison, their faces telling him that
they'd heard and were registering the seriousness of his
words.

With a nod of relief, Zach turned his attention back to business of finishing his breakfast. As his sisters talked softly to
each other about family matters, Zach's thoughts turned to
how he was going to get back inside the religious compound.
Leaving Teagan to deal with Daniel Mercy on her own was
not something he was willing to accept.

In fact, Daniel Mercy hadn't seen the last of him. As he
chewed the last of his breakfast, Zach decided to head back
up to the compound. He'd call the office and tell them to
expect him later. He'd also ask one of his deputies to do a
check on Daniel Mercy, shake the tree a bit and see what fell
out.

He intended to make himself a fairly regular visitor to the
religious compound. At least until he figured out why the hair
on the back of his neck insisted on standing on end whenever
he came in contact with New Jerusalem's charismatic religious leader.

Chapter Five

The oatmeal sat in the plastic dish, stone-cold and as lumpy as a laundry bag filled with unwashed socks. In fact, it tasted like unwashed socks.

Even worse, the bread was stale, and not even the act of toasting it and spreading a thick coating of cheap oily peanut butter could hide the moldy taste.

Teagan choked down a mouthful and then paused to watch the pregnant woman with an infant in her arms who sat across from her. In hushed tones, she tried to convince her overactive seven-year-old to sit still until breakfast was done.

The boy shoveled cereal into his mouth and jiggled up and down on the bench, vibrating the wooden plank from one end to the other. As soon as he scraped the bottom, he reached over and dug into his mother's bowl. With a tired smile, she pushed her portion in front of him, her hand coming up to stroke the back of his head.

Teagan slid her own bowl across the table to the woman, concerned that the mother was so thin she could have worn a child's dress and made it look like a muumuu. With one hand, she shifted the baby and glanced up in surprise. Her light eyes, the color of washed-out moonstone, ringed with dark circles, smiled her appreciation.

"Thank you," she mouthed silently.

Teagan nodded. Neither dared speak. Mercy had an iron

lad "no-talking-during-meals" rule, a blatant but familiar
echnique to help him keep the lines of communication closed.
Nothing was said without him knowing about it.

The woman dipped her spoon in and started eating the thick
oncoction, her jaw chewing through the lumps with a mind-
ess rhythmic motion. Teagan wondered how she managed to
eed the infant, let alone her unborn child, on the rations they
were getting. From the looks of things, she gave up a lot of
er own nourishment to feed the boy.

She glanced down the length of the table at the other tired,
wan faces. No one looked up. No one spoke. Everyone was
nore than a little weary after last night's fire.

A half bowl of oatmeal and a slab of toast weren't going
o hold most of them until lunch, and they still had a full day
f hard labor ahead of them. But not one of them had the
nergy to complain. They ate in silence and worked on com-
nand.

The seven-year-old finished his mother's cereal and ducked
nder the table before she could stop him. He giggled as he
cooted out the other side and ran for the door, never once
ooking back.

Picking up her empty tray, Teagan carried it to the dish
oom, and then headed for the door. Everyone had received
heir day's assignment earlier via a list posted on the com-
nunal bulletin board in each cabin.

Teagan hadn't found her name listed anywhere. Strange,
nd not what she'd come to expect. She couldn't help but feel
slight twist of anxiety in the pit of her stomach—a sensation
hat had nothing to do with the food and everything to do
rith not knowing what was going to happen next.

As hard as she worked to resist Daniel Mercy and his
hought-reform program, there was no denying its insidious
ffect. A change in routine was cause for concern, and she
vas luckier than most of the people inside the compound.

She was aware that a mind-control program was being used
n her. The others were blind to it. They had no idea why

they were plagued by uneasy or anxious feelings. Dani Mercy had managed to convince them that pressures from th outside—unbelievers and sinners questioning their way life—were at the root of their unease.

Teagan took a deep breath. Waiting was hard, but she kne the reverend would let her know when he was ready what h had planned for her. Besides, a part of her actually welcome the unexpected downtime. Although she'd completed a de tailed map of the entire compound, she still had two building that needed a thorough going-over.

Unfortunately, the two buildings left were the Temple an Daniel Mercy's private living quarters. Both were carefull guarded, and she knew that getting close wasn't going to b easy. But Teagan was confident she'd figure out a way to g inside undetected.

As she stepped out the side door of the dining hall, th sound of high-pitched voices hit her. The noise was startlin after the oppressive silence of the hall.

Curious, she walked around to the back of the buildin and located the source. A group of boys were running up an down a dusty patch of ground, engaged in a wild game basketball.

The makeshift court was used by the reverend to rewar the kids who followed directions and didn't make noise durin church services. Teagan had noticed that the kids gathere there every moment they had free, which, when it came rigl down to it wasn't often. Apparently a group of them ha snuck out right after breakfast to get in a few moments free play.

Two slightly listing poles with wicker baskets perched ne the top served as the hoops. The bottom of both baskets ha been cut out. Someone had gone into town and purchased ball—a bright orange one with the names of athletes sprawle all over it in black script.

The kids had organized themselves into two scraggly team a mass of wiggling, squirming bodies racing back and fortl

hoving and pushing to get the ball. There didn't appear to
e a lot of rules to this particular game.

A pile of shirts flung along the side of the field told her
ley were playing Shirts and Skins. Content to watch, Teagan
eaned against the side of the building.

In the midst of the pack, a skinny redheaded kid, covered
a sea of freckles and two scraped knees, jumped up and
own. "Pass it here, Billy! Pass it here!"

Teagan recognized him as the kid who had sat across from
er during breakfast. Apparently, there was a reason he'd
icked down his food so fast. He had wanted a chance to join
le older boys' game.

"Here! Give it to me!" He ran to the other side of the
ourt and bounced up and down again. "Me! Me! Give it to
1e!"

The older boys ignored him, almost running him down in
1eir haste to score a basket. Teagan couldn't help but respect
le little guy's determination. Apparently, giving up was not
1 option with this kid.

As the pack passed the boy again, someone elbowed him
the mouth. Another boy shoved a hand in the middle of
s back, sending him sprawling facefirst. For a moment Tea-
an thought he might burst out in tears. His lower lip trem-
ed, and he seemed to be blinking wildly to hold back the
ood of tears. But he didn't.

Instead, he struggled to his feet. But no sooner did he get
than the pack thundered past, knocking him flat again.
eagan winced. That must have hurt. The boy sat up again
id spat. A mouthful of dirt and a good scrape on his cheek
ere his reward for persistence.

Teagan pushed herself off the side of the building and
arted toward the boy. But then she stopped. Daniel Mercy,
eming to come out of nowhere, scooped the boy up and set
m back on his feet.

She watched in fascination as the man crooked a finger
ider the boy's chin, turning his face side to side as if check-

ing to make sure he hadn't gotten hurt. And then, as the crow
of boys ran past again, he reached out and deftly lifted th
ball out of their hands.

The game screeched to a halt as soon as the boys realize
the leader had confiscated their ball. A sense of uneasines
quickly settled over the pack. They stood with their hands a
their sides, their eyes wary and their bodies tensed for a quic
escape. There were no protests, no shouts of dissent. The
simply waited, resigned.

Daniel Mercy motioned to the younger boy, holding out th
ball and nodding his head toward the basket. The boy seeme
stunned, almost speechless. He dropped his gaze and shuffle
his sneakers in the dry dirt, sending up tiny puffs of dust.

"Go on, Kenny, give it a try," Mercy urged.

Kenny shook his head, suddenly shy. His little-boy bell
stuck out from between his T-shirt and shorts, and his red ha
spiked up wildly in all directions.

A few of the other boys giggled, but they stopped abrupt
when Mercy shot them a look of warning.

"Of course, you can." Mercy took the ball and placed
in Kenny's hands, guiding him down the court to the make
shift basket. They stopped a few feet from the basket.

"Okay, take your shot."

Teagan watched as Reverend Mercy stood behind the bo
guiding his hands into position and giving the ball an ext
push as it left the tips of Kenny's fingers. The ball hit th
rim, circled it once and dropped through. Kenny's mou
dropped open, and his eyes widened with delight. A few
the boys cheered.

Kenny turned on his toes and leaped into Mercy's arm
hugging him around the neck. The embrace was genuine a
sweet. Time seemed to stand still as Mercy's hands came
to wrap the boy in a hug. He held him close and whispere
something in the boy's ear. Kenny nodded eagerly, his arm
seeming to tighten even more around Mercy's neck.

Finally he set Kenny back down, and the boy looked up

im, his eyes brimming with adoration. Teagan marveled at the man's charisma. He had won the boy over in a matter of seconds. What had he said to elicit such adoration?

The boys gathered around Mercy, their former uneasiness soothed by his playful mood. One of the older boys, his face bolder than the scared expression he'd worn earlier, said, "Wanna play with us, Reverend Mercy?"

Another boy scampered after the ball, scooped it up and then threw it overhand to Mercy. "Come on, Father, play with us for just a little while?"

Mercy caught the ball with one hand and grinned. He whirled around and rose up on his toes. The ball swept up over his head and slid effortlessly into the basket. It never hit the sides, just a gentle swish and it dropped down to bounce in the dirt below. Not an easy feat considering the dilapidated condition of the wicker. The boys squealed with delight and scrambled for the ball, already shouting out who was going to be on Reverend Mercy's team.

But as quickly as he fanned their excitement about the possibility of a game with him, Mercy smothered it. He ruffled the scruffy mop of red hair on Kenny and turned away. "No time to play now, boys. I have a burning need to speak with Sister Teagan."

He glanced in her direction and smiled, a dazzling white flash of teeth that was almost blinding in its intensity. A predatory smile.

Teagan's stomach tightened. The wisp of darkness that seemed to hover in the depth of his eyes unsettled her, and she knew on some level that the boys felt the sudden change in the air, too.

They huddled together like an unruly flock of gulls, their easy chatter dying away. They seemed to move away from Mercy as one entity, their faces strained, cautious and closed. No one spoke. No one moved to start the game again.

There was no question in her heart that he'd known all along that she was watching, and deep down inside, she knew that his interaction with the boys had been for her benefit. His reason for wanting that was less clear.

He moved to stand in front of her, his body almost too close, too intimate. "Children are such a blessing, aren' they?"

Teagan nodded. "As long as you're not the one that has to tell them it's time to go to bed."

His gaze captured hers, holding her captive. "Strange, I've never had trouble getting children to do what they're told. I just takes a firm, loving hand." The gleam in his eye heated. "Much the same way as I handle my entire flock—children and adults alike."

"It doesn't bother you to always find yourself telling people—adults included—what to say? What to do?" Teagan held her breath, knowing that it was very possible that she was stepping over the line.

He raised an eyebrow. "Not at all. It's been my experience that most people are looking for direction. That they don't know how to act. How to live a spiritual life. In fact, most people are begging for direction." He shrugged. "I simply provide what they ask for."

Teagan was smart enough to know that she'd lose any religious or philosophical discussion she engaged in with Daniel Mercy. She was much more interested in getting him to talk about himself.

She nodded toward the court. "You're good. Did you play in college?"

"Actually, I never went to college." He shot her a quick glance, his dark eyes seeming to tear into her with a sharp intensity. "Does that surprise you?"

"Should it?"

Again he shrugged. "Some believe that in order to be a true teacher of God's word one must have a degree—a paper claiming you're worthy."

"I've met many intelligent and articulate people who never stepped foot inside a college classroom."

She stepped off to the side as if to get a better look at the boys. But in reality, what she wanted was to put some distance between them. Daniel Mercy's closeness seemed to press down on her, threatening to suffocate her or drown her in his overwhelming presence.

It was hard to erase the pain she'd suffered last night. Pain he had inflicted on her in his attempt to bend her to his will. And now she was witnessing the other side of him. The gentle soul who played with children and talked intimately with adults.

His behavior was disquieting—similar to the parent who severely punished his child and then sought the child out a short time later to soothe and pat him.

"You were very kind to the boy," she said, changing the subject.

"Kenny and his mother have been with me for a long time." The reverend motioned with a casual sweep of his hand. "Walk with me for a bit." Teagan fell in step beside him.

They moved in silence for a short time before he spoke again, "I've been thinking about what we should do about your dilemma."

"I wasn't aware I had a dilemma," she said softly.

"Of course you aren't. It's the reason you rely on me to watch out for your welfare." He turned his head sideways and graced her with one of his enigmatic smiles—a smile that didn't make her wonder what he was truly thinking.

"Your dilemma is Sheriff McCoy."

Teagan's heart beat a little faster, but she kept her surprise from showing. "Exactly how did Sheriff McCoy suddenly become *my* dilemma?"

He stopped and stepped closer, putting an arm around her and drawing her to him. He bent his head and whispered in her ear, "You do realize that any and all relationships are forbidden unless sanctioned by me, don't you?"

A chill shot up her arms but Teagan didn't pull away. "I

explained to you last night that the sheriff and I barely know each other. We have a passing acquaintance.''

"Ah, yes, you did say that, didn't you?" He smiled, his dark eyes sliding over her like a snake over smooth rock. "But casual friendships often strengthen over time, don't they?"

Her legs and shoulders ached with tension from her determination not to pull away from his touch. "This one hasn't. There's been no contact, Father." Teagan frowned, wondering where he was going with this. Somehow she had to keep Zach out of the mix.

"How long did you say it had been since you last spoke to him?" He dropped his arm and allowed her to step back a little.

"Last night is the first time I've seen or talked to him since college."

Mercy frowned. She could tell he wasn't buying this.

"Well over seven years. I wouldn't call that a close friendship." As she said the words, Teagan cringed inwardly. How sad. Her description of her relationship with Zach had a certain ring of truth to it. There had been no communication between them, no contact. Seven years of total and absolute silence on her part.

Not that Zach had made any attempts to contact her either. Somehow, on some deeper level, he had instinctively known that the only way to salvage what was left of his savaged heart was to leave quietly and cleanly, without making a scene or asking for reasons.

But deep down, Teagan knew that Zach had sacrificed a lot to stay away. To never pick up the phone and call her and ask for an explanation. She had seen it in his eyes last night— a familiar shadow of hurt that she'd seen in her own eyes whenever she was brave enough to really look at herself in the mirror.

But Zach had respected her wishes and given her the space she thought she needed. She wondered what it had cost him to do that. She knew it had cost her more than she'd ever thought possible.

Apparently unaware of her mental anguish, Daniel Mercy continued. "After much thought, I've decided that you're going to renew whatever kind of *friendship* you had with Sheriff McCoy. In fact, you're going to do everything in your power to make him feel welcome here. I want you to cultivate his interest and help him to see that he can be part of our little community."

"But why? You tell us that nonbelievers should be shunned and avoided at all costs. How many times have you told us that nonbelievers are dangerous?" As soon as the words slipped out her mouth, Teagan wanted to take them back. She was so focused on keeping Zach out of the picture that she'd forgotten that members of The Disciples' Temple never questioned their leader, especially when they were told what was expected of them in the way of service to the community.

Mercy reached across and grasped her elbow, turning her to face him. He searched her face as if seeing her for the first time.

Teagan's heart rate kicked up a notch. How could she have been so stupid? So amateurish? She was acting like a damn rookie. She needed to focus. To stop getting sidetracked every time her brain decided to take a detour to wonder about what might have been if she hadn't walked out on Zach.

"I'm sorry, Father. I should never have questioned your intentions."

"I detect a bit of reluctance in you, Teagan. Are you having a problem fitting in?" In spite of the soft, melodic tone of his voice, his gaze seemed to bore into her, demanding she acquiesce.

"No, Father. I—I simply wondered what the purpose was of cultivating a friendship with someone outside the faith."

The intensity of his gaze seemed to soften. "Do I ask you to understand? Do I require *any* of my followers to understand the purpose of my requests?"

"No, Father. You ask only that we obey."

He reached up and patted her cheek. "Good answer, Sister. Good answer."

One of the sentries shouted, "Truck approaching!"

Mercy smiled and cupped a hand under her elbow, urging her forward. "I have a feeling that your dear friend the sheriff has arrived."

"You asked him to come back?"

"I didn't need to." Smugness flickered in and out of his smile. "I knew he'd return. A young buck always returns to check on his doe."

The knot in Teagan's stomach tightened. No doubt about it, the reverend had tuned in to the vibes sparking between Zach and herself, and for some reason, he was seeing that interest as something to be encouraged and nurtured.

Her mouth went dry. What kind of trap was he setting for her? Or was the trap really for Zach, with her as the bait?

Apparently Zach hadn't been in a listening mood last night, because now he stood on the cult leader's doorstep, waiting to get in. And as much as she didn't want him here, Teagan couldn't deny that the thought of seeing him again created a pang of anticipation.

She clenched her hands, trying to force the rebellious feeling aside. Perhaps she was even more tired than she'd originally thought. But as much as she tried to deny it, Teagan knew that deep down she was glad Zach had come back. She wanted to see him again.

The thought of coming in contact with his steady, never-ruffled composure sent a spear of longing through her. Maybe seeing him again would reassure her that she wasn't in over her head after all.

Chapter Six

Zach was surprised that the main gate swung open even before he was out of his truck. Birdie bypassed his open door and jumped out the passenger's side window. Seeing Teagan standing next to Mercy, the two framed within the arch of the gate, made it too hard for Birdie to wait. She hit the ground running.

Zach had little doubt that the bird dog's powerful nose had picked up Teagan's scent as soon as they had entered the road leading to the religious compound.

But then he didn't blame the dog for her eagerness. He had fought his own feelings of anticipation while driving back up the mountain. Just the sight of Teagan was enough to tweak the sharp twinge of desire up another notch.

She wore the same kind of baggy overalls she'd had on last night, the cloth worn soft. They were too large for her, the sides hanging down below her waist. The brass fasteners gleamed almost gold in the early-morning light.

In contrast, her tie-dyed shirt appeared almost too small for her slender frame, the material drawn tight over her chest, and the hem a little too short. He could see a slice of tanned skin peeking out on one side. It gave her a slightly forlorn look, a certain vulnerability that almost seemed out of place with the woman he knew. But then he reminded himself that she was playing a role, the role of a submissive cult follower.

"Welcome back, Sheriff," Mercy greeted.

"Mornin', Reverend." Zach dipped his head. "Sister Teagan."

Teagan smiled wanly, her gaze more than a little wary. A small line of disapproval shot a groove between her dark, elegantly arched brows, and a twinge of regret shot through Zach. There was no other way to read that expression than for what it was—outright annoyance that he'd decided to crash her private party. No doubt she was seething beneath her placid exterior.

She bent forward to greet Birdie, and a shimmering sheet of hair swept forward and hid her face from him. His fingers itched to reach out and brush it back, to touch the strands that he knew would feel like threads of silk.

He shook himself mentally. Those kinds of thoughts were reckless and unproductive. She'd made it clear last night that she didn't feel anything for him, other than concern that he'd somehow mess up her current investigation.

Zach didn't blame her for the resentment she felt. Although he wasn't trying to horn in on her investigation, he did have an obligation to the people who voted him into office. Mercy and his organization were big unknowns. Ones that he needed to become familiar with.

If the townspeople and the religious organization could co-exist peacefully, then that was fine. But first he needed to learn everything he could about the group. And if Mercy's sudden show of openness was his way in, then Zach planned on taking him up on the offer. Besides, Zach was fairly certain Teagan was smart enough to understand that he was only doing his job.

"Sister Teagan has been badgering me all morning," Mercy said.

"Really? About what?"

"About when you were planning to visit again," Mercy said. "I told her she needed to have a bit of faith. That you'd be back."

Zach shot Teagan a quick look. She stared back at him, a bland, no-clue-here-what-he's-talking-about expression on her face. In fact, from the tight line of her lips, Zach figured that her seething interior had kicked into a full-fledged boil.

Nonetheless, Zach was intrigued. What had possessed Mercy to say Teagan was eager for him to return? And why the sudden open-door policy after months of secrecy? Something was definitely up.

"I thought I'd stop by and make sure everyone was fully recovered after last night's adventure," he said.

Mercy smiled. "My flock thrives on such challenges, Sheriff. It gives us an opportunity to pull together—to show our strength and commitment to handling whatever the good Lord throws our way." Mercy smiled. "After all, one never knows when the legions of the unfaithful will rise up and attempt to crush us. We need to be prepared for that day."

A chilliness brushed the back of Zach's neck. The man's smile never wavered. It seemed spooky. Almost beatific.

Teagan's assessment of the guy didn't seem far off the mark. The good reverend was teetering on the edge. And all Zach needed to do was figure out when that fall was going to happen, and to keep him from taking a few people with him—possibly even Teagan.

"In any case, I'm glad you're here. You're just in time to join us for morning worship." Mercy cocked an eyebrow. "You will join us, won't you?"

"Can't say that I've been to church in the middle of the week before. But I'm always open to new experiences."

The chance to penetrate the wall of secrecy around the religious cult was too tempting for him to refuse the invitation. He wasn't about to question Mercy's sudden change in policy about outsiders inside his compound.

Mercy rubbed his hands together. He didn't look the least bit surprised that Zach had taken him up on his offer. "Excellent. I consider this a challenge. A challenge to save your sinning soul, Sheriff.'' He darted a quick glance in Teagan's direction. "Isn't that right, Sister?''

Zach didn't miss the faint twitch of amusement that played at the corner of Teagan's mouth. But as quickly as it appeared, it vanished. He didn't doubt that she enjoyed the fact that he'd been labeled a "sinning soul."

Mercy herded the two ahead of him, closing in behind like a father shepherding his two children. "This really strengthens my belief that New Jerusalem and the citizens of Bradley can coexist peacefully."

"Bradley is always welcoming to new citizens," Zach protested.

Mercy quirked an eyebrow. "Really? Then I'm guessing that those aren't looks of suspicion I'm seeing on the townspeople's faces whenever we go into town?''

"All right, you've got me there. My only defense is that we're mountain people." He grinned sheepishly. "Sometimes we're a little reserved. But once you've been here a while, we tend to warm right up."

Mercy rubbed his hands together, an expression of pleasure transforming his face. "Excellent. Because I've decided we need to have a Day of Unity."

Zach frowned. "A Day of Unity?''

"Yes, a day to welcome new friends. A day to forge a deeper understanding and acceptance between Temple members and the townspeople." He nodded his head. "Yes, that's exactly what we'll do. I'll get my people on it right away. In fact, we'll hold it this weekend." He grinned at Zach. "Plenty of food. Music, perhaps. A bit of prayer. You'll help, of course, won't you, Sheriff?''

"I'd be happy to discuss it with you, Reverend. What exactly did you have in mind?''

Mercy shrugged. "Why, your presence and your seal of approval, of course." He stopped and slid an arm around Teagan's waist, pulling her in close.

A knot of muscle immediately marred the dimple in her

cheek, and a flash of displeasure flickered deep within her green eyes. It disappeared almost as quickly as it appeared. But it wasn't hard for Zach to guess that she resented the reverend's show of possessiveness.

Zach bit back his own surge of resentment.

"You'll have to excuse me, Sheriff, but I have a few things to finish up before morning service." As he spoke, Mercy's fingers slid across up the small expanse of bare skin at her side.

Zach's back teeth ached from clenching them. The man's thumb came to rest a mere centimeter away from the swell of her left breast. He seemed to be well aware of it because he stared back at Zach defiantly, as if daring him to say anything.

On the other side of Teagan, Birdie stood, a deep ugly growl issuing forth from her throat. Her brown eyes stared up at Mercy with a glint of unfamiliar malice.

"Sit, Birdie," Teagan and Zach said in unison.

Birdie sat, but she turned an accusatory glare in Zach's direction. She was making no bones about the fact that she didn't appreciate his failure to put a stop to the reverend's trespassing hand.

Mercy didn't appear pleased with Birdie's behavior. "That dog is safe, isn't she? We have a lot of children here at New Jerusalem, and I wouldn't want anyone to get hurt."

"She's okay, Reverend. She just seems to have taken a real liking to Sister Teagan," Zach explained.

"I certainly hope so. I wouldn't want one of my guards to see her behavior as a sign of aggression."

The man's tone was ominous, and Zach knew without question that it was a very real warning. "I'll keep a close eye on her."

"I appreciate that. And now, I'll leave you in the capable hands of Sister Teagan. She'll show you around, won't you, Sister?"

"Yes, Father." Her tone was flat, and a oddly eerie expression of total obedience occupied the fine lines of her face.

"She'll answer any question you might have about our little community." Mercy dropped his arm from around her waist and turned away, but then he stopped and turned back. Without saying a word, he reached out and gently straightened the strap of Teagan's overalls, his fingers skimming the blade of her shoulder. The touch was intimate. Possessive.

The hot breath of rage scorched Zach's throat, but he kept it from registering on his face. He knew without question that Mercy's gesture was for his benefit. A blatant gesture meant to signal one more time that Teagan belonged to him.

Mercy turned and smiled at Zach, and the pure glitter of triumph seemed to taunt him. To dare him to question the rightness of his touch. "Take your time, Sheriff. You and I will meet later to discuss your thoughts on my little paradise."

Before Zach could swallow against the black rage that thundered in his ears, Mercy took off in the direction of the largest, most meticulously tended building in the compound. It butted up against the rocky face of the mountain and hosted an imposing wooden cross over the double doors.

Zach figured it had to be the cult's actual place of worship. The Disciples' Temple.

Halfway across the compound, two men stepped out of the shadow of the watchtower and joined Mercy. They closed in on either side of the charismatic preacher and sheltered him with their bulk.

Without turning to look at him, Teagan snapped, "What the hell do you think you're doing?"

Zach laughed. "Tsk tsk, Sister, such language."

With Mercy gone, she obviously didn't feel compelled to hold back. Her eyes narrowed and she spit the words out from between clenched teeth. "I'm not joking, Zach. You need to take Birdie and get out. *Now.* You're compromising my mission."

"Relax. If you don't calm down, someone is going to think something is wrong."

He took a moment to survey the layout of the camp in

daylight. The watchtower stood inside the farthest front corner of the fence and seemed to loom over everything. Two men stood guard in the tower—one focusing his attention outside the wall, and the other observing the goings-on inside the camp. Apparently, Reverend Mercy was just as watchful of his faithful flock as he was of outsiders.

Although neither man standing in the tower appeared to be carrying a gun, Zach had no doubt that a small arsenal was hidden somewhere within easy reach of the guards. No one built a watchtower like that unless they felt they needed it for protection.

He nodded his head in the direction of the tower. "Ever been up there?"

Teagan shook her head. "Only the 'Chosen Elite' are permitted access."

"The 'Chosen Elite'?"

One of the men in the tower had stopped his careful pacing around the inside perimeter of the tower. He folded his arms and his gaze was locked on them. His expression wasn't one Zach would have expected to be on someone who was supposedly living a life of enlightenment and grace. It seemed closer to the look he'd seen on a few hardened drug dealers and lifetime criminals he'd dealt with over the years. The gaze was meant to intimidate.

Teagan nudged him gently with her elbow. "Don't get into a staring match."

"I wasn't staring. Just observing."

"Well, don't. People don't like it when outsiders get nosy. Come on. Let's get started with the tour."

Zach followed her, but didn't hold back on his questions. "Who exactly are the 'Chosen Elite'?"

"They're members of the group that Mercy has selected as the Lord's elite army. According to what I've been able to gather—from lectures, sermons and the occasional scrap of gossip—the 'Chosen Elite' are considered the most devoted and faithful of Mercy's religious family. They're responsible for identifying backsliders from among the other members.'' She glanced up at him. "You know—the ones who get too nosy and don't follow along without creating a few waves.''

"So what you're telling me is that they are there to spy on everyone else. To make sure everyone is toeing the line, right?''

Teagan nodded. "A fair enough description. But among the members, being selected to become one of the 'Chosen' is a pretty high honor. Mercy talks all the time about the 'Chosen Elite' as the ones who will be lifted to Heaven before the 144,000 pure and deserving. Guess that makes for a lot of competition for the few available slots.''

"Only 144,000 pure and deserving folks get to go, huh? How'd he come up with that number?''

"I guess you don't know your book of Revelation, do you, Sheriff?''

"Part of the Bible, right?''

Teagan nodded again. "According to what I've learned over the past few months, John, the apostle who wrote the book of Revelation, saw a vision of the lamb. Theologians believe the lamb represents Jesus.''

"Heavy-duty stuff.''

"You're telling me? I only had a crash course before entering the cult, so I'm not claiming to be an expert.'' She glanced around, obviously nervous about being overheard. "According to the experts, John's vision revealed that the lamb took 144,000 sealed believers with him into Heaven. The 144,000 are the faithful who wore God's seal rather than the beast's mark.'' She reached up and brushed back several strands of hair. "In case you're a virtual beginner at all of this, the beast represents Satan.''

"I gathered that. So I'm guessing that Mercy views me as one of the unfaithful, huh?''

"Anyone who isn't a member of Daniel Mercy's family is, in his eyes, 'destined to be slaughtered as God's judgment comes to pass.'''

"Sounds harsh…and more than a little painful."

"His name might be Mercy, but he doesn't have a lot of mercy when it comes to his sermons. The old fire and brimstone style of lecture comes to mind when I think of Daniel Mercy. You'll get your own taste of his style in a little bit."

"From your skeptical tone, I'm guessing you haven't yet been tapped to join the 'Chosen Elite,' huh?"

Teagan smiled crookedly. "Let's just say I'm not holding my breath. Hopefully, I won't be around long enough for that to happen. Most of the people who attain that kind of status have been with the reverend for years. They are a pretty close-knit group."

"Who knows—if you manage to convert me, you might get a promotion."

"I think Daniel Mercy has other plans for you. He's too smart to think he could actually convert you."

Up ahead, two women exited one of the long buildings, and Teagan stiffened. She pointed to the cluster of structures and said in fairly good imitation of a tour guide, "These are the living quarters for the members. Women and children occupy the three buildings on the right and the men live in the other three."

The two women passed and nodded silently to Teagan. Zach didn't miss the sideways glance of curiosity directed toward him, but when he touched his finger to his hat and murmured a soft "Good morning," both women lowered their gaze and continued on without speaking.

"None of the women will speak to you, unless given permission by Reverend Mercy," Teagan said. "Mingling among the sexes is pretty much discouraged around here—except when it comes to Daniel Mercy himself."

"Meaning what?"

"No sex for anyone except him—and maybe a few of his most loyal followers. As for the good reverend, I'm fairly certain he's sleeping with whomever he pleases—married or single."

"You mean he's sleeping with members of the cult?"

Teagan nodded. "He taps any of the female members he takes a fancy to. From what I've been able to tell, no one refuses him."

Zach could barely get the words out. "Has he bothered you?"

Teagan shook her head. "No, I've been exempt up to this point. I'm hoping he holds out until after I get this case finished. I have a feeling that if I rebuff his advances I'll be out of this place pretty fast."

"How do the male members of the cult handle this rule of no physical contact among the sexes?"

Teagan glanced over she shoulder, her eyes carrying more than a hint of anxiety. Her vigilance was more than keen. It was rabid. But Zach understood. Living under the tight constraints of any type of undercover work had to be difficult. Teagan lived under something worse—Mercy's tyrannical dictates.

"I get the feeling that it puts everyone on edge. But then lack of food, sex and sleep can do that to a person." She sighed. "Reverend Mercy tries to keep everyone off balance. There are night services, early-morning services, spur-of-the-moment services and more manual labor than the average person is used to doing. When people are allowed to sleep around here it's like the sleep of the dead."

"Sounds like a hard life."

Her eyes met his, the seriousness of her expression almost as chilling as Mercy's. "This is a hard place. Daniel Mercy never stops talking about the end of times—it's like he's obsessed with the book of Revelation." She started walking again. "He's reinforcing the compound like he expects us to be overrun by the United States Army at any moment."

Zach lowered his voice to just above a whisper. "Do you have evidence that they're stockpiling weapons?"

Teagan shoved her hands into the pocket of her pants. He

could tell that she was torn, concerned about how much to tell him about her mission.

"I'm almost certain he's got weapons, but I can't figure out where he's got them hidden. I've seen a few hunting rifles, and the men target-shoot out back near the obstacle course, but I haven't seen any automatic weapons or explosives."

"So why the feeling that he's preparing to be overrun?"

"Because the majority of our time is spent reinforcing the outer perimeter." She led him around the back of the bunkhouses. Zach was surprised to see an area filled with stack upon stack of cinder blocks and bricks. Off to one side, several piles of sand, complete with shovels and cloth bags, sat next to carefully stacked rows of newly filled sandbags.

"I can't tell you how many sandbags I've filled and placed along the wall this past week." Teagan reached up and absently rubbed the muscles of her upper arms. "I may never complain about working out at the gym again."

"Can't say that the minister of my local church has ever asked the congregation to fill sandbags or reinforce the church walls." Zach grinned. "We usually bond over the Thursday-night covered-dish dinners."

She ignored his attempt at humor. "Come on, I'll show you around the barn. I'm pretty familiar with it."

"Why? You think that's where they're stockpiling the weapons."

She laughed. "Not as far as I can tell. I just know every inch of the place because I've spent more than a few hours shoveling manure there."

She took off at a fast clip, her long legs in their baggy overalls eating up the ground. He followed at a slower pace, enjoying the view.

MERCY STEPPED into his cottage and paused to suck in a lungful of cool air. He sighed. Shortly after settling into the quaint little house, Mercy had ordered a few of the more skilled members to install central air. Since the humid heat of July had settled over his mountain paradise, he was glad he'd had the forethought to get it done.

He pulled his sweat-soaked T-shirt away from his chest and allowed the cool air to slip up beneath his shirt and fan his moist skin. The heat never used to bother him, but lately he found himself less and less tolerant of any type of discomfort, physical or mental.

So what if his flock had to deal with the oppressive heat, trapped inside the long, poorly ventilated bunkhouses? None of them dared to complain. They all knew he had earned the right to any and all luxuries. He was entitled. Hadn't he suffered enough for his people, trying to help them see the light? To straighten out their useless, sinning souls before they were forced to face the Lord's judgment?

As he shut the door, Mercy contemplated a pick-me-up to fortify him for the ordeal of morning worship. Hell, he deserved to celebrate. He was certain he'd hooked the country bumpkin of a sheriff. The guy couldn't keep his eyes off Sister Teagan, and since she was willing to do anything Mercy said, the sheriff was comfortably in Mercy's back pocket. He'd reel him in like a trout on a line.

He reached up and rubbed his forehead. He'd overindulged last night and a sharp pain had taken up residence between his eyes, pounding and aching until every brain cell seemed to scream for attention.

Maybe he needed more than a shot. Or perhaps he needed something stronger to help the words slide off his tongue with greater ease.

But before he could make a decision, Cyrus stepped out of his study. "Winston Chandler's on the phone for you. He's been calling all morning. He wasn't too happy to hear you weren't available."

"Our Mr. Chandler is a man used to getting his own way."

Cyrus closed the study door and walked over. "Well, he started out rude all right, but he backed off pretty quick. He ctually ended up apologizing." He gave Mercy a questioning ook. "What did you say to get his attention?"

Mercy smiled, savoring the moment. "I simply reminded im that he is a loving father."

He walked over to the small kitchen area set up just off the iving room. Things were definitely falling neatly into place. He had been trying to get through to the famous news reporter or days. Now the immensely popular news commentator of he blockbuster TV program *Hard Exposure* was calling him.

The sweet taste of victory surged through Mercy. Vengeance was finally within his reach. He'd have revenge for he smear job Chandler and his primetime news show had lone on the church and his reputation last year. The stories pread about him would be revealed to be exactly what they vere—outright lies. Soon all would see that he preached the oure truth for salvation.

It still infuriated Mercy that he had given Chandler unprecedented access to the Temple and his followers. He had opened his arms, his heart and his church to the man, and instead of portraying the good he did, the man had stabbed him in the heart and ripped him to shreds in public.

The show had highlighted the gripes and complaints of a few disgruntled and bitter ex-members of the Temple—backsliders and sinners all of them. Mercy wasn't about to forget uch transgressions. Retribution was near, especially now that he had Chandler right where he wanted him.

"How long has he been waiting?" He leaned down and opened a cabinet, retrieving a bottle of bourbon. As he plucked a glass from the sink drawer he decided to go easy on the hard stuff. He needed to stay sharp because the sheriff vas still on the premises.

"Another call came through a few minutes ago. I told him ou weren't available, but he said he'd wait." Cyrus shot him ne of his sharky smiles. "The man is definitely hot to talk o you."

"Tell him I'll be with him shortly." Mercy sprawled into

his lounge chair and took a sip of his liquor. "Tell him I'm busy conducting his daughter's private Bible study class."

A confused frown knitted Cyrus's heavy brow. "But his daughter isn't due in until later today."

"Ah, but Mr. Chandler doesn't know that, does he? And have no intention of wasting this perfect opportunity to turn the knife."

"He says he's coming up here to talk to you—alone."

"Of course, he's coming here." He rested his head back reveling in the buttery softness of the leather. "But he won' be coming alone. He'll be bringing his entire production crew."

Cyrus frowned, his confusion evident. "You *want* him back here with his cameras?"

Mercy rolled the smooth rim of the glass along his bottom lip. "I'm going to teach Mr. Chandler how a real news show does an in-depth interview—an interview that will shock the world with its wondrous revelations. Now go tell him that I'll call him later. Tell him I'm busy."

Lifting his head, he motioned Cyrus back into his study to deliver his message. While he waited, he sipped the bourbon enjoying how perfectly the tide had turned.

A few minutes later, Cyrus reappeared, his grin even wider "He won't hang up. He'd said he'd wait until you could come to the phone. I think he almost choked when I told him that you were with his daughter."

Mercy rested his head back on the soft cushion. "When exactly does his little darlin' arrive?"

"Today around eleven o'clock. But that brings up another problem."

Mercy lifted his head. "What now?"

"I got a call from Sarah. She says that the bus driver left the Boston retreat house several times this past week. She's not sure he's going to work out. Apparently he was gone for over three hours yesterday—alone."

Cyrus stepped farther into the room, his eyes narrowing

slightly as he warmed to the subject. "Both Sarah and I think something's up. He's done this once too many times. He's making Sarah nervous." He drew a hand through his dark hair. "Hell, he's making me nervous. Sarah says she doesn't think she can keep track of him anymore."

"Anyone have an idea where he goes?"

"His tail lost him in the downtown traffic. The guy is too quick."

Mercy nodded. "We'll take care of him when he gets here. After I'm done talking to Chandler, I want you to call Sarah and tell her to gather up the last remaining members and bring them on a bus tomorrow. Tell her I need her here. The time to act is getting closer."

"Who will take care of things down in Boston?"

"No one. We're closing the Boston retreat. I want everyone here. It's time to prepare."

Cyrus nodded toward the main compound. "What about that nosy sheriff wandering around the place?"

"What about him?" Mercy hid his smile behind the glass. It always amused him when his staff couldn't keep up with him. Or when they failed to understand his genius. Poor things. They missed the exhilarating rush that went with his kind of astounding creativity.

"He makes me nervous."

"Ah, but Sheriff McCoy is going to help me convince Mr. Chandler that it's safe to bring his whole production crew here."

"I thought he already told you that he was coming alone. That the issue of his daughter was personal and had nothing to do with his damn show."

"Oh, he did. But I think that when he finds out that the local sheriff and the town of Bradley have embraced me and the Temple, he'll change his mind about doing a live show from inside the compound of The Disciples' Temple."

"They've *embraced* us? Since when?"

"Since a short time ago. With the help of Sister Teagan's

beauty, I'll have Sheriff McCoy eating out of my hand in no time at all.''

Mercy allowed his lips to spread into a slow grin, noting the scowl on Cyrus's face at the mention of Sister Teagan. The man still hadn't given up on that delightful little piece of fluff. Not that Mercy blamed him. The woman truly was exquisite. He wouldn't mind a taste, either. But he was smart enough to know that little Teagan had much more important uses. For now anyway.

''Go back and tell Mr. Chandler that I'll be with him shortly,'' he said, tiring of the conversation.

Shrugging, Cyrus headed back to the phone.

Mercy took the final sip of bourbon and then tossed the empty glass in the sink. It clattered on the edge and shattered.

He didn't get up. No need. Someone else would take care of it. He had more important things on his mind. Like how he was going to organize his faithful followers for their final glorious clash with the hordes of unbelievers who wanted to overrun his paradise. Unbelievers and blasphemers who were destined to witness his greatness from the comfort of their living rooms.

Mercy smiled with satisfaction. Oh, yes, he intended to teach them all the lessons of his God, and he would assist them in understanding exactly how glorious and magnificent his plan for the final conflict was.

Chapter Seven

Teagan led Zach across the compound. The barn loomed in front of them, the double doors open. Birdie trotted ahead of them, her tail up and ears pricked forward as she caught the pungent smells wafting out the doors.

All around them, the compound bustled with activity. Five women hauled heavy laundry baskets filled with wet garments to the clotheslines set up behind the bunkhouses. As they hung the sheets and clothing on the lines, a pack of giggling children ran back and forth between the freshly laundered clothes. It was almost an idyllic scene of domestic life, but after hearing Teagan's take on life inside the compound, he knew that first impressions were deceiving.

Built on the back side of the compound, the barn was the closest to the lake. But even with its choice location, no one got a good view of the lake due to the imposing fence. Zach was beginning to wonder if the fence hadn't been built to keep in the inhabitants rather than keep out intruders.

With the watchtower and the guards posted along the perimeter, the place didn't look much different than a primitive prison camp. He wondered if Mercy was planning on installing barbed wire along the top of the wooden fence to complete the overall appearance of security.

"How closely do they watch you around here?" he asked.

"Close. If you're a newbie and you want to go anywhere,

it's always with a member of the inner circle. Step out of line and your infraction is immediately reported to Daniel Mercy.''

As they neared the doors, three women exited. They carried baskets filled with eggs. A thin woman carrying an infant smiled at Teagan and then shyly nodded her head in Zach's direction. Again, none of them actually dared to speak to him.

Teagan led him through the open doors, and the strong smell of hay, horses and chickens flooded Zach's senses. Born and raised a farm boy, Zach appreciated the immaculate condition of the barn. Bridles and harnesses hung neatly on hooks along one wall. On the other wall a wide variety of farm implements were carefully displayed. Overhead, the loft was stacked with hay and bags of feed.

Teagan pointed to the stalls lining opposite sides of the structure. ''We keep a small herd of milking cows, a few horses and about two hundred chickens. The chickens are in the coop out back.''

''Impressive.''

He walked over to one of the stalls. A sturdy workhorse the color of brown sugar, swung his head around and stuck his velvety nose into Zach's hand. Zach stroked the softness, smiling a bit as the horse blew a snort of warm air against his palm.

Teagan reached into a feed sack leaning against one wall and scooped out a handful of corn. She poured it into Zach's hand and he fed it to the huge beast.

''Oh, I almost forgot. I brought you a little present.'' He reached into his pocket and pulled out a small clear bag filled with strips of jerky.

''You darling man!'' Teagan snatched the plastic bag out of his hand and opened it before he could respond to the term of endearment. She glanced over her shoulder guiltily as she stuffed one end into her mouth. He watched in fascination as she tore off a hunk and chewed quickly, her small white teeth chewing and tearing with a ferocity that was unexpected.

She had barely swallowed before she bit off another piece. 'I'm sorry," she said around a mouthful. "I'm just so darn ungry all the time." She resealed the bag and stuffed it in er pocket. "I'll save the rest for later."

"Why the shortage of food?"

"No shortage as far as I've been able to tell. I think it's ust the reverend's way of keeping us in line."

"Where does he get the money to run this place?"

"Donations from the members. Once a person is hooked, hey're expected—no, make that *required*—to hand over all heir worldly possessions to the church."

She leaned over the top railing of the stall to stroke the orse's muscular neck. "Even the animals are donations. This s Elijah. He's a real cuddle bug. The kids love to ride him— ometimes three of them at a time. Not that they get much of chance to have fun very often."

She rose up on her toes, and leaned in closer to rub the orse's chest. Her shirt rode up a quarter of an inch, revealing he taut expanse of skin directly below her rib cage. Zach truggled to keep his attention focused on anything other than hat sweet stretch of honeyed skin, but it was nearly impos- ible.

For a moment, he was twenty again, making love to her nd running his fingertips over her smooth skin, whispering weet, silly words into her ear. She lay breathless beneath im, her skin flushed with excitement and her eyes slightly lazed. And in his mind, Zach remembered the feel of her ong legs coming up to wrap around his waist and hold him ght to her.

She waved a hand in front of his face. "Hello, Earth to ach."

He shook his head and met her cool, more than mildly mused gaze. "Sorry. Drifted off there for a second."

"Don't do that during Reverend Mercy's sermon or else ou might find yourself singled out for a reprimand." At his

expression of surprise, she added, "Relax, he won't pick o
you. You're an invited guest."

"What does he do if one of his members steps out of line?"

"Shames them. Ridicules them. Essentially makes the per
son feel like a social pariah."

She motioned for him to follow her to the back of the barn
and continued, "Use of public humiliation is a fairly common
technique around here. Daniel Mercy has developed it into a
art form. Members are timid, afraid to stick their necks out."

They entered a small shed built off the side of the barn
Several crudely built wooden boxes with wire doors were
stacked one on top of the other and lined one wall.

"What are these for?"

The words were barely out of his mouth when a tiny nose
sniffing and twitching, poked through the wire door. Teaga
unlatched the cage and pulled out one of the biggest rabbit
Zach had ever seen.

The fur was like black mink, sleek and shiny. As Teaga
lifted him, the rabbit's back legs jumped up and down fran
tically, until she pressed him close to her, cradling his bod
against hers.

"This is Snook. Short for Snookums." She lifted one o
the rabbit's paws and waved it at him. "Snook, meet Zach
He's one of the good guys."

"Cute. Who named him?"

"One of the kids."

He watched her stroke the animal's velvety ears, her finger
gently caressing the pink skin inside. Her nails were clippe
short and unpolished. Businesslike hands. Who'd have
thought such capable hands could be so gentle? So caring?

He reached out and stroked one of the ears, and for a brie
moment his fingers tangled with hers. "It's nice that Mercy
allows the kids to have a few pets."

She nodded and pressed her lips against Snook's neck, bury
ing her nose in his fur. When she looked up, there was a

finite look of sadness in her eyes, something that hadn't
en there a moment ago. Gone was the hard edge of anger.

"The rabbits aren't really pets. Although—" she carefully
aced Snook back in his cage before continuing "—Mercy
ncourages the kids to come up and play with them."

"Why aren't they considered pets then?"

Teagan didn't answer right away. Instead, she stuck her
agers into another cage. No pink nose poked through the
ire in response.

"This was Hank's cage," she said. "One of the kids told
e he used to nibble holes in the shirts of anyone who held
m. His favorite treat was baby carrots."

Her voice was soft, almost hypnotic, and a chill of suspi-
on skidded up the length of Zach's spine. "So what hap-
ned to Hank?"

"Mercy killed him the first night I was here."

"Killed the rabbit?"

She nodded.

"Why?"

She cocked her head. "It was a demonstration. A way to
ow the children who holds the power of life and death in
s hands here in the camp."

She dropped her hand and leaned against the side of the
ed. Her body seemed to collapse in on itself as she squeezed
r eyes closed tight. But she wasn't able to prevent the sin-
e, lone tear from slipping beneath her dark lashes and slid-
g down her cheek. It dropped onto her shirt, leaving a dark
ain.

"He strangled that poor rabbit in the middle of one of his
nting sermons. Right in front of the kids. And then he told
em that if they didn't follow God's word, the same would
appen to them."

"Aww, Tea, I'm sorry."

She shook her head and clutched her hands into fists. She
rned away and leaned her forehead against the wall of the
ed. For a brief moment her shoulders shook.

Zach stepped forward, turned her around and drew her against him, pressing her close. "He's a nutcase, pure and simple."

She took a shuddering breath. "I'm sorry, too." He felt the light brush of her lips against his shoulder as she spoke. "Usually something like this wouldn't reduce me to stupid tears, but lately I feel as though I'm hanging by a thread. I'm just so damn tired."

"It's understandable. You've been under a lot of pressure," he said. "Everything is going to work out. We're going to find the information you need and get you out of here."

She looked up at him, her eyes a dull metallic green. Her indecisiveness surprised him. It wasn't an emotion he associated with Teagan. She was always tough, always ready to jump in and take charge. This was something new.

"What's this 'we' stuff?"

He grinned. "I might not be your partner, but I'm willing to help in any way I can."

"And you can do that by steering clear of the compound."

He sighed. A glimmer of the old Teagan had emerged. Apparently, she wasn't about to give up on her campaign to get him out of the compound. "Have you forgotten how well I know the lay of the land around here? Maybe the firearms aren't even here in the camp. Maybe Mercy's hidden them somewhere outside the camp."

A spark of interest crept into her eyes. "You might be right."

"See. I might just be more help than you think."

She shook her head wearily, her hair brushing his chin and sending a shiver up his back. "Maybe I've listened to his doomsday psychobabble too long. It's beginning to get to me. I feel as though my brain has turned to mush."

He soothed back several strands of hair from her eyes. "That's all part of being subjected to brainwashing techniques. You're tired from fighting a war of words. But you

an get the goods on this guy if you just let me help.'' He
whispered the last few words in her ear.

She didn't respond, but instead leaned against him, her
warmth soaking through his skin like sun-soaked honey. He
an his hand up the center of her back and marveled at the
strength and beauty of its clean line.

His heart pounded against his chest, and he wondered if
he felt it, too. If she somehow knew how completely taken
e still was with her even after seven years.

He didn't want to dwell too long on it, but he had waited
long time for this day. A day when she'd be back in his
rms again, the warm caress of her sweet breath on his skin.
In his arms…

How many nights had he lain awake allowing his mind to
rift back to their time together? Torturing himself with the
memories? And then, when he had least expected it, she was
ere.

The green of her eyes darkened, her pupils dilated. She
pened her mouth as if to say something, and a fear that she'd
ull away—that she'd push him away with words—shot
rough him. He bent his head and pressed his lips over hers,
ealing the protest deep inside her.

He tasted the saltiness of that single tear on her bottom lip.
taste that vanished as quickly as it stung.

She stiffened, and he was sure she was going to pull away.
ut instead, she relaxed against him, and her lips melted be-
eath his like warm chocolate. Her fingertips pressed into his
ack, coaxing him to keep her in his arms.

He deepened the kiss, opening his mouth, and his heart
cked up another beat as she opened to him. She tasted the
ame. A delicious combination of spice and strength. Teagan
ad never done anything halfheartedly, and making love to
er had always been an adventure. Flashes of memory shot
rough his mind as he savored the taste of her.

The kiss went on and on, and he felt as if he were drowning
nd sinking into her. He pressed her up against the wall of

the shed, using his strength and height to overwhelm her, to keep her from pulling away. And she pressed back, her slender frame meeting the challenge of his with heat and passion. Her tongue and hands teased him, pushing him closer to the edge.

"Okay, Elijah, old buddy, food is coming, big guy."

They froze.

The voice floated in from the main part of the barn.

Teagan moved first. She pushed him away, stumbling sideways. Before he could speak, her finger went to her lips, silencing him.

She jerked her head toward the door at the back of the shed, motioning for him to go first.

On weaker knees than he cared to admit, Zach pushed the door open and stepped outside.

Teagan followed.

They stood at the back end of the barn, an area filled with piles of manure and old straw. The smell was pungent and heavy.

No one was around, and they were hidden from the main compound by the barn. A few yards away, a gate led to the lake. It was bolted shut from the inside.

Zach figured the back exit, large enough to drive a tractor through, was used to haul water in from the lake and herd the animals outside the perimeter to graze. Mercy hadn't planned particularly well with this gate in regards to protection of the compound. The barn partially blocked the watchtower's view of it. More than likely this was the gate Teagan had snuck in and out of when she'd come to see him up at the lean-to.

He watched as Teagan carefully closed the shed door and eased the latch shut.

"That was a mistake," she said, her voice harsh and raspy. Her breathing was like that of a runner who had just completed a marathon in the desert heat.

Zach nodded, not sure whether he wanted to trust his own voice. He braced himself against the side of the barn and ulped in some much-needed air for his own oxygen-deprived ungs. "It might have been a mistake, but it's one I'd gladly repeat."

"You wouldn't say that if someone had seen us."

He nodded, and held up a hand to show he didn't have any intention of repeating what had just happened. "Don't worry. realize that. And I'm sorry. I was way out of line back here."

"Let's just agree to leave our hormones out of this investigation." She yanked the strap of her overalls up higher on er shoulder. "Agreed?"

"Agreed."

She glanced over at him, her expression softening. Thanks."

"For what?" He was fairly certain her thanks had nothing do with the lengthy kiss they had exchanged.

"For understanding my indecisiveness a few minutes ago."

He shrugged. "In case you didn't notice, the feeling was mutual."

Before she could respond, the Temple bell sounded, its lear, melodic tones ringing out over the compound.

"That's our signal to worship. Now you'll get a firsthand aste of Mercy's own brand of gloom and doom."

He reached out and caught her arm. "Wait."

She paused. "What?"

"When are we going to meet again? I have a feeling that m going to be escorted off the grounds at the end of this ervice."

"We won't be meeting again, Zach. Not alone anyway."

"What about the lean-to? You were able to break away last me. We need to discuss where he might be hiding this stuff ome more."

Teagan shook her head. "I was caught coming back into amp last time. I can't risk another capture like that."

Zach tightened his grip on her arm. "You neglected to tell e that. Were you hurt in any way?"

"No, Reverend Mercy just let me know that he was going to use me as bait to snare you." Her expression turned puzzled. "For some reason he seems to think he needs you to pull off this Unity Day idea of his. Don't be fooled by him—the idea isn't a spur-of-the-moment decision. Everything this man does is carefully planned out."

She shook her head and the lines of puzzlement between her exquisite green eyes deepened with concern. "I don't know why he wants the people in this area to be more accepting of the Temple—he really doesn't need their acceptance, and it means opening his gates to them. But he's got a reason, and it worries me."

Before Zach could say anything else, Teagan stepped in close, her hand coming up to touch the center of his chest. It was similar to the way she'd touched him when they'd met at the lean-to the other night. But this time, it wasn't meant to push him away. Instead, her touch seemed intimate. Almost accepting, with a touch of regretfulness.

"Let's make an agreement. Let's agree not to push for something that we both know is impossible. I have a job to do and you have a town to protect. Let's not complicate things more than they already are, okay?"

He nodded even though his heart screamed at him to make no promises. Especially promises he wasn't sure he was capable of keeping.

"If you had any ideas where he might be stockpiling weapons you'd tell me, right?"

Her eyes softened and for a moment she looked like the woman he'd fallen in love with so long ago. Vibrant. Trusting.

His heart ached beneath the pressure of her hand, and he placed his own hand over hers, capturing it beneath the weight of his palm. It felt almost small next to his own. Too small to complete such a dangerous job. But inside him he knew there was no one more capable then Teagan when it came to accomplishing the impossible. She would do what she set her mind to do.

"You know I would."

She smiled gratefully and slid her hand slowly out from beneath his. Then, without another word, she turned and led him back out to the main compound. Zach followed, his mind already preparing to deal with the onslaught of Mercy's preaching. He couldn't help but wonder what the man would say that could so affect a person as it had Teagan.

PEOPLE FLOWED AHEAD and around them, streaming through the doors of the Temple. From inside the building, Zach could hear the sounds of a choir, the voices pure and strong, rising up and floating out the doors.

None of the hymns were strange or noticeably different than the ones Zach had overheard walking up the steps of his own community church. But once he stepped through the front doors of the Temple, he realized that the similarities ended there.

The absence of pews of any kind was slightly startling, but no one around him seemed unsettled by it. The cult members moved around and ahead of him, going to kneel on the dirt floor facing the huge stone altar and thronelike chair in the center of the long platform.

"We sit on the floor?" he asked out of the corner of his mouth.

"Everyone sits or kneels on the floor except for Father." Teagan shot him a wry smile. "He's kind of like The King in the *King & I*—no one's head is higher than his when inside the Temple. Unless you're in the choir, or if you're one of the 'Chosen Elite'. Then you're allowed to stand to sing or spy."

Zach raised an eyebrow. "Spy?"

She nodded toward the people standing along the edges of the crowd lining the wall on both sides of the huge room. Most were men, but there were a few women, too. Each stood at parade rest, their hands clasped behind their backs, a grim expression on their faces. They were clearly separated from the general cult members, wearing cloth vests made of a bright red material, edged in gold.

"Those are his private army, the 'Chosen Elite'. During service they wear the vests to identify themselves. If you have trouble or need to leave the service, you have to check with them first. They're there to watch for slackers and backsliders."

"What type of behavior identifies a person as a slacker or backslider?"

"Sleeping, talking or daydreaming during service. Just about anything other than listening to Father with rapt attention."

Zach nodded a polite greeting to the man in the red vest who was standing guard at the end of the row they were filing into. The man stared back, his eyes flat and expressionless.

"Friendly type," Zach said under his breath. He leaned down. "So, what you're saying is that they're Mercy's goon squad, right? The enforcers?"

Teagan nodded, her eyes scanning the crowd. Her gaze settled on a young boy who was weaving in and out of the crowd trying to reach someone three rows ahead of them. The woman was waving, directing the child to her.

Zach watched the boy skid to a stop in front of a woman holding a sleeping infant. "See, Mommy!" he said, his green eyes beneath a mop of unruly red hair lit up with excitement. "I told you Father said he was going to let me be one of the 'Chosen.' I told you!" He fairly danced on his toes in front of his mother, his grin of happiness contagious.

The woman ran the silky cloth of the vest he wore between her fingers. She shifted the infant to her other hip, her expression registering astonishment. Zach guessed that the woman hadn't expected the boy to become a member of Mercy's personal gestapo.

"I'm very proud of you, Kenny."

The boy slipped his hand into one of the deep front pockets "And see all these neat pockets?" He whirled around. "And gottem in the back too!'' He twirled back, around, and almost tripped in his excitement. ''Father says that they're for carrying God's message to the unfaithful.'' He lifted his face to his mother's, and his eyes sparkled with pride.

His mother glanced nervously toward the man standing along the wall before she turned back toward her son and gently took his hand. ''Hush now, Kenny. Let's go find a seat.''

Beside Zach, Teagan had watched the entire exchange with a studied intensity. She gave little away in her expression, but he could feel the tension radiating off her slender frame. She wasn't happy about what had just happened.

''What was that all about?'' he asked.

''It's a family I've gotten to know recently. Nice woman. I like the kid—he's got spunk.'' She leaned her head closer, her voice barely above a whisper. ''I watched the reverend with the boy this morning, and I wondered how he won him over. The vest explains a lot.''

''He looked pretty excited.''

''Being part of the 'Chosen Elite' is pretty intoxicating. It means special attention from Father.'' She jerked her chin toward the empty faces and exhausted bodies dragging themselves into orderly rows. ''When you're tired and beaten down, you'll do just about anything for a little recognition and privilege.''

''The kid said something about carrying a message to the unfaithful. What's that all about?''

''Good question. Daniel Mercy and his group have been alluding to the *message* for the past month or so. Everyone seems to know it has something to do with Mercy's interpretation of the Bible, but he won't tell any of us outside the inner circle exactly what the great event is all about, or when it's going to happen.''

''So, how do we find out?''

''I'm not sure. But his recent talk of a Day of Unity has me worried.''

He started to say something else, but she laid a warning hand on his forearm. A quick glance to the right told him that the guard at the end of their row had stepped forward and focused his dead-eyed stare on the two of them.

Beside him, Teagan knelt. Zach realized that they had been the only ones left standing as the rows behind them began to fill in.

When Zach met the guard's gaze, the man motioned for him to sit down. Zach gave him a conciliatory wave and then sat down next to Teagan, folding his long legs in front of him cross-legged.

"This isn't exactly comfortable," he griped, trying to adjust the butt of his revolver so it didn't dig into his side.

"Get used to it," Teagan shot back. "These things have the tendency to go on for hours."

"You're kidding, right?"

She shook her head. "Not at all. Yesterday we were here until lunch. And then we had to come back afterward for another two hours."

Zach laughed softly. "Must be an awful lot of sinning going on around here that you all need to spend so much time in church."

She shot him an exasperated look and shrugged. Her arm grazed the side of his chest and sent a sharp jolt of awareness through him. A remembrance of their surprising intimacy a short time ago—the silken touch of her fingers in his hair and the smooth sensuous glide of her lips over his.

"The reverend loves the sound of his own voice," she said as she shifted her body away from his. But the room was crowded and the bodies pressed in on all sides, and their shoulders touched again. This time she didn't move away.

In spite of her not moving, Zach could sense the tension in her, the tight guardedness. She was determined to keep herself from reacting to him like she had in the barn.

"What's today's topic?" he asked.

"They're all pretty much the same—the end time is near,

epent and prepare. The faithful shall be rewarded and the rest of us will bite the dust in the most unimaginably horrible way."

"Sounds pretty grim."

She didn't look at him, but her voice sounded weary. "Everything about this place is grim."

Before he could respond, a deep hush settled over the crowd and Mercy appeared on the platform. He was dressed in a simple white robe belted at the waist, and as he stepped to the center of the stage, a bright spotlight bathed him in golden glow, a light that seemed to give him a strange, otherworldly appearance.

Prepared for a show, Zach watched as Mercy raised his hands beseechingly and lifted his face into the warmth of the light. His eyes were closed as if praying, and his expression could only be described as rapturous.

"Am I correct in believing that a lighting bolt is going to appear at any moment?" Zach said out of one corner of his mouth.

Next to him, Teagan shot him a sharp look of reprimand, her gaze darting in the direction of the guard standing at the end of their aisle.

"Sorry," Zach mumbled.

But before Teagan could respond, Mercy's voice thundered from the stage, "It is time, people. Time for you all to stand up and be counted. Time to recognize the signs. Time to realize that your Lord God Almighty is coming. Coming to claim what is rightfully His and He isn't pleased with what He sees."

From the audience, several people shouted energetic *amens* and Zach noted that every face around him was fixed on the reverend. There didn't appear to be any slackers and backsliders in this bunch.

On the stage, Mercy raised a hand, pressed his lips to the microphone and rasped, "The beast is among us, children. He walks among us with his only desire to destroy each and every one of you.''

A chilled hush settled over the crowd, and they waited. Teagan leaned toward him and whispered, ''This is one of his favorite themes. It scares the crap out of everyone. You're in for a good show.''

As Zach settled in, preparing himself for a long sermon, he thought about the ramifications of listening to this kind of talk day in and day out. It was no wonder all the faces in the audience appeared dulled and shell-shocked. They believed what Mercy was feeding them, trusting each and every condemnation he heaped upon them.

It was like standing on the sidelines of the local carnival, watching the barker mesmerize the paying customers. The show was preposterous, outlandish and totally off-the-wall. But the people in the audience were buying every word Mercy was selling. They truly believed the man carried God's message, and in the midst of that message, they had lost their capacity to think and analyze for themselves. And the Reverend Mercy was obviously not above exploiting that very fact.

Chapter Eight

As they all filed out of the Temple, Teagan couldn't help but notice Zach appeared a bit dazed. Although he wasn't pale or rattled, he seemed more contemplative than usual. As she had anticipated, the reverend had put on a good show. A bit more toned-down than usual, but a good one nonetheless.

Zach didn't say anything, and she could tell he needed some time to mull things over. Obviously, Daniel Mercy's sermon about the approaching "end of times" and the need for all to prepare to meet their Maker had affected Zach as much as it had affected her the first time she'd heard it.

She didn't have the heart to tell him that today's sermon was actually one of Reverend Mercy's milder rants, lasting a mere hour and mentioning the final judgment only three or four times.

In fact, the cult leader had seemed more interested in stressing the theme of unity and cooperation between neighbors than ranting about the enemies that were trying to trample upon God's word and oppress the Temple—his usual theme.

For some reason, Teagan had gotten the feeling that the leader had been addressing much of his sermon directly at Zach. Knowing how the man worked, this suspicion made Teagan even more nervous. He was definitely up to something. Exactly what, she wasn't sure.

She walked across the compound with Zach at her side.

Around them swarmed the other cult members, the talk mainl about getting back to work. Most were too weary to eve think about unity and cooperation between New Jerusalen and their neighbor, Bradley.

Halfway across the yard, Mercy joined them. Cyrus an Eddie trailed a short distance behind him.

Mercy barely glanced in Teagan's direction. "So, Sheriff did you enjoy the service?"

"It was a very interesting experience," Zach said noncom mittally, his expression guarded.

"Interesting? Not enlightening or life changing? I must b losing my touch."

Zach laughed. "I think 'interesting' covers it for now."

"I can see that you're a cautious man, Sheriff. Perhaps yo need to come back again and spend a bit more time with us.'

"I'm sure I'll be back. After all, you mentioned the nee for unity among neighbors. I think that's a good thing."

Mercy's smile widened and a sickening jolt of anxiety hi Teagan's stomach. Zach was playing right into Danie Mercy's hands. This was exactly what he wanted. She coul only hope that Zach was aware of that and playing along.

"I see that you and I connected. Please—" he motione toward the gate "—let me walk you to your truck so we car discuss this further."

When Teagan started to follow, Cyrus stepped in front o her, his bulk pulling her up short. "Father wants you to ge back to work."

"But I don't have—" Teagan saw the reverend glance ove his shoulder at her, his eyes dark and vicious. He lifted his arm and slung it over Zach's wide shoulders, dipping his head in toward the tall sheriff, creating an air of complete intimacy. Teagan watched them walk away. One head as light and glowing as the sun overhead and the other dark and malevolent. A shadow passed over her heart.

Cyrus grabbed her arm, jerking her back to reality. "I said he doesn't need you anymore, woman. Now get moving or

I'll tell Father you need another taste of last night's discipline.'' He leaned in close and whispered in her ear, ''And this time Father won't be around to stop me.''

Teagan stiffened, bile rising up in her throat, and for a minute she forgot who she was and what she was trying to accomplish. Her hand tightened into a fist.

''Come with me, Sister,'' a soft voice said behind her. ''We need some help on the wall.''

Teagan glanced around, startled to see Kenny's mother, Ruth, standing behind her. The woman's washed-out eyes pleaded with her to come away. She kept her eyes carefully averted from Cyrus. All the women knew Cyrus was a man to avoid.

Realization of what she was doing washed over Teagan. *Get a grip,* she warned herself. ''Of course I'll help, Sister.'' She glanced back at Cyrus. ''Please excuse me, Brother Cyrus. I forgot myself for a moment.''

Disappointment entered his drab eyes. He had wanted her to resist, to challenge him. ''Well, don't let it happen again.''

She nodded meekly and followed Ruth over to the work detail stacking sandbags against the front wall. As she stood among the other women, she watched Daniel Mercy and Zach continue to head for the front gate.

Reverend Mercy talked enthusiastically, his arms striking the air to emphasize whatever it was he was spouting. Zach seemed content to give him his full rein.

Teagan chewed her bottom lip, dying to know what the two of them were discussing. Unfortunately, there would be no way to find out anytime soon. Not with Zach leaving, and her needing to focus completely on her mission.

Just as well. It was time to focus in and find Daniel Mercy's stockpile of weapons. Something told her that she didn't have much time left. As usual, his sermon had hinted at the approaching battle between the righteous and the unfaithful. The longer she stayed on the inside of the compound, the greater her risk of being found out and pushing the cult leader's paranoia into the stratosphere.

She had risked being caught just now with her careless response to Cyrus's bullying. Losing her composure was dangerous. She smiled ruefully. Who was she kidding? Her behavior in the barn had been ten times more dangerous. She wanted to kick herself for being so stupid, so indiscreet.

What had made her fall into Zach's arms like some kind of rank amateur, forgetting all the rules of undercover work? It wasn't something she did. Ever.

And the fact that the whole fiasco was all preceded by her getting a case of the shakes irritated her even more. She couldn't remember the last time she'd fallen apart like that. She was a professional and what happened earlier should never have happened.

She knew some of the male ATF agents called her the Ice Princess behind her back, and in all truth, she didn't mind. She had learned early on in her career to make sure her gender wasn't an issue. She accomplished that by being fearless. She made the men on her team forget she was a woman.

Sure it hadn't been easy, and sometimes she felt as though she'd been forced to turn off the most vital part of herself—the passionate, sexual part of her being. But she'd done it for a reason—a strong, unquenchable desire to prove that she was just as skilled, just as intelligent, just as quick as the rest of them.

She paused. She might have tried to shut it off, but it had taken Zach McCoy less than five minutes to unlock it with the ease of a seasoned lover. He'd turned her on like a dry match on a windless day. If someone hadn't walked into the barn and interrupted things, she wasn't sure where things would have ended up.

She bent her head and brushed the tip of her nose against the cloth of her shirt. Somehow his closeness to her had left his scent clinging to the soft fabric. The tangy scent of wood smoke and soap filled her nose, making her almost dizzy with emotion. Emotions she had thought she'd successfully buried a long time ago.

Angry, she straightened up. She needed to shake the useless feelings of nostalgia pulling at her. They were only complicating things. Making her job even more difficult.

She bent over one of the wheelbarrows and lifted a sandbag. With a soft grunt, she swung it up onto her shoulder and started for the front wall.

Her arms ached already, and the morning sun hit the back of her neck with a blazing heat. As she dropped the bag on top of another, she told herself that she'd lost control earlier due to her lack of sleep. Her fatigue was eroding her sharpness, destroying her usual caution.

SEVERAL HOURS PASSED as Teagan labored with the sandbag crew. She found herself bathed in a thick sheen of perspiration. Each new sandbag piled up against the wall had her hoping there'd be enough water, cold or hot, left in the tank by evening for a shower. Somehow a sponge bath just wasn't going to cut it this time.

As she headed back for another bag, the droning heat of the sun was broken by the sound of a horn outside the gates—two short toots and then a longer, more demanding one.

She paused and watched as the lookout in the tower signaled the men below to open the gate. Three men lifted the heavy log bolting the barrier, and two others hauled the gate open.

A battered refurbished school bus, painted forest-green with the bright yellow lettering New Jerusalem on the side, rumbled into the middle of the courtyard. Its brakes squealed a bit as the driver parked, and the front door swung open.

Teagan recognized the vehicle as the same one she'd traveled in for her trip to New Jerusalem. Apparently the new members from the Boston house had arrived.

Curious, Teagan maneuvered herself around the other three

women working with her and edged closer to the bus. New recruits were always an interest.

The doors of the bus swung open and people piled out. Everyone carried a variety of knapsacks, shopping bags, pillow cases stuffed with belongings and battered suitcases. There appeared to be quite a crowd this trip—forty or fifty adults with ten or so youngsters all under the age of twelve.

The kids immediately started exploring, but the adults stood together in a huddled group. The mothers called after the youngsters as they glanced about with a certain amount of awe.

The driver climbed down and stretched, his compact, wiry body uncoiling from the long trip. He wore jeans and the same black T-shirt worn by other staff members, but from beneath the hem of his pants, Teagan caught a quick glimpse of yellow socks. Banana-yellow.

Across the dusky compound his eyes met hers and then slid past. Not one tiny flicker of recognition crossed his face, but inwardly relief washed over Teagan. He had finally arrived— Miguel Lopez, a twenty-year ATF veteran, and her partner for the past three years.

Teagan bit back a small smile. He never went anywhere without his lucky socks. Once in L.A. when they were both pinned down in a warehouse by a gang of toughs running a meth lab, Miguel had rolled over onto his back to reload. As he lay on his back, gunfire ripping into the packing crates all around them, he'd smiled over at her and shouted over the racket, "Don't worry, we're gonna be fine. Rosie remembered to wash my lucky socks."

As he jammed a fresh clip into his gun, he lifted one leg to show her the blinding yellow of his socks. Of course, Teagan had been new to the veteran's sock routine and his reassurance hadn't gone real far in regards to comforting her. But now, three years later, the sight of those yellow socks sent a warm sense of comfort through her. Everything was going to be okay.

Her relief was palatable. They hadn't seen each other in over a week. She had known that having no contact with the outside world would be hard, she just hadn't realized how hard. With any other undercover operation she was sure she'd have been fine. But somehow, the atmosphere inside the religious camp was getting to her faster than any drug or firearms operation she'd ever been on. But now that Miguel had shown up, Teagan felt a sense of ease. There wasn't anyone she trusted more to cover her back than Miguel.

But as soon as that thought entered her mind, an image of Zach flashed into her head. Okay, so she'd trust him, too, and she knew on some level that she'd made it through the past two days because he'd been around. But now Miguel was here and she could turn to him for support and guidance through this ordeal with Reverend Mercy. He would help her figure out what the leader was up to.

Even more important than the support she knew she'd get from the veteran agent, Teagan knew that she needed to get information out to her supervisor, and Miguel was the conduit for that information.

Spending any more time with Zach would only lead to trouble. They had proved that fact this morning in the barn. Better to keep her mind focused. Miguel's presence would help that happen.

She heaved another sandbag over her shoulder, but watched from beneath lowered lashes as two of Daniel Mercy's men walked over to greet the new arrivals. They quickly organized the recruits into some semblance of order, the women and children on one side and the men on the other.

Their luggage was piled off to one side. Teagan knew from experience that the belongings would be thoroughly searched, and anything illegal or of value would be separated out. But after a few days inside the compound, none of the recruits would voice any concern about their disappearing belongings. Not after they became so tired, hungry and mentally exhausted that they wouldn't care.

"I'm starved," Miguel said, nodding to the two men. "Is there anything left over from breakfast?"

The taller of the two men checked his watch. "Just head over to the dining hall. The lunch bell will be ringing any minute now. Get yourself in line early."

Miguel nodded and wandered off in the general direction of the mess hall. His gaze never returned to hers; he knew better.

Teagan stuck a hand in her pocket and touched the edge of the crude but accurate map she'd drawn last night after returning from her encounter with Reverend Mercy. It hadn't been easy because the only light available came from a small light drifting into the room from the bathroom. But with a crayon lifted from a pile left behind by a group of children, and a scrap of white cloth, she'd drawn a fairly good rendition of the camp compound.

With the exception of Daniel Mercy's private cottage and the Temple, the map contained a detailed layout of the inside of the compound. Daniel Mercy's house and the Temple were pretty much off-limits unless she was in the company of a member of the man's trusted inner circle.

Her ATF supervisor was going to have to wait for the detailed map of those places. She needed a bit more time before she'd get access to them. But she also knew that things were heating up. The man's sermons were rambling more and more, were more paranoid. If they didn't want this thing to explode in all their faces, she needed to find out where the weapons were and what he had planned for them.

Teagan also knew that she needed to pass the map off to Miguel. He'd be heading back to Boston in the next day or so.

Out of the corner of her eye, she saw the reverend exit his cottage and head for the group of newcomers milling around the outside of the bus. He had dressed for one of his all-star performances. His dark hair hung loose to his shoulders and gleamed as if just brushed.

His ceremonial robe, a loose-fitting white shift belted at his waist with soft rope, hung on his lean frame. Teagan had decided early on that this particular outfit was his savior garb. People seemed to respond enthusiastically to this particular look, especially the newbies.

His two goons, Cyrus and Eddie, followed close on his sandaled heels. Mercy didn't bother glancing in her direction, but Cyrus shot her a quick scowl of disapproval. The message was clear: "Mind your own business, woman, and get back to work."

Like an obedient drone, Teagan picked up another sandbag and slung it over her shoulder. Although she managed to look busy, she kept a close eye on the group outside the bus.

As soon as Mercy reached them, several of the new arrivals surrounded him, their voices rising in excitement. Mercy accepted their adoration with ease. There was no evidence of embarrassment or discomfort as they lavished their praise on him. In fact, he seemed to lap it up, preening and grinning.

One woman reached out and gently stroked several strands of his hair, and her voice, choked with emotion, rose as she talked about her joy at finally arriving at New Jerusalem. She seemed almost overwhelmed, and tears streamed down her cheeks and spilled onto the front of her simple dress.

Mercy leaned in and said something to her, but his voice was pitched too low for Teagan to hear. But even as he spoke to the woman, his interest seemed to lay elsewhere. His gaze wandered over the group as if he was looking for someone. Suddenly, he paused and then brushed right past the woman trying to speak to him. He moved deeper into the crowd.

Finally, he came to a halt in front of a slender young woman with a wild bush of spiked blue hair. A tiny thing, she stood a shade short of five feet.

Accompanying the blue spikes were a series of body piercings—a right eyebrow, the side of her pug nose and a thick hoop through the center of her bottom lip. A black leather collar, cinched tight and studded with metal spikes, encircled her neck. Thick chains hung from her neck and waist.

The young woman seemed to be suffering a rather drastic and public identity crisis, and Teagan was fairly sure that Daniel Mercy's people wouldn't hesitate a second to use her confusion to the church's advantage. She appeared totally enamored with him.

He cupped her chin, a gesture similar to the way he'd touched the boy, Kenny, several hours earlier. It was a gentle, caressing touch. One that drew the girl's attention totally to him. He stared deep into her eyes, as if he had the ability to tune out the rest of the world and connect completely and absolutely with her alone. It was a fascinating performance to watch.

"Welcome, Becca," Mercy's gaze seemed to hold the young woman captive. "I've been awaiting for you." And the words were spoken in such a way that anyone hearing them would truly believe that Mercy had been waiting just for them.

"It's you," the girl said, her voice soft and breathy. "It really is you."

Her eyes lit up, and she stepped forward into his embrace, her head dropping forward to rest on his chest. Even from where she stood, Teagan could hear the soft sigh slip from between the young woman's lips. It was if she'd been on a long journey and finally found home.

The whole performance intrigued Teagan. What was there about the girl that attracted Reverend Mercy to her? It was as if he had excluded all the other new recruits to focus on the girl Becca.

His interest had to mean something. Who was the girl? Where had she come from? And how did she fit into Daniel Mercy's plans?

She watched as he wrapped his arms around Becca's slight body and hugged her close. They stood silent for a moment, an island unto themselves.

But then, one of the other newly arrived temple members tried to interrupt. She stepped forward and placed her arm on Mercy's shoulder. His sentries immediately cut her off.

When she tried to protest, she was led off to the side. No amount of sputtering protests had any effect. As Mercy led Becca away, she seemed slightly dazed and confused. Her steps were shuffling and hesitant next to Mercy's own sure stride. She leaned against him as if needing his support to keep herself upright.

Teagan sighed with weary relief when the lunch bell rang. She rubbed her upper arms, trying to relieve some of the ache. Joining the crowds of people headed for the mess hall, Teagan fell into step.

Hopefully, she would have a chance to get close enough to Miguel to pass him the map and make arrangements to meet later. Perhaps he had some insight into the young girl who had arrived on his bus. But even if he didn't, they needed time to discuss strategy before he left the compound again. And they needed to meet without Daniel Mercy's goons spotting them together.

THE MESS HALL was packed but as eerily silent as every meal. A large group of people stood in the food line, trays gripped tight in their hands and anxious looks on their gaunt faces. They were the ones who had arrived first, hopeful that they'd get through the line before the food ran out. It was every man and woman for himself when it came to eating.

The rest of the members had already dropped onto the long benches around the plank tables. Most sat with their elbows on the table, propping up their heads. They kept their eyes downcast, their weariness evident in the slump of their shoulders. Most knew that they might lose out if they didn't get into line, but they were just too tired to care.

Teagan sniffed the air and her stomach growled. Vegetable stew. She hid her disappointment. At this point she would have promised her firstborn for a piece of real beef or even a few measly scraps of chicken.

Grabbing a tray off the cart sitting along one wall, she stepped in behind the last man in line. When he turned around Teagan's eyes widened slightly, but she kept her expression neutral. Miguel had maneuvered himself into the spot ahead of her.

"Something's up," he said softly under his breath.

Teagan kept her gaze on the opposite wall. "What's wrong?"

The line moved a few shuffling inches as the cooks started dishing up the food. Miguel turned half away from her.

"They've closed down the Boston church and retreat house."

A shot of concern ripped through Teagan's belly, and it didn't have anything to do with hunger. She dipped her head and moved closer. "Do you have any idea why?"

"No." He grabbed a spoon out of the container set in front of the serving line. The line moved several more inches. "Something is up but I can't find out what."

"Are you scheduled to go back to Boston?"

"It doesn't look like it."

He held his tray up to the server behind the counter. The cook set a bowl of stew on his tray, and Miguel grabbed two slices of homemade bread off a metal platter. When he laid them on his tray, the woman reached across and took one slice back.

"Sorry, Brother, only one slice." The woman tempered her comment with an apologetic look.

Miguel sighed and moved on down the line, stopping in front of the huge institutional jug of lemonade.

As Teagan moved along behind him, her heart tightened with concern. This information wasn't a good sign. Reverend Mercy was definitely planning something, but what? If he closed things in Boston then there was no other place to re

ruit new members. And no new recruits meant no new influx
▪f money.

New Jerusalem was nowhere near self-sufficient. They
▪rew vegetables and had a few chickens. That didn't bring in
nough money to feed ten people, let alone the three hundred
urrently living inside the compound.

Teagan held her tray up for a bowl of veggie stew. A quick
▪ook told her that calling the liquid "vegetable stew" was a
▪tretch of the imagination. Floating around in the thin, yellow
▪roth was a single chunk of carrot.

As she lifted a piece of bread off the platter, she considered
▪he possibility of breaking the bread up and dunking it in the
▪tew. She needed something to help fill her up. She moved
▪p beside Miguel again.

"Who's the girl you brought in? The one with the blue hair
▪nd body piercings?"

Miguel added some extra sugar to the pale lemonade and
▪tirred it. "I don't know. But she's someone important. When
▪he arrived at the Boston house, she was never left alone."

"Well, there's no missing Daniel Mercy's interest. And for
▪nce I don't think it's just his hormones kicking in."

Miguel moved off as the person behind her stepped up to
▪he beverage container. Teagan helped herself to a cup of
▪emonade and then glanced around. Her eyes swept over the
▪illing crowd, looking for Miguel. None of the "Elite" spies
▪eemed interested in her or anyone else. They were pretty
▪nuch tied up getting their own trays and wolfing down their
▪wn lunches. One good thing about the low rations is that no
▪ne paid much attention when they were trying desperately to
▪ll their empty bellies.

Miguel had taken a seat at the back of the mess hall, leaving
▪ne spot open next to him. Weaving her way down the
▪rowded center aisle, Teagan pretended to search for a seat.
▪Vhen she arrived at Miguel's table, she quietly dropped into
▪he seat next to him.

She sipped her lemonade as Miguel's hand slipped over to

touch the side of her leg. She knew he was leaving her a note. Opening up her napkin, she reached down and draped it over her thigh, smoothly palming the note and sliding it into her pocket. Without missing a beat, she resumed eating.

"Pass me the salt, please," Miguel said.

Teagan grabbed the plastic shaker and passed it over to him. She glanced at the people around them, but no one seemed interested in them. Their spoons dipped repeatedly into the thin stew, scooping it up as fast as they could shovel it into their mouths.

She leaned closer to Miguel. "Are you going to be able to get out of here at any point?"

"Your guess is as good as mine." He lifted his head and glanced around, his dark eyes assessing the crowd. "We're going to have to regroup because it doesn't look like I'll be making any more runs to Boston or anywhere else. Mercy is definitely hunkering down, getting ready for something big."

That said, he stood up and picked up his tray. As he walked away, Teagan spooned another mouthful of the soup into her mouth. She barely tasted the watery concoction as it slipped down her throat.

No more outside runs. That meant no more contact with their supervisor. It isolated both of them inside the religious compound. Teagan knew that Miguel had enjoyed much more freedom on the outside—the "Chosen Elite" weren't able to follow him every minute like they could here on the inside. She felt as if Daniel Mercy's velvet noose was slowly closing in on them.

ZACH PUSHED OPEN the front door of his office and stepped into the main reception area. The institutional gray chairs lining one side of the wall were empty. Apparently no one had business with the Essex County Sheriff's Department at the moment.

He breathed a sigh of relief. He had enough work to do this afternoon without the usual problems piling up on him.

"Sheriff! I'm so glad you finally got here." His secretary, Candi Talbot, bounced cheerfully out of the small break room at the back of the reception area.

She held a diet soda in one hand and a bowl of something that smelled delicious. Her bright red hair, cut too short and emphasizing her chubby cheeks clung to her head like a shiny helmet.

She held up the bowl. "I just heated up some lunch. You want some?"

"No, thanks." He hung his hat on a hook right inside the front door. "Smells good. What is it?"

"Chicken pot pie, with a real homemade crust." Candi winked.

"Those cooking lessons must be paying off, huh?" Zach shot her a teasing glance. "Tommy Jackson been over to the house to give them a try yet?"

Candi's china-white skin flamed bright red, and she flopped into her desk chair with a squeal of embarrassment. "Of course not. You know he's dating Marsha Hawkins."

Zach laughed. "Doesn't mean a man can't stop by for a nice helping of homemade chicken pot pie."

"That's what I keep telling her," another voice said from the doorway.

Zach glanced up to see his second in command, Deputy Drake Matthews, standing in the doorway. "Guess we'll have to have a chat with Tommy, huh, Drake?

Drake nodded solemnly. "Definitely, Boss."

Candi stood up, alarm written all over her face. "Don't you dare. I don't need you two screwing up my chances."

Both men laughed. Candi was a favorite around the office, and she was a good sport about all the teasing she got.

"Did you have any luck getting that information I requested?" Zach asked, getting serious.

Drake grinned and hung up his hat. "You know me, Boss. I don't give up easy. It took me most of the night, but I was able to come up with some interesting stuff." He nodded toward his desk. "I've got a file started."

"Good. Get it and bring it into my office. We'll take look."

A few minutes later, Drake was settled in the chair across from Zach's desk. He waved a thin blue file. "Every scrap of information I could get on Daniel Mercy is right here."

"Anything interesting? Anything unusual?"

Drake grinned. "Lots." He held up the top sheet. "First off, his name isn't Mercy."

"No big surprise there. What is it?"

"Stewart Thomas Crane. Born forty-seven years ago, in Trenton Falls, Mississippi. His mama was Dorothy Ross Crane—deceased."

"Father?"

Drake shook his head. "No daddy on the birth certificate. But I made a few calls down there to Trenton Falls, and they remember Stewart and his mama real well. Seems that Dot— that's what they called his mom—was a little touched in the head."

"She was mentally ill?"

Drake shrugged. "Not real sure on that. According to the sheriff down there, Dot's parents kept her out of school, homeschooled her. They were real religious people—church every day and twice on Sunday. According to the sheriff, Dot would walk around town talking to herself. Claimed she heard the voice of God."

"In most cases that would qualify you as mentally ill. Did the sheriff know who Mercy's father was?"

Drake shook his head. "Everyone suspected it was some tent revival preacher who blew into town for a week, but it was never proven. The grandparents raised the boy along with continuing to take care of his mama. Seems that they looked on the boy as a punishment for past sins."

"Must have made for a pleasant childhood," Zach said dryly. "The background information fits though with Mercy"

rrent infatuation with religion. Did the sheriff have any in-
rmation on Mercy as a kid?"

"Loner. Got teased a lot as a kid. The grandparents tried
homeschool him but finally gave up when he was eight.
ey sent him to the local public school. Apparently, he was
bit of a hellion."

Zach raised an eyebrow. "What kind of student was he?"

Drake laughed. "According to the report card they faxed
e, he was a hell of a lot better student than I was. Quite a
ience student from the looks of things. He won some kind
award in the eleventh grade—the All County Science
ward in Chemistry."

"So why did the local sheriff label him a hellion?"

"Guess he was a brain but a troublemaker—especially
hen he reached adolescence. A lot of swearing, fighting,
inking and truancy. The sheriff said that if that wasn't bad
ough, he graduated pretty early to girls."

"Graduated to girls? In what way?"

"Apparently the guy was a babe magnet. They flocked
ound him like bees to honey. And he took advantage of it.
ccording to the sheriff, he took off at age nineteen after
tting a sixteen-year-old girl from a locally prominent family
egnant. No one in Trenton Falls has seen him since."

Drake looked up, his expression pensive. "The sheriff did
ention that Stewart knew his Bible up one side and down
e other. He could outquote any of the local ministers by the
e of eight. Guess his grandparents made him memorize
rses as punishment when he was bad."

"Any idea where he went after he left Trenton Falls?"

Drake's grin widened. Zach knew his deputy relished the
pportunity to showcase his investigative skills. "Took me a
hile, but I finally got a lead on him. After leaving Trenton
lls, he headed west and ended up in L.A."

"How'd you track him there?"

Drake's grinned even wider. "Our boy has a record."

Zach sat up. "What kind of record?"

"Seven moving violations early on. A trunk full of parkir
tickets." Drake looked up from the file. "All unpaid for unt
they finally picked him up and squeezed the money out
him. Then there's a few D.W.I.'s over the next few year
Seems that his boozing behavior continued even out there
L.A."

"Not model citizen behavior by any means, but hard
earth-shattering. Nothing any juicier than that?"

Drake grinned. "Well, nothing for ten or twelve years. B
then it seems that our guy found religion again. Apparent
he hooked up with a fundamental Christian church o
there—" he pulled a sheet out of the file "—a place calle
the Holy Church of Redeemers."

"Guess his interest in religion stuck with him even out
L.A."

Drake nodded. "But what's even more interesting is th
he got popped for a couple of misdemeanors while a memb
of the church. And get this, the charges were filed by churc
elders."

"Church elders? How does a person disturb the peace
get disorderly in church?"

"Good question." Drake held up a finger. "It just so hap
pens that I called out there and talked to the current pastor.
He reached into his back pocket and fished out his noteboo
He flipped it open to his notes. "The pastor remembers Stev
art Crane well. Says that Stewie could talk any member
the church under the table with his knowledge of the Scri
tures—including the former pastor."

"So because he knew his Scriptures, they filed charge
against him? That doesn't make sense."

"Well, that's not the whole story. Apparently he was ve
well liked when he first joined the church. He started a you
group, enlarged their shelter for the homeless and increase
the local corporate gifts—food and clothing donations real
picked up under his watch. He also conducted some very po
ular Bible study classes for adults."

Zach frowned, leaning forward to rest his forearms on his desk. "So, why were the charges filed?"

"Hold your horses, I'm getting to that." Drake flipped to the next page. "Apparently things began to unravel when Stewart's head started to swell. He got to thinking that the people saw him as more of an expert than their own pastor. He started interrupting services, actually standing up to correct the pastor during a service. And more than once he jumped up and started preaching his own sermon. They tried shutting him up, even tried kicking him out, but Stewie wouldn't back down. Finally, the pastor got sick of it and filed charges. But Stewie kept coming back."

"Pretty mild stuff."

Drake shrugged. "I guess things really escalated when some of the elders got nervous with his antics with the women of the congregation."

"What kind of antics?"

"The pastor didn't have specifics, but he said that Stewie was pretty slick. None of the women—or young girls—who flocked around him ever accused him of doing anything inappropriate. But the elders decided they wanted him out."

"But none of the charges they brought against him ever amounted to anything, right?"

"Exactly. They'd file charges and Stewie would be back in the front pew, bugging them the next Sunday. But the straw that finally broke the camel's back was when Stewie made an outright attempt to take over the church."

"A takeover? He tried to push out the pastor and the elders?"

Drake nodded and sat back. "Yep, he pulled a mini religious revolution. But the pastor and the elders were able to quash it. By the time they were done, Stewart was out."

Zach started to comment but Drake held up his hand. "Wait, there's more. When Stewie left L.A. for Boston, he took about fifty of the Redeemer parishioners, and more than a few of them were the more wealthy members of the

church.'' Drake snapped his notebook closed. ''A short tim
after he appeared in Boston, The Disciples' Temple spran
into existence.''

''You did a good job.'' Zach sat back, trying not to let hi
disappointment flavor his praise of Drake's hard work. But a
much as he tried to hide it, he couldn't deny a certain feelin
of being let down. The background search hadn't turned u
anything unexpected or surprising.

Drake shot a triumphant smile across the desk at him
''Hey, don't be congratulating me too soon. Wait until yo
hear the rest.''

''There's more?''

''I dug a little deeper and found out that Stewie worked fo
the Ubee Construction Company while in L.A. He apprentice
with their explosives expert and got licensed as a demolitio
contractor.''

An icy finger of dread crept up the back of Zach's neck
He sat forward, his chair snapping up against the middle c
his back. ''Were you able to talk to anyone who knew hir
at the job?''

Drake nodded eagerly, opened his notebook and flipped t
a page. ''According to a foreman who remembered him, Ste
wie was a natural. Better even than some of the guys the
had on the payroll who'd had military training with explo
sives. They were sorry to see him go.''

Zach reached up and rubbed the spot between his eyes tha
had suddenly developed a serious ache. This was not what h
wanted to hear, but it would explain a lot. Especially abou
ATF Special Agent Teagan Kennedy's appearance inside th
New Jerusalem compound. It was very possible that the AT
suspected that Reverend Daniel Mercy was stockpiling mor
than just guns. Perhaps they suspected him of making or sto
ing dangerous explosives.

If that was the case, it meant that Teagan had told him onl
part of her mission. That she had left out the part concernin
the possibility of explosives. But whatever the case was, Zac

tended to get to the bottom of things. Teagan wouldn't be
tting him off so easily in the future. She had a lot to answer
r.

HE EVENING services droned on endlessly. Teagan knelt in
e back, biting the inside of her cheek to keep from falling
leep. Several times she'd actually drawn blood in an attempt
keep herself alert. But after a while, even the effectiveness
the pain was beginning to wan. If things went on too much
nger, she was afraid she'd simply curl up in the middle of
e row and start snoring.

She glanced down at her watch. It was going on midnight.
iguel had wanted to meet her in the barn at midnight, but
w they were both tied up here. No way were either of them
e to get up and leave. Every member of the compound was
uck inside the Temple.

She glanced over the heads of the row in front of her,
arching out Miguel, trying to reassure herself that he was
ill nearby. He was closer to the front, about three rows back
om Reverend Mercy's platform. Although she couldn't see
s face, just a glimpse of his broad back sent a tiny wave of
lief through her.

She sighed. Reverend Mercy had been talking since they'd
ished dinner. The bell had rung, calling them all to the
mple around 6:30 p.m. The reverend had started off the
ening by announcing the closing of the Boston church and
plaining the need for them all to draw closer and take shel-
r in New Jerusalem.

He had then moved on to reading to them from the *New
rk Times*—pausing every once in a while to rant and rave
out the level of violence in American society. People in the
dience kept themselves awake by shouting out the occa-
nal "Amen!" or "Praise, God!"

By the time 9:00 p.m. had rolled around, the comments had
ased and everyone appeared to have slipped into a dazed
ma. They now stared straight ahead, their eyes blank. Up

to this point, no one had fallen asleep. But Teagan figure
that was because they all knew what the consequences wer
if they did—ridicule and a lengthening of the already-endle
sermon.

Focusing back on Reverend Mercy, she watched him pa
restlessly back and forth on the platform. His waved his arn
and shouted into the microphone about the governmental co
spiracy to discredit him and the government's attempt to co
vince them—the faithful—of the uselessness of fightir
against hordes of sinners pressing in on them from all side

And his voice droned on, fading in and out. Exhaustic
pressed down on her. Her eyes closed and then snapped ope
again. Maybe if she just let them stay closed for a few secon
she'd wake up rejuvenated. Her head dipped and her chin sar
onto her chest.

"You!" Reverend Mercy shouted. "You, asleep in t
back!"

Teagan's head snapped up and she glanced around. B
Daniel Mercy wasn't talking to her. He was pointing to
older man, who had slumped over onto his partner.

The old man, his gray hair rumpled and in disarray, glance
about in confusion, his eyes blinking behind thick glasses
he tried to focus. His partner, a slender woman of about six
or sixty-five, was trying frantically to prop him up.

"Stand and face me." The reverend stood at the edge
the stage, his hand outstretched, pointing out the sinner. Th
slacker. Two of the "Chosen Elite" stepped into the row ar
jerked the old man to his feet. "Explain yourself. Tell the
good people why *you* are different. Why you should be pe
mitted to sleep while they pray and make plans to save o
world."

"I—I didn't mean—" The old man's voice trembled wi
age and fear. His hand shook as he raised it up in protest.

"What's your name?" Reverend Mercy demanded, cuttir
him off.

Teagan pressed her nails into the palms of her hands. She

n this drill before. It was the reverend's way of indoctri-
ing the new members into the way of the cult. Established
mbers were expected to gang up on the new member, be-
e and admonish the individual. But it also meant that the
ire service would be prolonged. She could almost feel the
sion of everyone in the room increase several more
ches.

"Alex, Father. Alexander Jacob." The old man glanced
wn at his wife, his face confused. Pleading. She started to
up to comfort him, but one of the "Elite" shoved her
k down.

The old man's face crumpled. "I—I didn't mean to fall
ep, Father. I was tired from the bus ride. We got up so
ly this morning to come here. I—"

"Silence!" Reverend Mercy roared. "I'm sick to death of
ur useless, petty excuses." The crowd shifted uneasily.
ey knew the focus had shifted off the old man to all of
m. "Your stupid pleas for understanding and forgiveness
gust me. None of you—" he jabbed his finger at the con-
gation "—not one single person in here is willing to make
necessary sacrifices."

A cry of protest went up from the members of the audience,
Jo, Father. We're ready!"

"We're not slackers, Father."

"We are willing to make the sacrifices!"

Reverend Mercy waved a hand, dismissing their pleas for
ognition. "Useless promises. Broken commitments. All I
ar from you are complaints and grumbling."

He hefted the microphone and paced to the opposite end
the stage. When he turned to face them again, he had trans-
med his face into a petulant expression. He said in a mock-
, whining voice, "But, Father, my soup is cold."

He moved to the center of the platform and leaned forward
in. "But, Father, my back hurts. Don't make me lift any
re, Father."

The crowd shifted uneasily again; a few people exchang‹
nervous looks.

"Are *those* the voices of God's warriors? Do God's wa
riors say things like that when they've been called upon
rise up and defend the word of God?"

A loud chorus of noes rippled through the crowd. Even t‹
old man who had a moment ago been reduced to tears h‹
straightened his spine, his face a fierce mask of newfou‹
determination and commitment.

Reverend Mercy paused and every person in the audien‹
leaned forward, waiting for his next words. No one was slee‹
now. They were all wide-awake and on edge—unsure of wh‹
would come next.

"I only say these things, children, because we are enteri‹
a new time. A dark time. And I need to know that I can tr‹
you." He raised his hands as if beseeching them with eve‹
ounce of his being. "I need to know that when the trait‹
makes himself known to us that you will see that person f‹
what he is and come to me—tell me who has betrayed us a‹
our Lord."

Again the members' voices rose up in a chorus of conce‹

"You can trust us, Father."

"Show us the traitors, Father!"

The reverend turned around and walked slowly back to ‹
chair. He eased himself into the thronelike chair and slump‹
down as if the weight of every sinner pressed down upon ‹
shoulders. He sighed into the microphone, the sound vibrati‹
and throbbing through the overhead speakers.

The audience shifted uneasily, knowing he wasn't hap‹
with them or their responses.

"People…people…people, *you* are the ones who m‹
point out the traitor to *me*. It is you who will come to ‹
with names of the sinners. Look at your neighbor. Search ‹
faces of your mothers, fathers, sisters, brothers. Question e‹
erything your friends do. Scrutinize the actions of your ch‹
dren. It is you, not I, who will discover the Judas."

Up near the front, Miguel partially turned and glanced back
her. The worried look in his eyes told her what he was
nking—things were now escalating out of control. She
ew he was as concerned as she was that Reverend Mercy's
cture might be a signal that he knew there were agents inside
e compound. Perhaps he had even identified them.

Around them the crowd moved and shifted again. Glances
distrust and suspicion darted among them. Their faces were
shed with excitement as they warmed to the subject of trai-
s. What better way to get people to do your bidding than
ratchet up the paranoia factor another few degrees?

"Time grows short." The reverend stood again and pointed
finger at the crowd, sweeping it across the room to include
m all. "Every one of you will be tested over the next few
ys. Each of you will be asked to perform. To act and dem-
strate your faith."

"We are ready, Father."

"Test us, Father."

Reverend Mercy seemed oblivious to their shouts now. He
emed to be in his own trance, his eyes glazed and the mi-
phone waving back and forth in his hand. Teagan won-
red if the cup he'd been sipping from during the evening
vice contained alcohol or some kind of drug.

A heavy silence settled over the crowd. Everyone waited,
ir faces frozen with anticipation, waiting for Reverend
ercy's next order, unable to move until he told them what
do. Teagan cautiously watched their faces, unsure what
uld happen next.

On the platform, the reverend didn't move. He sat slumped
his chair, the microphone drooping in his hand, his eyes
sed.

Finally, when Teagan didn't think that she could kneel one
re minute, he raised his head and said softly, "Go to bed,
ldren. Go back to your cabins and go to sleep. But stay
rt. Be ready for my call to action because the end is nearly

upon us. And when I call upon you to serve, I expect to
obeyed.''

His head dropped back against the back of his chair and
didn't speak again. Teagan accompanied the crowd leavi
the Temple for the bunkhouses. The murmur of exciteme
rippling through the cult members told her that as exhaust
as everyone was, it would be a while before they all got
sleep. Her rendezvous with Miguel would have to be delaye
No doubt the night was going to get even longer than anti
ipated.

Get FREE BOOKS and a FREE GIFT when you play the...

LAS VEGAS
GAME

Just scratch off the gold box with a coin. Then check below to see the gifts you get!

YES! I have scratched off the gold Box. Please send me my **2 FREE BOOKS** and **gift for which I qualify**. I understand that I am under no obligation to purchase any books as explained on the back of this card.

382 HDL DVEP   182 HDL DVE5

FIRST NAME	LAST NAME

ADDRESS

APT.#	CITY

STATE/PROV.	ZIP/POSTAL CODE

(H-I-01/04)

The Harlequin Reader Service® — Here's how it works:

Accepting your 2 free books and mystery gift places you under no obligation to buy anything. You may keep the books and gift and return the shipping statement marked "cancel." If you do not cancel, about a month later we'll send you 6 additional books and bill you just $3.99 each in the U.S., or $4.74 each in Canada, plus 25¢ shipping & handling per b and applicable taxes if any.* That's the complete price and — compared to cover prices of $4.75 each in the U.S. and $5.75 each in Canada — it's quite a bargain! You may cancel at any time, but if you choose to continue, every month v send you 6 more books, which you may either purchase at the discount price or return to us and cancel your subscrip

*Terms and prices subject to change without notice. Sales tax applicable in N.Y. Canadian residents will be charged applicable provincial taxes and GST. Credit or Debit balances in a customer's account(s) may be offset by any other outstanding balance owed by or to the customer.

Chapter Nine

he next morning, Teagan found herself standing on a moun-
ain trail several miles from the compound. Concern and
orry ate at her. Miguel's note, the one he'd passed to her
uring lunch, had made arrangements for them to meet in the
arn sometime after midnight. Teagan had waited over two
ours for him, crouched against the back wall of one of the
orse stalls. But Miguel had never shown up, and she'd finally
een forced to return to her bed.

At breakfast, she had searched the mess hall and compound
or him. But she had come up empty-handed. It was if he had
anished off the face of the earth. She didn't dare question
nyone inside the camp for fear of them reporting her interest
in the bus driver.

When she discovered that she'd been assigned to a job out-
de the camp, her concern had skyrocketed. New members
idn't typically get assignments for outside work. With Mi-
uel among the missing, the assignment only served to make
er more uneasy.

She paused to study the group spread out along the trail
head of her—four other women from the Temple and their
hildren, the boy, Kenny, his baby sister and two other eight-
r nine-year-old girls she'd seen running around the com-
ound. They were all busy stuffing handfuls of fresh blue-
erries into canvas bags slung over their shoulders.

A member of the "Chosen Elite" had dropped them of earlier, gruffly instructing them to fill as many bags as pos sible. He then mumbled something about being back aroun dinnertime to pick them up.

Teagan bent down and grabbed a handful of berries off th bush and stuffed them in her bag. She couldn't help but worr about Miguel. What if someone had seen them talking yes terday during lunch? Guilt tore at her as she considered th possibility that someone had found the map of the camp she' given him. Such a discovery would put him in the worst pos sible position with the reverend. The man was parano enough without finding a detailed map of his camp.

She dropped another handful of berries into the bag slun over one shoulder and straightened up. It was only 9:00 a.m and the temperature was already up in the eighties. By noo it would hit ninety. She wiped a fine sheen of sweat off h forehead.

She glanced over at the two jugs of water they'd taken o the truck and carted over into the shade. Water but no foo Oh well, there were enough berries to fill the canvas bags an the children's stomachs, as well. Even the adults would get chance to eat heartier than usual—if they allowed themselv the luxury. Teagan planned on feasting on them first chanc she got. She just wasn't too sure about the other adults.

She paused. Had she done something wrong that had gotte her sent on this detail? Perhaps it wasn't her conversation wi Miguel that had gotten her sent outside the compound. May someone had witnessed her kissing Zach and reported it Reverend Mercy?

She pushed the thought aside. No, not likely. Even thoug there were spies galore inside the camp, she was positive i one had been nearby. Their indiscretion had been ill-advise but she was positive that no one had seen them.

She stretched, a hand pressed to the base of her spine she tried to get the kinks out. Sunlight drifted down throug the leaves overhead, hitting her face and lips with its warmt

s touch triggered a memory of Zach's lips on hers, and she
n the tip of her tongue along her bottom lip, hoping that
e could still capture the taste of him.

She knew the thought was ridiculous. Silly even. But she
ill longed to savor the steamy taste of him. A familiar twinge
heated passion she'd tried so hard to tuck away and forget
ashed over her.

What had made her believe that she was actually capable
walking away from Zach? Had she really been so naive
at she'd thought that she could erase the memory of him?
ot a chance.

"Hey!" Kenny shouted from somewhere up the trail.
Look down there!"

Startled, Teagan snapped out of her daydreaming. A short
stance away, Kenny stood on top of an oversize boulder.
om previous hikes on the trail, Teagan knew Scopes Falls
y just beyond the trail. A steep ravine with the water cas-
ding over a rock ledge, Scopes Falls fell into a deep pool
water below.

A thick rope secured to a low hanging branch at the side
the ravine reminded Teagan that more than a few adrena-
e-seeking hikers got their thrills by swinging out over the
vine. Once out in the middle of the ravine, they'd let go
d drop straight into the pool below.

Teagan grinned. She had even tried the leap one hot after-
on a long time ago. A time when Zach had egged her on—
allenging her to "let go and fly."

The fall had been fast and furious, but the plunge into the
e-cold, nearly bottomless pool below had been the thing that
ok her breath away. She had chalked the experience up to
e craziness of youth and her ever-present need to prove she
as just as tough as him. As tough as any guy—her biggest
wnfall.

Of course, the warmth and heat came later when they got
ck to his lean-to and Zach had gathered her up and rolled
em both into his flannel-lined sleeping bag.

"Kenny, get down from there," his mother demanded. S
ran back down the trail and grabbed his arm, trying to ya
him backward off the rock.

Kenny pulled away, his sneakers skidding on the smoo
rock face. "Wait, Mom. Look! There's a guy down there.

Frowning with parental skepticism, Ruth stepped arou
the rock to take a look.

"People jump off this cliff all the time," Teagan said, a
then she paused. Maybe it wasn't such a good idea to ta
about jumping off cliffs to such an impressionable and ov
active seven-year-old. "However, jumping is *not* a smart—

Ruth's high-pitched scream ripped through Teagan's d
sertation on safety. The baby began to cry immediately. S
grabbed Kenny's arm and pulled him back from the edg
whirled around to face them, her eyes wide with shock. "(
my God, someone's fallen! There's a man on the ledge do
there."

Teagan pushed past the other women, stepping around t
boulder to get a better look. The drop was dizzying, she
rock lining the sides of the ravine and tons of cascading wa
spilling down over the falls.

About twenty feet below, on a narrow ledge, both le
twisted at an odd angle, a man lay facedown.

Teagan's breath hitched in her throat. A hint of yello
peeked out below the hem of the man's pants.

Her heart sank. Even as she told herself not to jump
conclusions, she knew it was Miguel Lopez lying on the led
below.

There was no reason for him to be out here. Teagan kne
he hadn't been hiking. This was no accident. His odd positi
on the ledge told her that he was either unconscious and bad
injured or dead.

She laid a hand on the Ruth's arm, and although both t
woman and the infant stopped screaming, Teagan felt the
olent tremors rocketing through Ruth's thin frame.

She squeezed her arm gently and spoke slowly, "Go ba

ut to the main road, Ruth. Take the baby and the kids with ou. Flag down a motorist.''

Ruth looked up, her eyes slightly dazed. Teagan squeezed er arm again, trying to get her to focus. ''If the person has cell phone, have him call 911. If he doesn't, have him take ou to the nearest house to call for help.''

''B-but we're not supposed to talk to outsiders,'' one of ne women protested.

Teagan turned to the woman, anger making her tone lipped, ''Forget the damn rules for a minute.''

The women all drew in an audible breath, and Teagan aved her hand in apology. ''I'm sorry. I didn't mean to ffend anyone. I'm just upset.''

Ruth nodded her head in understanding, clutching her baby ɔ her chest, but the woman who had spoken out against talk-ıg to outsiders didn't look as forgiving.

''Look, a man's life is at stake here. He could still be live,'' Teagan said. ''Would you prefer we leave him down ıere to die rather than talk to anyone outside the group?''

The woman shrunk back, her expression turning contrite. N-no, of course not.''

''I didn't think so.'' Teagan motioned to Ruth and the chil-ren. ''Go on now. Get some help.''

Ruth hustled the children ahead of her back down the trail. reta, followed, her face pale and drawn.

''What are we going to do until someone gets here?'' the keptic asked, her hands clenched in front of her.

''Gail, right?''

The woman nodded.

''You're going to wait right here. When the paramedics get ere, you're going to point them to the ledge. And while ou're waiting, you and Tami are going to help me.''

''Help you?''

''I'm going to climb down and see if I can assist that man.'' eagan bent down and rolled up the baggy length of her pants. 'amn, if she only had some rubber bands to hold them in

place. If she didn't end up falling and killing herself, it wou[
be a miracle. But she couldn't leave Miguel down there alo[
until the rescuers arrived. He could still be alive, and they ha[
no idea how long it would be before Ruth found a motori[
willing to stop and help.

"You can't climb down there," Gail wailed. "You'll fall.[

"I won't fall." *Hopefully,* Teagan thought. She nodded h[
head toward the other woman. "Not if you and Tami wat[
out for me."

She slipped a small pocketknife out of her pocket, and tri[
to ignore Gail's gasp of shock. Great, not only was she goi[
to have to deal with Miguel's death and the possibility [
finishing this case alone, but if Gail's reaction to her havi[
a knife was any indication, when she got back to the co[
pound she was also going to have to confess the fact that s[
was carrying an illegal weapon.

The thought of crawling on her hands and knees in fro[
of Reverend Mercy, asking for his forgiveness, didn't [
much to improve her mood.

She boosted herself up the tree and started to saw the ro[
off the limb near the knot. She'd have to do a single-stra[
rappel down the side of the ravine. With no belay device [
take the friction, she was left with the traditional body rapp[
It was the only thing around to help her get down the side [
Miguel. She owed him this and more.

A FEW MINUTES later, the rope secured as her anchor, Teag[
tied a loop around the opposite end. It would serve as a hand[
to hang from if she wasn't able to reach the ledge.

Slipping the rope between her legs, and then up her ba[
and over her shoulder, she grabbed the end in her hand. [
was lucky she was wearing pants, because she knew the fri[
tion of the rope between her legs would be brutal. But wi[
a little luck and skill, she'd get down to the ledge witho[
slipping.

The most difficult part of the entire feat was that the ro[

appeared too short to lower her all the way to the ledge. She'd have to drop down as far as the rope would allow her and then jump the rest of the way. The possibility of falling was too real.

She glanced down at her sandals. The soles were too slick to give her any kind of grip on the rock face. She kicked them off. Bare feet would serve her better. Hopefully, she wouldn't tear up the bottoms of her feet too badly.

"You're going to slip and fall," Gail said, hovering too close and wringing her hands. "Wait until help comes. You can't do anything for that poor man."

"We don't know that. He could be hurt and in need of immediate attention." She played the rope through her fingers, checking for fraying. "Besides, with you and Tami up here holding the rope, I'll be fine."

Gail stumbled backward. "I'm afraid of heights. I—I can't do anything."

Teagan grabbed her arm. "I'm not asking you to climb down there. I just need you to keep me from falling if I slip."

"But I don't know how to do that. I'm not strong enough."

"I'll show you how. You'll be strong enough." Teagan wrapped the rope around Gail's narrow hips. "All I want you to do is let the rope out slowly while I climb down. Keep the rope taut. That way, if I slip, I won't fall very far."

She motioned Tami over next to Gail. "You let the rope out. Gail can just use her body to help anchor things."

Tami nodded. She was small, but there wasn't any fear in her face.

"B-but what if you slip and pull me down with you?" Gail wailed.

"That's not going to happen." Teagan struggled to keep impatience out of her voice. "Sit down on the ground and brace yourself against the tree with your feet. You'll be fine."

The two women did as they were told. Neither looked very convinced, but at least Tami's mouth was clamped shut with a determined twist to it.

Teagan yanked on the rope. "Keep it taut. But feed it out to me smoothly."

Both nodded rapidly. They looked more afraid than she felt.

Teagan stood on the edge of the cliff and carefully placed her feet a shoulder's width apart. She focused on the rock face below, trying to figure out where her feet would go next. She knew well the importance of planning each movement carefully.

It had been a while since she'd rappelled, but she knew enough to lean out, effectively jamming the soles of her feet against the cool, smooth rock. She knew from experience that the farther she leaned out, the more secure she would be.

As she disappeared below the lip of the cliff, she heard Gail start to whimper softly. She ignored the woman, concentrating on her descent, reminding herself not to jam her toes into any footholds or tiny ledges. They would only unseat her as she unweighted the rope on the way down. Better to focus on the effectiveness of her lean.

The rope cut at the palm of her hands and ripped at the skin between her legs. Even her overalls didn't totally protect her from the friction of the rope. She tried to ignore the pain, keeping her eyes on the ledge below.

As she got closer to the end of the rope, she realized that she was going to be several feet short of the ledge. She twisted her hand around the rope several times and grasped it tight.

She tilted her head back. "Tami!"

The woman's pale face appeared over the rim.

"I'm going to have to drop down to the ledge. Don't jerk on the rope. Hold it steady."

Tami nodded.

Teagan saw her own fear mirrored on the woman's face.

Biting her lower lip, she let go of the rope with her other hand, allowing it to slip over her shoulder and back through her legs. Her body dropped and the rope jerked. It felt as if it might pull her arm out of its socket. She held on, hanging by one hand.

Grasping the rope with both hands, she started downward, hand over hand until she reached the loop at the end. She slipped her hand through the loop and allowed her body to drop another few feet.

A quick glance told her that she was still two or three feet above the ledge. Damn. She rested her forehead against the rope. Her arms screamed with pain.

Was she going to be able to do this? She had to either let go and hope she didn't lose her balance and tumble off the edge, or she needed to climb back up the rope to safety.

The ache in her arms told her that she didn't have any reserve strength left. Climbing back up was not an option. But she also knew she couldn't leave Miguel alone on the ledge.

She closed her eyes for a moment, summoning every last ounce of courage. Then, opening her eyes, she counted to three and let go of the rope.

She dropped, and her feet smacked the ledge with a jarring jolt. Her fingers scraped across the rock face searching frantically for something, anything, to grab on to. Fragments of rock came away in her hand.

Her legs folded and she fell sideways, her shoulder hitting the ledge. She rolled and her left leg swung off into space. Her right leg followed.

Her heart lurched. God help her, she was going over.

From above, she heard Tami scream.

One minute she hung suspended on the lip of the ledge and the next she was dangling over the side, her fingers clinging frantically to the edge.

"Are you all right?" Tami yelled down. "Can you hang on?"

Teagan didn't bother answering. There wasn't time. Her strength seemed to be leaking out the tips of her fingers like water out of a punctured canteen. Every muscle screamed in protest. Too much longer and she'd fall into the ravine below.

Stretching one hand up, she searched for a hold. She shoved her fingers into a small groove and pulled. Using her last bit of strength, she swung one leg up and hooked it over the edge. A sharp rock cut into her shin, slicing the skin, but she ignored the pain.

Her body felt like lead. She grunted, pulling upward with everything she had, until she was able to boost herself back up on the ledge.

She flopped down facefirst and gasped for breath.

"Are you okay?" Tami shouted down again.

Teagan waved a hand, signaling she was okay. Not that Tami or Gail would have been able to do anything if she wasn't.

The tips of her fingers stung, and she lifted her head to examine them. Her nails were broken and torn, blood seeping out from beneath them.

Hugging the wall of the ledge, she wiggled over to Miguel, reaching out to touch his head. He didn't move. She slid one hand down the side of his face to touch his neck, checking for a pulse. Nothing. No steady beat, no flutter of movement. His skin was cool.

A terrible grief welled up inside her, and Teagan dropped her head down to touch the top of his head. Tears threatened to spill, and she gently pressed her lips into the softness of his hair.

All for nothing. He was already gone.

"I'm sorry, Miguel," she whispered softly. "I should have been there for you."

She rested against him, not wanting to sit up and face the fact that he was gone. How had they gotten suspicious of him? Miguel was a consummate professional, and she wanted to believe that he would have known if they were on to them. What had they managed to get out of him before they killed him and dumped his body over the side of the ravine?

Hatred for Reverend Mercy and his henchmen flooded Teagan's entire body and settled into the pit of her belly. And along with the hatred came anger, a desire for revenge. They would not get away with this.

"Is he alive?" one of the woman yelled from above.

Teagan couldn't answer. She sat up and wrapped her arms around her knees and leaned her head back against the rock face. Her fingers dug into the skin of her opposite hand as anger fought with sadness.

She had failed her partner, and the success of their mission was seriously compromised. She was left with no way to communicate with the outside. Miguel had been her one and only means of outside communication. With her connection severed, she knew her supervisor would tell her it was time to get out.

But Teagan knew that if she abandoned the cult, the ATF or any other law-enforcement agency would never get anyone back inside, and all the work she and Miguel had done would have been for nothing.

Reverend Mercy had grown too paranoid. He was pulling back, building a huge wall around himself and the people who had chosen to follow him. He had closed the Boston church in order to cut off the outside world. He would never again trust a newcomer. Somehow she had to come up with a plan to remain on the inside.

LESS THAN thirty minutes later, Zach slammed his patrol car into park and jumped out. One of the Bradley fire department's vehicles was parked in the trail pull-off, the back doors open. It was the mountain rescue vehicle. Zach figured the rescue team had already started up the trail.

The call for the rescue of an injured hiker had come in ten minutes ago. Zach had been on his way over to the county jail when the call had come in, but something had niggled at him until he turned his vehicle around and drove to the site of the accident.

An ambulance from Bradley had followed close on his heels and it pulled in behind him. The siren burped once before shutting off. Zach didn't bother waiting for them but instead ran up the trail.

Less than a quarter of a mile up the path, close to Scopes Falls, he saw the cluster of rescue workers. They had just raised up a rescue basket with a person inside.

Off to the side, a group of women and several children from the Temple huddled together, identifiable by their trademark coveralls. Their faces were a mixture of anxiety and defensiveness. The expression was familiar. It was one Zach had seen on every Temple member's face when they came to town.

He searched the group to see if Teagan was among them. He knew there was only a slim chance, but he hoped nonetheless. She wasn't.

Returning his attention to the rescuers, he focused on their leader, Will Hayes, a hulking giant of a man with fiery red hair.

"What do you have, Will?" Zach asked, stepping into the middle of the group.

The mammoth firefighter jerked his head toward a metal rescue basket they had just hauled up over the lip of the ravine. "Some guy took a tumble. Dead." Will leaned in close to Zach and whispered, "You might want to take a closer look at him. Someone throttled the poor guy before they chucked him over the side."

Zach stepped closer to the body and pulled back the blanket. A small-framed yet heavily muscled man with black hair streaked with gray lay beneath. He was dressed in jeans and simple T-shirt. A raw-looking welt encircled his thick neck. His tongue, swollen and purple, protruded from his mouth.

Bending down, Zach checked the man's hands. The knuckles were cut and the nails were bleeding and torn. "Looks like he put up quite a fight." He stood back up. "Don't let anyone touch the body until we get some scrapings from under those nails."

Will nodded and jerked his head toward the ravine. "A woman is still down there."

Zach raised an eyebrow. "Another victim?"

"No, it's one of the women from the group over there."

Will jerked his chin in the direction of the cluster of Temple women. "Damn fool climbed down there thinking the guy might still be alive. When Pete went down, she insisted that he take the dead guy first. Pete figured it wasn't worth getting her all upset so he did what she asked."

"Gutsy move on the woman's part." Zach stepped over to the edge of the ravine and looked down. "What the hell—"

His heart lurched.

Teagan stared up at him from the ledge, the fingers of both her hands wedged into the rock crevice to keep herself anchored.

"Are you just going to stand there gaping at me, Sheriff? Or are you sending someone down to get me up?"

"You know her?" Will asked, his surprise evident.

Zach shook his head in amazement. "Yeah, we've met."

"Look, do you two mind saving the chitchat for later and sending another rope down for me? I'd like to get out of here sometime today."

Will shot Zach a concerned glance. "Even with a harness, I don't want her climbing back up. She needs to come up in the litter."

"I don't need the litter," Teagan protested from below.

"You'll do what the rescue team tells you." Zach grabbed a harness off the pile of equipment lying on the ground.

"Whoa, wait a minute, Zach. Didn't you just say the rescue team calls the shots?" Will said. "That's my job."

Zach continued to strap himself in. "I'm a volunteer fireman just like you, and I'm pulling rank. I'm the one going down."

Will held up his hands in surrender. "Fine by me. I'll be your backup." He rummaged through the equipment and came up with a small emergency pouch. "Slap a bandage on her leg so she doesn't bleed to death before we get her up here. I'll be right down after you."

Zach nodded and then lowered himself down over the lip of the rock face, letting the rope out slowly.

A few seconds later, he landed on the ledge next to her. "I thought you knew better than to play around Scopes Falls."

"Some idiot showed me this place a long time ago. He had this incredible urge to play Tarzan."

Zach grinned. "And don't tell me—you played Jane to his Tarzan, right?"

"Very funny. Let's concentrate on getting me out of here. My legs are about ready to give out."

For the first time, Zach noticed the pasty whiteness of her face and the fine sheen of sweat dotting her forehead and upper lip. "You don't look so hot."

"Gee, thanks. You're just full of cheerful thoughts." She gave him a haggard smile. "Low rations and no sleep have finally caught up with me. It's like my energy has been zapped." She sucked in another shaky breath. "I was a fool to attempt the climb in the first place, but I couldn't leave Miguel down here without checking to see if he was alive."

"Miguel?" He reached out and grasped her upper arm. "Are you telling me that you know the guy they hauled out of here?"

She swallowed hard and then ducked her head to wipe her forehead on her sleeve. When she looked up again, the emotional pain he had seen a moment ago had disappeared, replaced by a fragile shell of hardness.

"He's been my partner for the past three years."

Zach's gut tightened. "Damn, Tea. He was your outside contact, wasn't he?"

"Yes." She glanced up toward the top of the ledge. "But let's talk about that after you get me out of here. I'm not sure how much help I'm going to be. My arms and legs are about the consistency of warm Jell-O right now."

"All right. Hang on and relax into your harness. I need to get on the other side and take a look at your leg."

"Forget my leg. Just get me out of here."

"Hey, I'm the rescuer." He pointed a finger at her chest. "You're the rescuee." Zach pushed off the ledge and swung out behind her, switching sides. As he set his feet on the ledge, he said, "The rescuee's job is to keep quiet and co-operate. Think you can manage that?"

He grinned at the knot of muscle that appeared in the side of her cheek. He hoped she wasn't grinding her teeth too badly. "Just do what you have to do," she said.

Zach knew her well enough to know that was about as close to a concession as he was going to get out of her.

Within a few minutes, the firemen at the top had lowered down the basket and Zach and Will securely strapped Teagan in. It worried him that she didn't once attempt to tell him how to do things. She was entirely too quiet. As they began to haul her up, she laid her head back and closed her eyes. Her complexion was disturbingly pale and drawn.

As soon as the rescue basket was safely over the lip of the ravine, Zach signaled the men to start bringing him back up. He felt a heightened sense of urgency.

Teagan's contact was dead. Murdered. And he wanted answers. After she was taken to the hospital and checked out, he was going to demand some answers. He wanted to know what was going on inside the New Jerusalem compound and why the ATF was so darn interested in the Reverend Daniel Mercy. This time he wasn't taking no for an answer.

Chapter Ten

As Zach climbed out of his harness, he heard Teagan arguing with the paramedics.

"I don't need a hospital," she protested as the two men tried to lift her out of the rescue basket and onto an ambulance gurney.

Zach sighed. Nothing ever changed. Apparently her precarious trip up the side of the ravine in a metal basket had revived her and fired up her defiant spirit. He didn't know whether to be relieved or annoyed that she was back to her usual uncooperative, stubborn self.

"We're not going to argue about this, Sister Teagan," he said, walking over to stand near her.

He was aware that her fellow cult members were standing off to the side watching everything with wide eyes. "You're going to the hospital."

She stared defiantly back up at him, two red spots of anger highlighting her cheek against the paleness of her skin. "No, I'm not. I have a simple cut. They need to wash it out and put a bandage on it." She shot an appraising look in the direction of the two paramedics. "They look like bright, capable boys. I'm sure they can handle that."

"Your leg needs to be looked at by a doctor, miss," one of the paramedics said.

Teagan shook her head and swung her feet over the side

of the stretcher. "I'm not going to tie up a spot in the emergency room for a little cut."

The two paramedics looked at Zach and shrugged. They were smart enough to know when to quit. Resigned, Zach nodded that it was okay for them to back off. There was no sense in making a scene.

"What Sister Teagan needs to do is to return to camp with us," one of the Temple women said, stepping into the circle assembled around the stretcher.

Zach glanced at her, and his attention seemed to give the woman some degree of confidence. She pushed her way through the group of firemen, and planted herself in front of Zach. Her expression was taunt and nervous, her gaze jumping back and forth between Teagan and Zach.

"I'd appreciate it if you had one of your men call the Temple and let them know we're down here. They'll send someone to pick us up. Someone at the camp will take care of Sister Teagan's leg."

Zach shook his head. "Sorry, but no one is leaving until I've had a chance to interview you. We'll be conducting the interviews down in Elizabethtown at my office."

The woman's lips thinned, and two straight lines of disapproval jumped into existence between her dark brows. "You can't force us to come with you." She glanced around at the other officials standing around. "You can't hold us against our will. I insist you bring us back to the camp. Reverend Mercy needs to be informed of—"

"Of what?" Zach asked calmly. "That you are all possible witnesses to a murder and need to be questioned by the police?"

"M-murder?" Another woman in the group blurted out. It was the woman Zach had seen at the Temple. The one with the young boy, Kenny. "I—I thought the man fell. Or—or jumped. No one said anything about murder." She pressed Kenny's head against the side of her hip as if to protect him from what was being discussed. She glanced around the group, her face fearful.

"A person doesn't strangle himself, ma'am, and then jump off a cliff," one of the paramedics said dryly.

The woman stroked her son's head, her face whitening to the color of bleached bone. "Strangled? The man was strangled?" She glanced about wildly. "Y-you can't possibly believe that any of us had anything to do with it?"

Beside him, Teagan reached out and lightly touched his arm. He glanced down at her.

"There isn't any need to scare them any more than they already are. They don't know anything."

The color of her eyes darkened, and he could see the slightest hint of pleading in their depths. He knew how to read her even after all their years apart. Her sudden gentleness surprised him, but he didn't question it. He could tell that she was banking on him to do as she asked without argument.

"What do you want me to do?" he asked softly. "I need to take a report."

"Just have one of your deputies drive them back to the compound," she said. "I'll go have a doctor look at my leg and then you can ask me all the questions you have about what happened."

"All right." He glanced around. "Drake, take these people back up to New Jerusalem. Get a statement from each of them before dropping them off."

The self-appointed leader of the women, the sour-faced, bossy one, didn't look at all pleased with the change in plans. In fact, Zach thought that she looked as though she had sucked down a bushel of lemons. He was fairly certain she didn't like the fact that Teagan wasn't in the group scheduled to return to the compound.

But she also seemed to realize that no amount of arguing on her part was going to change his mind. She clamped her mouth shut and glared pointedly in Teagan's direction.

The glare didn't bode well for Teagan. No doubt she'd have a lot to answer for when she returned to the camp.

Deputy Drake Matthews nodded and started herding the group of The Disciples' Temple members ahead of him down the trail.

ONCE THEY WERE settled in his car, Zach paused, his hand on the shift. "You do realize that Mercy isn't going to be happy when he finds out you went with me rather than the other deputy, right?"

Teagan nodded and snapped her seat belt with a firm click. "If he's worried, he'll come for me. I kind of like the idea that he'll be forced to step outside his little cocoon."

"You're playing a dangerous cat-and-mouse game with that man, Tea. The death of your partner attests to that."

She glanced up. "Do you really think I'm so naive that I don't realize that?"

He stared across the short distance separating them, studying her for a moment. "Not naive. Just too damn ballsy sometimes."

"Would you have rather I went back with them?"

He shook his head and shoved the car into reverse. No, he didn't want that. Never that. Truth be told, he wanted her right were she was, next to him. Safe. Out of harm's way. But he also knew that wouldn't last for long.

The back wheels spun a bit on the gravel, but he ignored it and jammed the shift into drive.

She waited until he was out on the highway before speaking again. "What makes you so sure Reverend Mercy killed Miguel?"

"Come on. Who else could have offed him?" he scoffed. "The guy was murdered when someone inside the compound found out he was an agent." He shot her an exasperated glance. "And that probably means he knows you're an agent, too."

She glanced over at him, her expression calm. "It's possible."

He hit the steering column with the heel of his hand. "Could you say that with any less concern?"

She smiled without much humor. "Look, Zach. It's a very real possibility that Reverend Mercy suspects me. Do I think so? Not really. Personally, I don't think he would have let me out of his sight if that was so."

She scrunched down slightly in the seat and rested her head back against the headrest. Her hair, dark, flowing and like midnight silk, spread out against the worn vinyl. Zach struggled to ignore the urge to reach out and touch it, to run his fingers through the soft strands.

He focused back on the road, his fingers grasping the steering wheel so hard they ached. He needed to get a grip.

"What if Miguel talked?" he asked.

She sat up straight, her hair sliding over her shoulders like a black shawl, her expression darkening. "That didn't happen. Miguel would have never given me up."

"Relax. I'm not trying to dirty up Lopez's honor. I'm just posing questions. Besides, you don't know what happened. I get the distinct feeling that Mercy can be pretty persuasive."

She seemed to realize she'd overreacted and melted back against the seat again. "I agree. But I also believe that if the reverend suspected I was a federal agent, he would have never let me outside the camp this morning. He would have simply made me disappear."

She shifted on the seat, as if trying to get more comfortable. She winced slightly as her injured leg moved. "I'm more inclined to think that he's watching all of us, waiting to see who makes a wrong move. Miguel must have done something to arouse his suspicions."

"Did any of his goons see you with Miguel at any point?"

She glanced over at him, her expression irritated. He could tell this had crossed her mind and she was probably beating herself up with guilt. "Your concern is touching, Zach, but eally do know how to conduct myself during an undercover nvestigation. Miguel and I didn't stand out in the middle of he compound, discussing strategy.''

"Of course not. But you're a risk taker, Tea." He jerked ais head in the direction of her injured leg. "As demonstrated very nicely by your crazy climb this morning."

"Hey, I made it, didn't I?" She glanced away again, a sense of sadness seeming to settle over her. "Besides, I owed t to Miguel to check on him." She studied the passing scenery for a few minutes before speaking again. "I had lunch yesterday with Miguel, but he was careful to make the arangements seem entirely accidental. No one would have noiced anything out of the ordinary."

"Did he speak to you at any point?"

"Not really. He passed me a note, letting me know he wanted us to meet last night."

"And did you?"

A shadow passed over her eyes and the tenseness around ner mouth tightened even more. "No, I waited for him, but ne never showed."

"Mercy must have already caught him at that point."

She nodded but didn't speak. He knew she was laying the guilt for her partner's capture at her own doorstep.

"Don't you think that by not returning with the rest of them you've put yourself at risk?" He slowed for a stop sign, putting his turn signal on to take a right toward Bradley. "At least if I had hauled everyone in, you could have been part of the group. Not hanging out there alone."

"There was no reason to scare the women and children more than they already were, Zach." She scrubbed her face with the palm of her hand, her weariness evident in every move she made. "Those people—especially the children—are under enough pressure just living under Reverend Mercy's thumb. No need for us to add to it."

"I'm all for making their lives easier, Tea. But what about you?"

"I'll be fine."

She cracked the window and leaned her head back against the seat. The late-morning sun hit her face, and Zach was struck by her pale, almost fragile beauty. It was in stark contrast to her no-nonsense, downright stubborn attitude almost the whole car ride. How could two such opposing realities live within the same slender body?

Zach shook his head. What made him think that he'd ever understand her? She was more of a mystery now than she'd been those years ago when she dropped out of his life. Nothing he saw up to this point made him believe that she was any more readable now than she was then. She'd had years to practice. Years to reinforce that damn wall around herself.

He glanced down at the bandage the EMT had slapped on her leg before they'd left the mountain. Her overalls were still rolled up to about midcalf. The center of the pristine white gauze had turned bright red, telling him that she was still bleeding.

"Look, Tea, I don't—"

He stopped talking. Beside him, her shoulders had slumped and her lips had softened, opening slightly. She drew in a deep breath, exhaled and then took in another one. The tense lines of her face had relaxed, making her seem younger.

"Tea?"

No answer. Her chest rose and fell evenly. She had fallen asleep midconversation.

Zach stepped on the accelerator. He needed to get her to town and on to his sister's examining table soon. He wondered how much longer she and the other residents of New Jerusalem were going to be able to survive Daniel Mercy's regimen of "healthy living."

THE KNOCK at his bedroom door roused Mercy out of a light sleep. He rolled over onto his back and blinked. He'd slept heavier than he'd expected.

The drapes were closed, making the room dark, almost

cavelike. The air conditioner, stuck in the wall on the far side of the room, whispered coolly. The clock on his bedside table read 1:00 p.m. It was early; they'd only retired to his room an hour or so ago. Maybe he was getting old. He seemed to get tired out quicker than usual. Of course, part of that was due to all the services he'd been conducting lately. He felt as though he didn't have enough time to finish his mission. Time was pressing down heavily on him.

He slipped his arm out from beneath Becca's neck and sat up. She sighed softly and rolled up on her side. The knock, soft but insistent, came again. Mercy reached back and pulled the sheet over Becca's bare shoulder.

"Come in," he said.

The door swung open. Cyrus stood in the doorway, his expression carefully neutral. Mercy had trained all his disciples well. He didn't like interruptions, not when he was preaching and certainly not when he napped in the afternoon. If they needed to interrupt him, they knew the reason needed to be a damn good one.

"What?" he asked.

"The body was found exactly as you wanted."

Mercy bent over and picked his jeans up off the floor. He pulled them on and then brushed past Cyrus, padding barefoot out into the living room. Cyrus quietly shut the door and followed him out.

"Fix me a drink," Mercy ordered, walking over to the large window overlooking the compound. "Are all our little sheep back safe and sound?"

Ice cubes tinkled merrily as Cyrus dropped them into the crystal tumbler. He poured a healthy splash of whiskey over them and then handed it to Mercy.

"All except Sister Teagan."

Mercy raised an eyebrow. "Really? And where has my wayward Teagan disappeared to?"

Cyrus shrugged. "Who knows? That ferret-faced woman, Sister Gail, says that she refused to come back with the others.

Apparently she was taken back to town for medical attention." Cyrus went back and poured himself a glass. "The ferret seems to think that she was getting too cozy with the townspeople—especially the sheriff." Cyrus paused to take a sip of whiskey. "She said that she reminded Sister Teagan that she could get medical attention back here, but the girl ignored her."

Mercy smiled and sipped his own drink, savoring the sharp, clean slice of flavor sliding across his tongue. He didn't get to indulge often enough. "How badly was she injured?"

"Nothing serious. A small cut on her leg. Something she got while trying to climb down to Lopez's body."

Mercy turned around, a smile cutting across his face. Damn, but the woman was gutsy. If he didn't have little Becca to focus on right now, he was fairly certain that Sister Teagan would be warming his bed.

He walked over to the couch and sat down. That would happen soon enough. But first he needed to teach Becca' daddy a lesson in humility, and then he could move onto bigger and better prey. Any woman he wanted actually—that would be his reward for serving his Lord. For bringing about the ultimate judgment upon those who scoffed and ridiculed.

It didn't surprise him in the least that Teagan had climbed down the side of Scopes Falls to get to the body. Her air of servitude seemed to cloak an underlying sense of steely purpose. It was a dichotomy he intended to investigate further.

He glanced up at Cyrus. "I imagine Sheriff McCoy showed up."

Cyrus's scowl deepened. "Of course. According to Sister Gail, the guy couldn't volunteer fast enough to go down the side of the wall to bring Sister Teagan back up."

Mercy swirled the amber liquid in his glass, watching it coat and color the crystal. Things were progressing better than even he had anticipated. The sheriff's attraction to Teagan was strong, growing every time he came in contact with her. By the time he was done throwing the two of them together, the man would be so besotted with her that he'd do anything Mercy asked. Including supporting Mercy's attempts to draw in the townspeople.

He sipped his drink, and allowed one of the ice cubes to slip into his mouth. He sucked it contemplatively as he considered his plans for a Day of Unity. The more witnesses he had to the destruction of The Beast, the better. The sheriff would bring him his witnesses, and the man's reputation would deliver them right into his hands.

"Do you want me to go into town and get her?"

"Perhaps, but first I have something else for you to do." Mercy settled back against the black, butter-soft leather couch, the cushions curving luxuriously around his body. "I want you to go wake up Becca. Have her call Daddy Dearest, and make sure she tells him how hard she's struggling to do what is asked of her. Have her tell him about how hungry she is."

Cyrus grinned, something nasty and predatory. "What kind of hunger are we talking about here, Reverend?"

Mercy allowed his expression to go cold. "Don't play with me, Cyrus—just get her to make the call." He swallowed the final ounce of whiskey and stood up. "I'm going to get something to eat. When you're done, find me and we'll discuss how you're going to go into town to collect my wayward little sheep."

Cyrus's gaze skittered away from his, his expression telling Mercy that he had realized that he'd overstepped the carefully drawn line between them.

Cyrus didn't do it often, but when he did, Mercy didn't hesitate to put him in his place.

TEAGAN JUMPED when Zach's hand touched her shoulder. She blinked in confusion.

"Sorry, you fell asleep," Zach said. "We're here."

"Here?" She wasn't exactly sure where and what "here" was. She sat up and looked around. Her mouth felt dry as dirt and she wondered if she had embarrassed herself by snoring.

Every bone in her body ached and a steady throb of pain ha
settled into her left leg.

Zach put on his turning signal. "This is the doctor's offic
Remember, you didn't want to go to the hospital?"

She nodded and glanced out the window. Her brain wa
still filled with cobwebs, but they were starting to clear.

The doctor's office sat in the middle of Bradley's mai
street, right between Dobson's Pharmacy and the tiny Fier
bergh Public Library. It was a neat, cottage-style house re
modeled into a small but bustling medical clinic. The flowe
boxes and yellow shutters with the cutout hearts at the botto
probably meant the place had once been someone's actua
home.

A line of cars took up the majority of parking spots on bot
sides of the street, and people streamed in and out of the fro
door.

Zach pulled into the driveway, parking behind the dar
green Jeep Cherokee with the M.D. license plate.

"Maybe you shouldn't block the doctor in," Teagan saic

Zach grinned. "Not a problem. I happen to know the docto
personally, so she'll see you right away." He jumped out an
came around to her side of the vehicle, opening the doo
Teagan swung her legs off the side of the seat, gritting he
teeth against the sting in her left leg.

Zach's frame filled the doorway. "Wait, let me carry yo
No need for you to put more weight on that leg than neces
sary."

Teagan planted her good foot flat against the front of hi
muscular thighs and pushed him back. "As much as I appre
ciate the offer, that would be a bit much. I'll walk."

"Gee, why am I not surprised?" He grabbed her arm a
she stood up. "At least you could pretend to lean on me."

"I'm fine. Stop fussing." When her left foot grazed th
pavement, a wave of pain washed over her. Her fingers tight
ened down on the hard muscle of his forearm, steadying her

elf. Okay, so maybe she should have taken him up on his offer.

Hopping on one foot, she braced herself as he wrapped an arm around her back, his hand coming to rest right over her left hip. He pulled her close and the heat of his body immediately soaked through her clothing.

She felt warm and sweaty, and she worried she smelled less than fresh. But she was also weary, and she wasn't about to agonize over a bit of simple sweat and how he was going to react to it. For a moment, she allowed herself to rest against him, savoring in the delicious but familiar feel of him along the length of her body. God, she'd missed him.

He half dragged her up the front walk and into the comfortable waiting room. Everyone looked up from their magazines, and a few greeted Zach, their expressions registering obvious interest in who the woman hanging all over him was.

But Zach took it all in stride. He politely greeted each person in the waiting room and then walked up to the door leading to the back.

The middle-aged woman with a head of tight red curls and a pair of serious-looking spectacles opened up the receptionist's glass. "Hold it right there, Sheriff. Where do you think you're going?" She glanced down at the appointment book in front of her. "I don't have you or the young lady scheduled to see Dr. Wade."

"She doesn't have an appointment, Pat, but she needs to be seen."

Pat gave Teagan a quick assessing look. "Not if she isn't bleeding to death, she doesn't. Doc is out straight today."

Teagan started to turn away, but Zach didn't let go. "I'm putting her in the back room, Pat. Helen will see her."

Apparently no one crossed him when he made an announcement like that because the receptionist didn't blink an eye when he opened the door and marched Teagan down the hall to a small examining room. He whipped open the door and waved her in. More than a little amused, she walked in and took a seat on the end of the examination table.

Within minutes, a pretty dark-haired nurse bustled in. She smiled at Zach as she checked the dressing on Teagan's leg and then carefully took Teagan's vitals. They waited patiently as she charted them in a file.

"Dr. Wade will be with you shortly." She dropped a sheet of paper on Teagan's lap. "Please fill that out for the doctor."

She was out the door before Teagan had a chance to ask how long "shortly" was in Doc Wade's world.

She picked up the paper and glanced over it. Standard history. "Got a pen?"

He patted his pockets. "Sorry, must have left them in the patrol car."

She shoved the history onto the table next to her and sat back. It wasn't as if she'd ever be back here for treatment.

Across the room, Zach propped himself up against the wall. He looked as tired as she felt. Several strands of thick blond hair lay plastered against his forehead, and his tan uniform shirt was marked with half circles of sweat under both arms. It hugged the width of his broad chest, and Teagan felt her mouth go dry. Figures. She had a gash on her leg that needed stitches and her libido was kicking into overdrive.

"Did I thank you for saving me?" she asked.

He grinned, a slow, easy stretch of his magnificent lips over white teeth. Damn, she'd forgotten the devastating effect that particular smile had on her. She wouldn't have believed it but the years hadn't diminished the effect of that smile on her one bit. She was grateful for the tiny air-conditioning unit blowing a cooling breeze over her.

"I think at one point you told me to get the hell off your ledge so they could haul you up."

"Sorry. I was beginning to worry that Reverend Mercy was going to show up and find us lounging around down there."

He pushed himself off the wall and stepped closer. She

wanted to tell him to stay on his side of the room, but it was too late.

He leaned one hip on the side of the examining table, and his hand brushed the side of her thigh. The white paper on the table crinkled beneath her, giving off a warning.

He smelled of sweat and pine, a stinging, intoxicating combination. She bit the inside of her cheek and tried to ignore the devastating effect his closeness had on her.

Suddenly, the air-conditioning unit didn't seem to be cooling her. Heat radiated off his body with the intensity of the sun and drowned her in its warmth, making her wish she was someplace cold and frozen.

Desperate, she grabbed at anything. "How long do you think we'll have to wait?"

"Doc Wade isn't the type to be rushed. She'll mosey in here on her own good time." But he hastened to add, "She's a good doctor, though. Her waiting room is always packed."

"So I noticed."

"You sure you're okay?"

Teagan nodded and shifted her upper body, trying to put some space between them. She bumped the side of the wall with her hip, and the zing of pain up the side of her left leg reminded her not to move too quickly.

He laid a hand on her arm. His touch—the curl of his fingers against the bare flesh of her forearm—was both intense and intimate at the same time. "Easy, Tea. You don't want to get that cut bleeding again."

The concern and compassion in his voice tore at her defenses, and she fought to keep the inevitable sweet meltdown—the one that threatened to surge through every nerve and cell of her body—from happening. But deep down, Teagan knew she didn't have the reserve of energy to fight him. His gentleness, his downright bullish, single-minded determination to treat her with sweet concern, did her in every time. The sensation washed over her and swept her sideways, allowing her to slip up against him as she melted into something the consistency of gold honey.

Without speaking, he reached up and gently brushed back several strands of her hair, his flesh warm and rough on the smoothness of her cheek. His fingers skimmed along the top of her ear and slid effortlessly into the thickness of her hair at the nape of her neck. A chill ran up her back as his fingers tunneled deeper into her hair.

Her eyes closed and she sighed softly, not daring to look directly into his face. She knew what would happen, how she would lose the precarious grip she now held on her defenses. If she met his gaze, the risk was too great that she'd succumb to his power. That she would somehow connect to the depth of feeling he had for her.

Teagan struggled to concentrate on what he saying and not what he was doing to her body with his exquisite touch. But she could feel her defenses dissolving, deserting her.

"This is wrong," she protested. But even as she spoke, her body trembled, and her head, as if of its own free will, dropped back into the center of his palm, and she allowed him to cradle her.

"Look at me, Tea," he ordered, his voice as rough and raspy with feeling.

Slowly, she opened her eyes and met his gaze. The blue was so brilliant it was almost painful, and for a moment, she believed that he could reach inside her and sear the memory of this moment into her brain.

Time seemed to stretch out between them, and it was as if all past wrongs vanished in an instant. The hurt between them disappeared in a swirl of hot, undiscovered emotions.

A tiny sigh escaped from between Teagan's lips, and the heaviness in her heart seemed to lift. It was like stepping from darkness into light, and she tasted the intensity, the burning heat of her own need. She wanted him. Wanted his strength and his goodness. She wanted everything he had to offer. And then, when she thought she could wait not one more minute he leaned forward and kissed the corner of her mouth. Her lips softened beneath his, and he gently, tentatively ran the tip of his tongue along the length of her lower lip, as if testing her resistance.

But there was none left in her. Her resistance had deserted her before she had even opened her eyes. She desired him so much that she couldn't imagine a time without his touch, without his hard gentleness pressing in on her, forcing her to recognize and accept her own breathless need.

She opened to him and he delved deeper, seeming to sink into her as she melted against him. She reached up and wrapped her arms around him, wanting him closer and desiring the one thing she knew she wasn't supposed to have. Or even want.

Zach. Her lover. Her heart. Her missing piece.

As their kiss deepened, every sane, coherent thought slipped from Teagan's mind. She took what he offered, and she gave back that tiny portion of herself she had always believed had faded from existence seven years ago when she left him.

Chapter Eleven

They both jumped when the examining room door swung open.

Teagan froze and Zach stepped back, lifting a hand to casually scratch the back of his head. Teagan didn't think either of them could have had a guiltier expression if they tried.

A tall woman, her blond hair shot through with strands of silver, stood in the doorway. Her own expression of surprise was almost as comical as Zach's attempt to appear nonchalant.

Apparently finding the Essex County sheriff wrapped in the arms of one of her patients wasn't what Dr. Wade had expected to find when she opened the door to examining room 5.

She nudged Teagan's chart open in her hand and dropped her gaze down to study it through a pair of delicate gold-rimmed reading glasses perched low on her pert nose. When she glanced up again, her facial features had been schooled to reveal nothing, but Teagan didn't miss the sharp assessing look in the blue eyes.

She brushed past Zach. "You can go."

Her tone was dismissive, and surprisingly, Zach didn't argue. He moved to the door. "I'll be right outside the door. Yell if she gets out of line. But I've discovered that her bark is definitely worse than her bite."

Teagan bit back a grin. Apparently Dr. Wade had some

story with Zach. In spite of her having about ten or twelve
years on him, she wondered if the two were romantically involved, or had been at some point. She was certainly beautiful
enough to catch the handsome sheriff's attention.

Teagan regarded the woman with renewed interest. She was
tall, with long shapely legs peeking out from beneath her long
white lab coat. Her thick, honey-colored hair was in a neat
french braid at the back of her neck, and the gold spectacles
only added to her sharp, intellectual look.

A tiny twinge of jealousy ripped through Teagan, surprising
her. What had she thought? That Zach would have lived the
last seven years as a monk? More than ridiculous.

The words *Zach* and *celibate* didn't go together. The man
was flesh and blood. Flesh and blood that was packaged quite
a bit nicer than the normal, everyday man walking the street,
and Teagan didn't doubt that the doctor and more than a few
other women in the town had noticed that fact.

When the examining room door clicked shut behind him,
Dr. Wade held out her hand. "I'm Helen Wade."

Teagan reached across and shook it. A firm, no-nonsense
grip to go with the doctor's firm, no-nonsense approach.
"Teagan Benson." In spite of her brains being scrambled
from Zach's kiss, she had the foresight to remember her cover
name.

"And why are you here, Ms. Benson?" Dr. Wade's voice
was stiff, almost cold.

Teagan shifted on the table. "I was hiking out at Scopes
Falls and—" She stopped, understanding dawning. "When
you asked me why I was here, you weren't interested in how
I got hurt, were you?"

Dr. Wade pulled on a pair of disposable gloves. "Very
perceptive of you." She bent down and unwrapped the bandage around Teagan's leg. "I was actually more interested in
knowing what brought you to our little town of Bradley."

"I'm a member of The Disciples' Temple."

The doctor poked the edge of the cut and a tiny bubble of

blood oozed out the side. Teagan sucked air through clench
teeth. "Careful. The damn thing stings like a son of—" S
bit back the rest of the sentence.

Dr. Wade looked up, one blond eyebrow arched. Her g
held a slightly mocking twist to it. "A religious woman w
swears like a sailor. How unexpected."

"Can't say I expected your lack of bedside manner,
ther," Teagan countered.

Dr. Wade laughed and dropped the strip of soiled gauze
the medical waste container hanging on the wall. "Touc
It's a nasty cut. Deep enough that it's going to require a f
stitches to close it up."

"Are you sure you can't just seal it up with a few butt
flies?"

Helen Wade sniffed and opened one of the drawers i
huge metal cabinet. She pulled out a package wrapped in li
green paper, a sterile syringe and a small vial, setting it
on a wheeled bedside tray.

As she rolled it over next to the examining table, she sa
"Unless I'm mistaken, you came to me requesting medi
care. Anytime you want to leave and take over your own ca
feel free." She tilted her head and raised one eyebrow qu
tioningly. "So, what's the verdict, are we going to do this

Teagan nodded.

"Good. I'll give you a local and then sew it up." S
opened the syringe package and drew up some of the cl
liquid in the vial. She worked in silence for a few minu
and then asked, "You seem to know Sheriff McCoy rat
well."

"We've known each other for a while," Teagan said n
committally.

"He's well liked around here. Not many people would
preciate it if anyone came in here and ended up hurting him

"I imagine not." Teagan cocked her head. "You don't p
any punches, do you, Dr. Wade?"

"Not when it comes to my little brother."

Teagan stiffened in surprise. "Little brother? Zach's your brother?"

Dr. Wade nodded but didn't glance up. She slid the needle under Teagan's skin and injected the anesthetic. With studied patience, she concentrated on putting a neat, tidy line of stitches in the wound. Several minutes passed in silence.

Finally, she knotted the last stitch and used the scissors to cut the ends. Grabbing a clean piece of gauze, she slapped it on the newly closed wound and taped it in place.

Teagan watched as the woman silently cleaned up her mess. She wasn't sure what to say next, but she figured Dr. Wade would lead the way.

When done, Dr. Wade slipped the needle into the red medical waste container. Then she stepped back and folded her arms, giving Teagan a sharp assessing glance.

"Several years ago, my brother fell in love with a young woman named Teagan—for the life of me, I can't remember her last name." There was no softness in her blue eyes, no forgiving curve to the tight lines bracketing both corners of her mouth. "Unfortunately, I never met the young woman—I was away doing my residency in Cincinnati."

Teagan slid her legs off the table and sat perched on the edge, waiting. She wasn't terribly comfortable with the direction the conversation had taken. Discussing the past with Zach hadn't even been an option she was willing to indulge in up to this point, and the thought of going there with his sister was even more uncomfortable.

"When I came home, I saw firsthand the results of their breakup. To say my brother was devastated is an understatement." She shoved her hands in the pockets of her lab coat. She didn't appear too comfortable with the topic, either, but there was a stubborn tilt to her chin. "Zach threw himself into his work and wasn't willing to talk about what happened. But I knew it had to be pretty bad because he isn't the kind of man who hurts easy."

The muscle in her cheek tightened into a knot, and her gaze

maintained an harsh steely quality to it. This was a woma
who wasn't afraid to defend her own.

"It's taken him a while to get back to his old self. B
fortunately for us, it's happened over time. I like seeing hi
happy, and I'd like to see him stay that way."

Teagan glanced down, studying the smudges of dirt stainir
her pants. She smoothed the tips of her fingers over the so
worn material.

How was she supposed to respond? She couldn't deny h
part in putting that particular kernel of hurt in Zach's hea
Nor could she deny that she'd left without settling things wi
him all those years ago.

As hard as it was for her to believe that she'd done anythir
or said anything that could diminish Zach in any way, the
was no denying the genuine anger and wariness in his old
sister's eyes. It was pretty clear that she wanted Teagan
stay clear of her brother.

"Are we coming to some kind of understanding here, M
Benson?"

Teagan lifted her head, meeting Helen Wade's gaze dea
on. "We understand each other perfectly, Doctor. I can on
promise you that I'm not here to hurt Zach. I live at the Ne
Jerusalem complex and don't plan on venturing out muc
You have nothing to worry about."

Dr. Wade straightened up, her smile formal, downrig
chilly actually. "Excellent. Then we have nothing else to di
cuss in regards to this particular topic, do we?"

Teagan shook her head no.

Zach's sister pushed the bedside rolling tray up against tl
far wall. "I'd appreciate it if you didn't mention our conve
sation to Zach." She flashed another one of her chilly smile
"My brother has never been too keen on his older siste
sticking their noses into his business."

"He won't hear anything from me."

As she reassured Zach's sister, Teagan's throat tighten
against the surge of emotions that threatened to overwhel

r. What would it have been like to have a family that cared
r her as much as Helen Wade obviously cared for Zach?

Would things have been different for her if she'd had a
ving, compassionate clan of people who knew everything
ere was to know about her and yet loved and protected her
ithout question?

Hot emotions scalded the back of her throat and threatened
choke her. But she pushed them back, refusing to submit.
he didn't have time for this.

She had hurt Zach, but he had managed to get over it—
en his sister had said he was happy. Who was she to come
d mess all of that up? He had a loving, protective family
take comfort in.

Family. Teagan rolled the word around inside her mouth.
ch a strange, unfamiliar word. Something she knew little
out. Her own family was made up of a mother who had
ent a lifetime checking in and out of psychiatric institutions,
ying to stay sane. Mostly she had failed.

Of course, Teagan knew that as hard as it was, she had
arned to accept and tolerate her mother's deep, gut-
renching depressions and her wild manic phases. But on the
her hand, her father, an exacting man who believed in dom-
ating anyone and anything that stepped into his world, had
ver quite found the same ability to accept his wife's fail-
es.

His demands for perfection and cold rage when his expec-
tions weren't met, crushed his emotionally fragile wife. And
e day, when Teagan was nine, he simply walked out.

Within a few months, he had replaced Teagan's mother
ith a newer, more streamlined model, a woman who knew
ow to complement the crisp military perfection of his uni-
rm and enhance his career. When Teagan's mother crum-
ed under her grief, Teagan's father returned, but only for as
ng as it took to gain full custody of his daughter through
e courts.

For some reason, Colonel George W. Kennedy never re-

alized the impact his behavior would have on his impressio
able young daughter. But Teagan learned early in life nev
to complain, never to whimper or cry. People left you wh
you clung too hard. Better to be the one who left first.

Of course, years later, when Teagan went to college a
some backwoods mountain man from the tiny town of Bra
ley, New York, showed an interest in her, Colonel Kenne
had been less than impressed. Especially when the young m
had no other ambition than to work in local law enforceme
Ambition and discipline were everything to the colonel.

It hadn't taken him long to realize that Teagan and Za
weren't involved in a brief "college fling." When he reco
nized the seriousness of their relationship, he issued an ul
matum. An ultimatum that forced Teagan to face the fact th
as strong as she thought she was, she wasn't strong enou
to refuse him. She caved, leaving Zach and her heart behi

Swallowing back the bitter taste of regret, Teagan stoo
and touched her injured foot gingerly to the floor. She wigg
her toes. "Not bad. You do good work, Doc."

Helen didn't answer, but instead, opened the door. Sh
didn't seem surprised to find Zach leaning up against the w
right outside the door.

She sighed. "You can come in now."

"She's okay?" Zach asked, his gaze jumping back a
forth between the two of them.

"She's fine. I sewed up the cut. She needs to keep it clea
If she comes back next week, I'll take out the stitches."

"I'm sure someone at the camp will be able to take the
out," Teagan said.

Helen snorted. "I'm tired of everyone around here thinki
they have a medical degree. When I tell a patient to co
back, I expect them to listen."

Amusement tugged at one corner of Teagan's mouth, a
she held up her hands in surrender. "I'll stop back at the e
of the week."

Helen nodded briskly. "Good. I want you to use an an

iotic ointment when you change the dressing.'' She made a
uick note on Teagan's chart and then continued. ''I think I
ave a sample around here somewhere. I'll get it. After that,
ou're free to go.''

Teagan nodded and watched her leave. From the stiffness
f her posture as she brushed pass her brother, Teagan had
o trouble guessing that she was letting him know that she
idn't approve of him returning to the room.

Zach glanced after his sister and then back at Teagan. He
ave her a sheepish grin. ''You'll have to excuse her. She
an be a little overpowering at times.''

''You didn't mention before that she was your sister.''

''I didn't?'' He shrugged and stepped back into the room.
I guess I forget sometimes that everyone doesn't know the
xtent of the McCoy clan.''

She didn't answer right away. Instead, she reached over and
arefully smoothed out the wrinkled paper on the examining
ble. There was no point in telling her that someone would
e in to tear the sheet off and throw it away, and a fresh new
heet would be pulled down for the next patient. Teagan
asn't an idiot—she realized that. But she did it anyway,
usying herself with something other than him. And Zach
idn't say anything to stop her; he simply waited.

When she finally looked up, he could feel the wall standing
etween them again, and he wondered how she had managed
o rebuild it brick by brick in the few short minutes she had
een out of his sight. No doubt his sister had said something
o get it erected again in such a short period of time.

''You okay?'' he asked.

''Fine. A small cut is all.'' She hooked her sandal with her
oes and pulled it closer. She shoved her foot into it and then
ent down to gently ease the strap up over her heel.

Zach tried not to stare, but the sweet curve of her back,
isible through the soft material of her shirt, sent a pang of
onging through him. A pang so deep and swift that it took
im by surprise. Damn her. He'd worked so hard over the

past few years to purge Teagan from his system, and she h
walked back in as if she'd never left, bringing back a flo
of emotions he'd thought were long gone. His body still hu
gered for her, responded to her as if she'd never left his sid

"We need to go somewhere and talk about what's happe
ing up there at the compound," he said.

"I also need to get to a phone," she said, straightening u

He nodded. "You can use the one at my office."

"I'll need some privacy. I can't have anyone seeing n
make a call to the outside."

"My office is private. All anyone has to know is that you'
a witness I'm taking a statement from."

One of her overall straps had slid down, hanging off h
shoulder and giving her an unexpectedly vulnerable look. I
pushed aside the urge to reach out and slip it back into plac
knowing inside that what he really wanted was to feel th
graceful sweep of her shoulder blade beneath his fingers.

But he didn't move. He knew she didn't want to tha
Didn't want to feel anything.

"That'll work. I've got to let my boss know that Miguel
dead. He's going to have to call Linda." She glanced up
him and he noticed the flicker of anguish darkened her ey
for a moment. But she swallowed and continued. "That's h
wife—Linda. They have two girls—eight and ten."

She glanced away, and for a second, Zach was sure th
her eyes welled up with tears. But when she looked bac
again, her eyes were dry and her gaze steady. The same o
Teagan—hard as nails and blessed or haunted with a dete
mined will. It depended on how one wanted to look at th
whole issue of denial.

He stepped closer, putting his hand on her shoulder. "Yo
know, it really is okay to cry. You lost a good friend. I
watched your back and you watched his. In my book, th
makes for a pretty intense relationship."

Sparks of anger flashed in the depths of her eyes. "Don

ell me how to feel, Zach. I don't need it.'' She shrugged out
from beneath his hand.

"Somehow, I think you do."

"Look, I cared about Miguel more than you'll ever know."
She yanked her hair back away from her face with one hand
and slipped a rubber band around it, securing it at the back
of her neck. It was her "let's get down to business" gesture.
A gesture meant to tell him to back off. "But wallowing in
grief isn't going to get me where I need to be right now. I
need to be finding out what Reverend Mercy and his cult are
up to."

"And in spite of that, you're not permitted to be human
for one minute and allow yourself a little time to mourn someone you cared for a great deal?"

Teagan froze, her fingers curling into fists. Her knuckles
turned white and he knew her nails were biting into the palms
of her hands. He had hit a nerve.

Her breathing was short and uneven. "Everyone mourns in
their own way." The words were clipped and cold.

"Not when they're always running away."

She pulled back, stung by his words. "I didn't run away.
I left because the direction we were headed didn't make sense
for us."

He knew just as she did that the conversation was no longer
about the loss of her partner. A giant crack had split down
the middle of her newly constructed wall.

"Made sense for whom?" He used his foot to swing the
door shut, cutting off the bustle of staff and patients in the
hall. The closeness of the tiny examining room seemed to
press in on them, making it seem as if they were the only
people in the world. "Are you telling me that you knew how
I felt back then?" he asked. "Because I don't recall you ever
actually asking me how I felt."

She didn't answer for a moment, a legion of emotions—
anger, despair, fear, all fighting for dominance at once. Although Zach knew he was pushing her past her limit at a time

when she was terribly vulnerable, he couldn't back off. He
had to know. Had to understand what had happened to them

"You left, Tea. Just walked out without even saying good
bye. At least you could have stopped to see if we could have
worked things out. Instead, you decided for both of us."

She swallowed hard, her throat working hard. But in spite
of the regret in her eyes, there was no missing the tiny in
dentation at the corners of her lush lips. The familiar sign that
she wasn't about to back off or change her mind.

She shook her head. "I'm sorry, Zach. It was a long time
ago and maybe I wasn't thinking too clearly. I can only plead
ignorance. I thought I was doing the best thing for us at the
time. If I was wrong, I apologize. Leaving is never easy on
anyone."

Zach shook his head, suddenly weary of battling with her
over words. If she didn't want to talk about what had hap
pened to them seven years ago, then there was little sense in
him forcing the issue. He needed to accept that he was prob
ably never going to get a satisfactory answer.

"Yeah, you're right. Leaving's a bitch. Forget I ever
brought it up. We have other things to deal with." He grabbed
the doorknob and yanked the door open. "Look, I'll go get
the ointment from my sister. I'll meet you up front."

That said, he turned and walked out.

ZACH FOUND HIS SISTER in the back supply room, rummaging
through a cabinet filled with a variety of drug samples. She
glanced up when he walked in and he could tell from her
expression that she had immediately picked up on his mood.
It didn't surprise him. She was the more perceptive of the
McCoy sisters, or at least she seemed to be when it came to
him.

"Well, if that isn't a familiar Zach McCoy expression,"
she said, grabbing a sample box and straightening up. "Don't
tell me, the two of you have already started to argue, right?"

"I just came to get the medicine, Helen. I don't need a well-meaning but ill-timed sisterly lecture."

Helen laughed, but the sound had a bitter ring to it. "What are you doing, Zach? The woman is trouble. Didn't you suffer enough the first time around?"

"Drop it, Helen. You don't even know what you're talking about." Zach reached out and took the box from her hand.

As he turned to go she pressed on. "Look, I'm not an idiot. I can see how beautiful she is." She stepped closer, her hand touching his forearm in an expression of concern. "But she's wound up so tight that she looks about ready to snap. And so do you. Neither of you need this."

Zach gently placed his hand over his sister's and squeezed, wanting to reassure her. "As much as I adore you—and you know I do—this isn't any of your business. I appreciate you seeing her today and taking care of her. You're a good doctor and an even better sister."

Helen shook her head. "You're making a mistake, Zach."

"Well, it wouldn't be the first time." He turned to leave and then stopped. "You look tired, Helen. When are you going to start taking care of yourself instead of worrying about everyone else?"

Although Helen obviously knew it was an outright ploy to get the subject off of himself, she smiled. "Funny you should mention that. Alex and I are taking a weekend for ourselves. We're going to go down to New York to see a few shows. Dr. Penner over in E-town is going to cover for me."

"Who's going to watch the girls?"

Helen laughed. "Don't worry. I'm not planning to deposit them on your doorstep."

"Hey, you know I'd take them in a New York minute. But I can't this weekend with the case I've got going."

Helen held up a hand to halt his protests. "Relax. I've got Pam Springer coming over to sit. Mom is going to stop in to check in on them, and you can poke your head in a couple of times this weekend just to see that they're not destroying the place.''

Zach frowned. ''Pam Springer is a flake. Couldn't you get anyone else?''

''Actually, no. But I plan to leave her a very specific list of the dos and don'ts. They'll be fine.'' She glanced at her watch. ''And now, I've got to get back to work. My waiting room is filled.''

Zach allowed her to slip by him into the hall, tolerating her quick peck on his cheek as she passed.

''Make sure Mom stops in more than once, and make sure Pam knows that I'm planning to swing by unannounced. That way Pam won't have any unauthorized guests over,'' he said

Helen turned around and hit him with one of her unflinching, no-nonsense stares. ''Maybe you need to start worrying more about yourself. I have a feeling you just walked back into the jaws of a very beautiful but deadly barracuda.''

''You don't know her, Helen.''

''No, you're right. I don't. But I know very well the pain you went through seven years ago. And call me a busybody, but I love you too much to see you go through all that again.''

''It's not going to happen.''

Helen nodded, studying him for a minute. ''I sure hope not, for your sake.'' She turned, and walked to the door of the next examining room. As she plucked the chart out of the box hanging next to it, she glanced back at him. He could read her concern as easily as he read her determination not to pressure him anymore. She waved and opened the door, stepping inside without another word.

Zach stood alone in the hall, the muted sounds of voices coming from the rooms lining the hall. He threw the small medicine box up in the air and caught it. No, he wasn't going to be hurt again. He planned to make sure of that. But he was going to find out why Teagan had left him, if it was the last thing he did.

A SHORT TIME LATER, a sample tube of prescription ointment tucked in her back pocket and a bill in her hand, Teagan stepped out onto the front steps of Dr. Wade's medical clinic. Zach followed close on her heels.

A quick glance in the direction of the driveway told Teagan that the trouble she'd been expecting had arrived. One of the Temple's vans, a battered, barely drivable drab green vehicle, sat at the end of the driveway, blocking Zach's patrol car in. But it was the two men next to the van that worried her more than the fact that they were blocked in.

Cyrus, his arms folded across his chest and an impatient frown on his brutish face, scowled at the two of them. Eddie, seated on the back fender, stood and glanced anxiously at Cyrus. He was obviously looking to the other man for some kind of direction.

"Let me take care of this," Zach said, brushing past her.

A sharp retort about her being able to take care of herself threatened to slip out, but Teagan bit it back. He was right. She was supposed to be in his custody. It would look better if she allowed him to handle the reverend's two thugs.

She took her time getting down the steps as Zach strolled across the clinic's front lawn to face Cyrus.

"We came to pick up Sister Teagan," Cyrus said. He motioned for Eddie to open the side door of the van. "Reverend Mercy wants her back home."

Zach stopped a few feet from the van. "Nice of you to drive all the way down for her, but she's not quite done here. The doctor just checked out her leg, and now I'm taking her on over to my office to get an official statement." He turned around. "Sister Teagan, I'd appreciate it if you'd get in my patrol car, please. We'll be leaving in a moment." He turned back toward Cyrus. "Just as soon as these nice gentlemen move their van."

"I ain't moving anywhere." Cyrus moved as if to walk past Zach.

Zach held out a hand to stop him.

"You best not go against the Father's will, woman," Cyrus shouted around Zach.

Teagan knew how to play the part. She paused, glancing anxiously back and forth between the two men. "Perhaps should return with Brother Cyrus, Sheriff."

"You need to get in the car, Sister," Zach said without turning his head. "Brother Cyrus is about to be cited for a misdemeanor if he doesn't move his car."

Cyrus paused, indecision on his face. Apparently he didn' have permission from the reverend to get into any legal trouble.

Teagan quietly slipped into the front seat of Zach's patrol car and then watched in the side mirror, keeping an eye on the situation behind her.

Zach waited, his weight balanced on one hip, his arms folded. She couldn't see his expression, but she was fairly certain it was unflinchingly calm. The man was a rock. If Cyrus didn't realize that there was no way he was getting past Zach, than he was stupider than she had thought.

Finally, Cyrus backed down. He motioned for Eddie to get in the van and then he climbed in. He backed the vehicle up squealing the tires on the hot pavement. Zach climbed into the patrol car and shot her a cocky grin as he turned the keys in the ignition. There was no missing the fact that he liked winning.

He backed out and she glanced in the direction of the green van; Cyrus glared at her through the windshield.

"He's going to follow us back to your office," she said.

Zach shrugged. "Who cares? He doesn't dare start anything at the police station, and I was up-front about you coming down to give a statement. Let him follow."

They headed out of town, the van following a short distance behind them. The silence between them was heavy, and Teagan had a strong feeling that Zach was trying to decide how to speak to her about the issues bothering him. She knew without him opening his mouth that he wanted more information on her mission inside the camp. And something told her that he wasn't going to settle for the brief explanation she'd given last time.

As if on cue, he asked, "Don't you think it's about time that you told me why the ATF is so interested in Mercy and The Disciples' Temple?"

Teagan glanced across and met the endless Caribbean blue of his eyes. They seemed to demand an explanation, their sincerity and trust boring a hole through her defenses.

Did she dare tell him? She sighed inwardly. How did she dare *not* tell him?

With Miguel's death, Zach had become her only viable contact with the outside. There wasn't time for her superior to get another agent installed inside Mercy's organization. She was alone, totally cut off. She didn't have any other option than to trust Zach. She had to put her life in his hands and come completely clean about what they suspected. She had to trust that he wouldn't jeopardize the mission by talking with others about the sensitive nature of her assignment.

She took a deep breath and plunged in. "About eight months ago, a man was arrested in Boston for a series of armed robberies. The gun was unregistered, and ATF agents ran the gun down—found out it was sold by a small gun dealer in the Worcester area. He didn't have his paperwork in order and the agents leaned on him hard."

"And they found out he'd been selling more than a few unregistered guns, right?"

Teagan nodded and reached down to turn the air-conditioner vent so that it blew right on her. Apparently the county patrol car's cooling system wasn't top-notch. The breeze coming out of the vent was paltry.

"The guy was a regular old-fashioned gunrunner. It was unbelievable what he managed to run in and out of that little shop. We got the Justice Department to cut him a deal for information about who he was selling to. Reverend Mercy's

name was on the list—he was the one who bought the most
substantial number of guns—a cache of semiautomatics.''

''Which red-flagged him in a big way, right.''

Teagan nodded. Telling Zach all this wasn't easy. A part
of her screamed that she was stepping over the line, that she
should wait until she got the go-ahead from her supervisor.
Sharing intelligence with local law enforcement *was* done, but
only when the supervising agent in charge gave permission.
And even then, the information was carefully filtered.

But Teagan knew that she owed Zach this information. He
had stuck around, helped her out of a tough situation. And he
might be her only lifeline left right now.

''We're pretty sure the guns were shipped up here.''

''How do you know that?''

''Process of elimination—we can't find them anywhere else
in Boston.''

''And your boss won't go in and search New Jerusalem
because he's worried he's going to create an uproar that will
result in things escalating out of control, right?''

She nodded. ''We have to be sure the guns are actually
here before stepping in. No one wants to take the risk of
touching off another Waco. The profilers have done an exten-
sive file on Daniel Mercy using all the information we have
on him. They feel that he's pretty close to the edge.''

''And the fact that he's a certified explosives expert makes
you doubly nervous, right?''

Teagan shot him a quick look, a small smile playing with
one corner of her mouth. ''You've been busy doing your
homework, haven't you?''

''I'm not a county bumpkin, Tea. My staff may be small
compared to the ATF, but they're good. So what's the deal
with explosives?''

She shrugged. ''We're not positive, but we think he might
have been able to get his hands on some explosives in addition
to the guns.''

Zach shook his head. ''Great. The guy's a certifiable loon

sitting on a cache of guns *and* explosives.'' He glanced over at her. ''What kind of explosives are we talking about?''

''Titadine.''

His foot must have slipped off the pedal because the speed of the patrol car dropped dramatically. Teagan glanced in the side mirror and watched the van inch closer to their back bumper. ''Uh, mind picking it up a little? Otherwise Cyrus is going to end up sitting in your back seat.''

Zach's grip on the wheel tightened and he hit the accelerator. The patrol car shot forward.

Teagan ventured a glance in his direction. She wasn't surprised to see the muscle in his cheek tighten into a hard knot. The news about the explosives hadn't gone over well. He didn't speak for a few moments.

Finally, he said, ''When exactly were you planning to let me know this? Or was this going to be your little secret?''

''You know that keeping this all secret wasn't my decision. It's standard operating procedure.'' She kept her eyes forward, not wanting Cyrus to figure out she was having a regular gab fest in the front seat of the local police cruiser. ''I'm taking a chance even telling you now.''

Zach nodded but he didn't look convinced. He wasn't pleased about being left in the dark about the severity of the situation at New Jerusalem, and Teagan couldn't say she blamed him.

Although the site was fairly remote, and Reverend Mercy's paranoia kept his little religious order essentially isolated from the residents of Essex County, Teagan knew that Zach was thinking about all the women and children he had seen living inside the walls of the compound.

No doubt he was thinking about Reverend Mercy's talk about establishing a bond of friendship with the townspeople of Bradley. Who wanted to be friends with a man who was sitting on a pile of automatic weapons and a cache of Titadine dynamite?

Chapter Twelve

Twenty minutes later, Zach pulled into the county seat of Essex County, Elizabethtown. In the rearview mirror, he watched as Cyrus followed close on their heels. He wondered if the man intended to sit outside his office until Teagan was released. If he did, Zach vowed that it was going to be a long wait. He liked the idea of the man having to cool his heels outside the sheriff's office.

Taking a right onto the main drag, he passed a few shops and then the county government buildings. He wondered if the buildings looked as quaint and small townish to Teagan as they suddenly did to him.

Over the years, he'd checked up on her. The majority of her professional career had been out of Boston and Washington, D.C. Which meant that since she'd left Plattsburgh, she had spent much of her life in large metropolitan areas. He knew it must seem strange to her to find herself back in the small, rural community surrounding Sunset Lake.

He pulled into his reserved slot behind the government buildings and climbed out. Teagan stepped out of the passenger side and paused to look around.

She glanced at him over the roof of the car. "Cyrus pulled into Stewart's across the street."

"Hope he's prepared for a nice wait."

She grinned. "At least he'll be able to get a good cup of

coffee.'' She glanced around, taking in the sight of the tiny community hospital a short distance away. "Remember when you broke your big toe on that climb up Pocco?"

He nodded.

"We took you there, right? To that little hospital."

He nodded again. "The operative word being *little,* right?"

She shot him a puzzled look, but Zach didn't bother to explain. Instead, he headed toward the side door of the County Sheriff's Department. "Let's go inside."

As soon as he pushed open the door and stepped inside, Candi spied him. She motioned the man at the front counter to wait, and she hurried over to him.

"Boy, am I glad to see you." She gave Teagan a quick glance, her expression revealing her curiosity, but she continued. "Dave Springer from over in Bradley has been calling all morning. He said he needed to talk to you as soon as you came in."

"What does the mayor want?"

Candi shrugged. "He called all excited about this Day of Unity thing you've got planned with that religious place up by Sunset Lake." She shot a quick glance in Teagan's direction, her expression revealing that she was well aware that Teagan was from the very place she was talking about. "I guess he just called to say he was on board and thought it was a great idea."

"Okay, thanks. If he calls again, tell him I'm tied up for the day and I'll get back to him later." He stopped, his brain racing. "Do me a favor, Candi and call my sister's office. Tell her to remind the mayor's daughter Pam not to take the twins up to the Day of Unity celebration on Saturday. Let my sister know that I'll explain later."

He pushed open the swinging gate and motioned Teagan through. "My office is straight on back, Miss Benson. I'd appreciate it if you'd go on in and have a seat. I'll be with you in a moment."

As Teagan started back toward his office, the side door

opened and Drake walked in. He was studying a piece of paper, his expression so intense that he didn't even notice them.

"Everything okay, Drake?" Zach asked. Out of the corner of his eye, he saw Teagan pause on her way to his office.

Drake looked up, startled to see him. "You gotta see this." He held up the piece of paper. "They're up all over town."

Zach took the paper, giving it a quick look.

AN EVENING OF PEACE & HARMONY
The Disciples' Temple invites you
to
CELEBRATE A DAY OF UNITY
When: Sat. July 22nd
Time: 7:00 p.m. to 11:00 p.m.
Where: New Jerusalem
Refreshments, music and camaraderie will abound

Drake leaned over his shoulder and pointed to the statement typed at the bottom of the page. "Did you give them permission to put that?"

Zach frowned. At the bottom of the poster, in bold type, it said:

Sponsored
by
The Disciples' Temple & the Essex County
Sheriff's Department.

A warning chill settled into the pit of Zach's stomach. Mercy had been a busy man. What did this mean? Was Mercy already using his assumed close relationship with Zach to manipulate things? The question, however, was why? What was he going to get out of holding the Day of Unity and enticing the townspeople to participate? There was no doubt in Zach's mind that by putting the Essex County Sheriff's Department's name at the bottom of the poster that more people would go to the event. They trusted him. His name meant something in this county. But what was the reason? The fact that his name was on the poster didn't mean that people would convert to Mercy's religion in one afternoon. In fact, most people would go to the event only out of curiosity.

He glanced up at Drake. "I didn't give anyone permission to post this or to include our name on the bottom as a sponsor."

"Want me to go up to that place and have a little chat with them?" Drake asked.

Zach thought for a moment and then shook his head. "No, I'll take care of it." He folded the poster in half and stuck it in his back pocket. "Are there a lot of posters up?"

Drake laughed. "They're on every post, tree and store window between here and Bradley. I'm sure if I drove over to Lewis or Westport I'd find them all over the place there, too." He cocked his head. "Want me to get them pulled down?"

"Yeah, get them down. Unfortunately, I'm sure they've been seen already."

"Well, if anyone asks, we can make sure they know that it's a mistake."

"True, but at this point, there's not enough time to print a retraction. We'll just have to do a bit of damage control." Zach turned to Teagan. "If you'll follow me, miss, we'll get that statement finished up." He led her into his office and gently closed the door behind him.

"What do you think that was all about?" she asked, taking a seat in one of the chairs across from his desk. He could read the relief in her face as she sat down. His sister might have treated her injured leg, but until she got a decent night's sleep and a belly full of nutritious food, she was going to be wiped out.

He held up a hand and reopened the door. "Candi!"

His secretary looked up from her desk. "Yes, Sheriff?"

"Call Bub's and order a pepperoni-and-mushroom pizza

with extra cheese and two large colas." He started to close the door and then reopened it to add, "Have them send over a quart of homemade macaroni soup, too."

"You got it." Her red lacquered nails were already flying over the keys of her phone as he closed the door.

Turning back to Teagan, he didn't miss the look of gratitude in her eyes. "Bub's pizza. You're a saint, Zachary Mc Coy. My mouth is watering just at the thought of biting into some of Bub's pizza."

He laughed and moved around his desk to sit across from her. He would have preferred to sit right next to her, but he was willing to follow the rules she'd set down about him keeping his distance. He pulled the paper out of his pocket and passed it over to her. "Got any thoughts on what he's up to?"

She read it over again and a small frown of concentration popped up between her eyebrows. She caught her bottom lip with her teeth and gnawed on it gently. Finally, she looked up. "There has to be a reason behind this, but for the life of me, I can't figure out what he's up to. With his paranoia, it doesn't make sense that he'd just invite a bunch of unknowns into his living space."

"I agree. But somehow he's thinking that if he uses my name—or the name of the Essex County Sheriff's Department, the event is somehow sanctioned by us. And that means more people will go. The question is, why would he want people there?" Zach leaned back. "He has to know that he isn't going to convert anyone in one evening."

Teagan's frown deepened, her expression intense. "And he couldn't want them there as hostages. He has over three hundred people already inside the compound. Any more than that and the number becomes too unwieldy—in fact, the number is *already* unwieldy. Daniel Mercy's smart enough to realize that."

Frustrated, Zach straightened up and pushed his phone across the desk at her. "Why don't you make that call now

We'll try to figure this out after you've talked to your supervisor. Maybe he's got some insight."

Teagan shifted forward and grabbed the receiver.

He watched as she quickly punched in a number and then sat back, waiting for the connection. Her eyes met his across the desk and he knew without her saying anything that she would have preferred some privacy. But he gave her a lot of credit for not asking him to leave. He figured it was because she knew him well enough to know that he wasn't about to leave. Whether she liked it or not, this case had now become as much his as it was hers.

Getting connected to her supervisor, Allen Paine, took less time than she had expected. He must have been anticipating the call because she had no sooner identified herself to the person answering the phone than she was patched through to Paine's office.

"Where are you?" Paine asked as soon as he picked up the phone.

"I'm in the local sheriff's office. I don't have a lot of time."

"Are you alone?"

Teagan glanced over at Zach, and he stared back across the desk at her, raising his eyebrow with a touch of amusement. She knew he wasn't about to budge. "No, Sheriff McCoy is sitting right across from me."

There was a moment of silence on the other end. Teagan knew that Paine was weighing what she had said, considering possible courses of action.

"Special Agent Lopez is dead, sir," she said quietly.

"When? How did it happen?" Paine asked, his voice calm. If she didn't already know how close Paine was to Miguel, Teagan was sure she would never have known it from the flat, matter-of-fact tone of his voice.

"He was murdered, sir. Strangled and then dumped over the side of a ravine. I found him earlier this morning. The sheriff brought me back here to take a statement. I had to tell him about my role inside the compound."

Teagan swallowed nervously, unsure how Paine was taking all of this.

"Has your cover been compromised?"

"I don't think so, sir."

"Is the sheriff familiar with Mercy?"

"Yes, sir. For some reason, unclear to the both of us, Reverend Mercy has been trying to cultivate some kind of alliance with the sheriff. He seems to think he needs the sheriff's approval in order to establish some kind of cooperation between his commune and the local community."

"Put me on speakerphone, Kennedy," Paine ordered.

Within a few minutes, the phone call was diverted to the speakerphone and Zach was introduced to Teagan's supervisor.

Paine quickly made it clear that there was no chance that he'd be able to insert another agent anywhere near the compound as a backup for Teagan. They all knew that the circle around Mercy had gotten much too restrictive.

After a few minutes of fast talking, Zach made it clear that he was volunteering as Teagan's new backup, and Teagan knew without anything being said, that Paine wasn't totally comfortable with that plan.

Federal agents weren't known for actively seeking out the assistance of the local police unless they were forced to. Recruiting help on a need-to-know basis was fine, but intimate involvement in a case was not common practice. But Paine wasn't a dumb man, and he definitely hadn't gotten to the level he was at without breaking a few rules once in a while. He knew that things were heating up and he needed to keep Teagan inside the compound. She was the eyes and ears of the whole operation, and there was no way he could leave her on the inside without backup. So, that meant that Zach was in.

"We have a pretty good idea what Mercy has got planned," Paine said.

Teagan glanced at Zach, unable to hide her surprise. "What would that be, sir?"

"Are either of you familiar with the name Winston Chandler?"

"The television anchorman?" Zach asked, his expression puzzled. "Isn't he the guy who hosts that TV news show *Hard Exposure?*"

"That's the one, Sheriff McCoy. Chandler came to us several days ago through other channels. He told us he'd been in contact with Reverend Daniel Mercy."

"Didn't Chandler do an exposé on Reverend Mercy and The Disciples' Temple last year?" Teagan asked.

"Yes, but it wasn't a very flattering story on the man," Paine stated. "According to Chandler, Mercy approached him with a request for another interview. But this time he came packing a bit of persuasion." Paine paused as if considering his next statement carefully. "Mercy has let Chandler know that his daughter is living inside the cult, and that unless Chandler agrees to broadcast one of his sermons on national television, he'll never see his daughter again."

Teagan slid to the edge of her seat. "Do we have a picture of the girl, sir? I might have seen her."

She could hear Paine shuffling through papers on his desk. "I have a photo here. I can fax it to you."

Her palms suddenly warm, Teagan rubbed them across the top of her pants. "By any chance is the girl petite with blue-colored hair and lots of body piercings?"

"Bingo, Kennedy, you hit it on the first try," Paine said. "I'm guessing that means you've seen her inside Mercy's compound, right?"

"Yes, sir. The girl arrived yesterday—on the very bus Lopez drove up from Boston."

Paine swore softly. "We need to get her out of there. Chandler won't agree to stall the broadcast as long as Mercy has his daughter in his custody." The supervising agent cleared his throat. "In fact, Chandler's on his way there with a camera crew to do the broadcast Saturday night."

Teagan and Zach's gazes met again.

Zach gave a low whistle. "It can't be coincidence that the broadcast is scheduled for the same day Mercy's holding his so-called Day of Unity."

"Day of Unity? What the hell is that?" Paine asked, his voice rumbling over the phone line.

Zach quickly explained how Mercy had proposed a day of peace and unity between the Bradley townspeople and the Temple members. He expressed his own confusion as to the reason behind this plan.

"Sounds to me like he's stacking the deck—getting as big an audience as he can for his national debut," Paine offered.

"No disrespect, sir, but why?" Teagan asked. "I mean he's got a captured, dedicated audience in the members of the cult. Why bring in outsiders? It just doesn't fit with his typical paranoia."

"Is it possible that he's doing all of this in order to position himself as a more mainstream religious leader?" Paine asked.

Teagan shook her head, her hands tightening into fists. How could she get Paine to understand how out of character this current behavior was for Daniel Mercy, how on edge it was making her feel? "I don't think so, sir. If anything, his latest sermons seem to indicate that he's more off the wall than ever—more out of the mainstream."

Zach shifted restlessly in his chair. "Look, we could speculate about this all day. But the reality of the situation is that we won't know until Mercy tells us or until we actually see for ourselves his reason." He got up and started to pace. "In any case, we need to concentrate on finding the guns and explosives. Those are the things that make him the most dangerous. He isn't going to kill anyone with words, but he can with those weapons stashed on the compound site. Do you agree?"

Teagan nodded. ''I'm going to need more time inside the compound.''

Paine grunted in agreement. ''All right, I'm prepared to give you both until Saturday afternoon. After that I want you out. And if you can get Chandler's daughter out with you, all the better.''

''At this point, Mercy is still letting me enter the compound fairly freely,'' Zach said. ''I'll keep a close eye on her. Do we let the Day of Unity celebration go on as planned?''

Paine was quiet again as he considered the question. Finally he said, ''I say we let it go on as planned. But I'll use the occasion to send in a contingent of agents posing as townspeople and *Hard Exposure* staffers. Mercy will never be able to tell the difference, and their presence will give both of you more backup.''

Within a few minutes, the three wrapped up their conversation. Before hanging up, Zach agreed to be the one responsible for maintaining contact with Paine. Teagan felt a sense of relief that he'd keep her supervisor apprised of her progress toward locating the weapons and explosives.

Now she had to find what they were looking for. The thought of going back inside the cult sent a twinge of anxiety shooting through her. Even with Zach as her backup, Teagan knew that Daniel Mercy was up to something, something she nor Zach had figured out yet. And whatever it was that he had planned, it was going to happen sooner than they all expected.

Chapter Thirteen

As they pulled out of the sheriff department's parking lot once again in Zach's truck, Zach quickly checked Stewart's lot for a glimpse of the Temple's beat-up van. But it was gone. No doubt Cyrus and his sidekick, Eddie, had gotten tired of waiting and returned to New Jerusalem.

Heading out of town, the two of them rode in silence for a good fifteen minutes. The late-afternoon sun beat against the front windshield, hitting them both with its brilliance. Zach flipped down his visor and grabbed for his sunglasses.

As he slipped them on, he nodded toward the glove compartment. "There's an extra pair in there if you'd like."

Teagan nodded and leaned forward to rummage through his junk. Her position put her in the direct path of the air conditioner. He grinned as she stayed bent over, seeming to savor the feel of the cooling breeze on her face.

His gut tightened in response to the vision of the dark strands of hair whipping back from her elegant features. She grinned and closed her eyes, allowing the air-conditioning to wash over her. Even hot, tired and sweaty from her long day and perilous climb, Teagan managed to look desirable. It was strange how feelings like this one seemed to catch hold and shake him when he least expected it. But no matter how much he desired her, she'd made it perfectly clear that there was no way she could return those feelings. He forced himself to focus his attention back on the road.

A short time later, he turned on to Sunset Lake Road. He tried not to dwell on the thought of what waited for Teagan once she walked back through the gates of New Jerusalem.

He knew even without any concrete proof that her partner had been executed by Mercy and his men. Now he was agreeing to assist the ATF in their plan to insert her back into the dangerous cult. A part of him wanted to make a U turn and head back down the mountain. Instead, he was now part of the plan to place the woman he still loved back into the nest of dangerous vipers.

But the other part of him, the lawman part of him, knew that he couldn't back off. He knew that he had to think of all the innocent lives still living within the confines of Mercy's compound. All the families that had no clue of the danger they were in. And he also knew, deep in his heart, that Teagan would never agree to back away from what she believed was her duty. It was that fierce dedication that only cemented his love for her.

"I'll be up again in the morning," he said, swerving slightly to miss a crazed chipmunk's dash for the opposite side of the rutted road.

She nodded and concentrated on the road ahead.

"Are you sure you're ready to go back there?" he asked.

She glanced over at him. "No, I'm not ready yet."

Her voice was soft, pitched so low he almost missed it over the rumble of the vehicle's engine. He glanced at her, not quite sure he had heard her right.

"What did you say?"

She sighed and leaned back, resting her head against the headrest, her hair loose and flowing, her eyes closed. Her lashes spiked along the upper line of her cheekbones, shielding her eyes from him and the invading sun. Her hands lay loosely in her lap.

"I said, I'm not ready to go back yet." She rolled her head

toward him and met his questioning gaze with her own. "
think we need to talk a little before I go back inside."

Zach pulled over, not quite trusting himself to discuss thi
surprising development while driving. His heart hammere
against his ribs, and although he felt as if he had waited
lifetime for this moment—this sudden willingness on her pa
to open herself to him—he knew only too well the possibl
cost to them both.

Could she really believe that stalling now was the righ
thing? If she didn't return soon, how would Mercy react?
was possible that the preacher would take steps to see tha
she ended up like Miguel—on the cold, hard autopsy table i
the Essex County morgue.

"You don't even know what you're saying. We've put yo
at enough risk by not sending you back with Cyrus. Let m
walk you in. Talk to him and explain."

She stared straight ahead, her eyes seeming to search th
road for some unanswered question. Finally, she turned bac
to face him. Her gaze was steady, totally open, and sh
reached up to gently touch his face as if memorizing the shap
of it with the tips of her fingers. The gesture seemed oddl
vulnerable, as if she were asking him for his protection. Ye
Zach knew she would never do that.

Once she reentered New Jerusalem she was totally at th
mercy of a madman. Mercy would use Teagan any way h
pleased, and that fact tore at Zach's gut. Made his inside
rage against the very thought.

"We need to push Daniel Mercy outside his comfo
zone."

Zach turned off the ignition and cracked his window. /
light breeze slipped through the crack and filled the cab wit
the scent of wildflowers and pine. "Look, pushing him ou
side his comfort zone is one thing. But setting a fire unde
the guy is suicide. If you don't show up soon, he's going t
go bonkers. And there's no telling how he'd react."

Teagan shifted around, and cocked one leg up on the edg

f the seat. She leaned forward, her expression intense. "I've hought a lot about this, Zach. Up to this point, you and I have done everything Reverend Mercy has wanted. He figures he's got the both of us wrapped around his little finger. All he has to do is jerk the string and you and I jump." She leaned in closer. "Well, I think now is the time to turn the tables on him. Shake him up a little. If he expects me to be back inside he compound before dark, I say I should show up later. He knows I'm with you. So, he's going to worry what we're doing, what we're thinking."

"Oh, he'll be worrying, all right. What makes you think he won't send someone after you?"

She shrugged. "He might, but I'm guessing he won't. Not with everything he needs to get done between now and Saturday. But—" she reached across and pressed the flat of her hand against the middle of his chest "—the whole time, he'll be thinking about how much control he has over you and me."

Zach tensed, determined not to jump as the pressure of her fingers seemed to burn down to the core of his belly. He shifted slightly, conscious of the tightening in his groin.

If she moved her hand lower, he'd be the one who was worrying. Worrying he'd lose control and pull her into his arms whether she wanted him to or not. He forced himself to focus on what she was saying and not what was going on below his waist.

"All that gets us is Mercy at his psycho best," he protested. "And in turn, it puts you more at risk when I bring you back."

Teagan shook her head, her expression frustrated. "Don't you see? We *want* him angry. Pushing Daniel Mercy off balance increases the chance that he'll make a wrong move. We both know that we don't have much time left. If he's planning something for the Day of Unity, we only have two days to figure it out. We have to force his hand."

"So you're thinking that by extending your curfew, you' force his hand?"

She shrugged. "It's possible."

"Okay, I can see where you're going with this, but I can' say that I like it."

She reached out again and laid her hand lightly on his thigh her expression imploring. "I can't say that I'm crazy about either, Zach, but it's all we have left right now."

Zach struggled to process what she was saying. On on level, he wanted desperately to move away from her touch To escape the wild sensations she was creating inside him But on another level, he wanted to savor the sweet hunger caused. He realized with a pang of regret that she still ha the power to seduce him with a single brush of her hand.

"I hope we don't regret this later," he managed.

She laughed without much humor. "You and me both."

Zach started the truck and shoved it into gear. As the zipped past the turnoff for the compound, he felt his gu tighten. No doubt the sentries would note they had passed b the turnoff. It wouldn't be long before Mercy knew she wasn' returning immediately. He wondered how the religious leade would take the news.

A FEW MINUTES LATER, at the site of his lean-to, Zac watched Teagan pace back and forth in front on the newl built campfire. Every restless movement of her long limbs wa a testament to her nervousness.

She had talked about wanting Mercy to sweat a little, bu at the moment, Zach thought she looked as though she wa the one who was about ready to burst into flames.

He leaned over and picked up the coffeepot. "Want cup?"

She shook her head. "No, I'm already too keyed up."

"No kidding?" he said sarcastically, and then dipped hi head to hide a smile.

She paused midpace. "Oh, smart guy, huh? Maybe you'v

rgotten that I'm the one that has to walk back through the
tes at the end of all this?''

"Nope, I haven't forgotten. But I also remember that you
ere the one who thought this was such a great idea.'' He
ted his head. "Getting cold feet?''

She grinned and shook her head. "No. Not when I know
at Reverend Mercy is down there sweating it out.''

He stood and walked over to stand in front of her, forcing
r to meet his gaze. "I have the perfect home remedy for a
d case of the nerves.'' His grin was wicked, a flash of white
the gathering dusk.

She couldn't help but smile in return. "And what exactly
this perfect home remedy?''

He reached out and slid his hand beneath the weight of her
ir, his fingers caressing the warm skin of her neck. She
aned back a little, testing the strength of his grasp, but he
lled her to him effortlessly. "Oh, it's a little something I
arned from the mountain men around these parts. It's been
own to make a woman weak in the knees, but it's a surefire
re for the jitters.''

Teagan molded her body to his, allowing her arms to slip
ound him. As he pulled her closer, pressing her to him, his
igh nudged between her legs, applying the most exquisite
essure to exactly the right place. She moaned softly and her
ad fell back. His lips settled on the pulse at her throat,
ating her blood to a slow, roiling boil.

She reached around him and pulled at his shirt, freeing it
om his pants, and then slid her hands beneath, following the
raight, sleek length of his spine. Air hissed between his teeth
her hands moved over him, and she marveled at the smooth
owerful glide of his muscles beneath her fingertips. As he
ted her closer, she felt him hard and ready against the soft-
ss of her belly, and she knew she wanted him right then,
ght there.

He reached between them, his hands sure and quick. The
raps of her overalls fell to her waist, and she shivered with

need as his hand crept up beneath the hem of her shirt, slidi
over her skin to cup her left breast. The rough calluses of l
hand teased and tormented her sensitive nipple, making h
bite her lower lip to keep from begging.

"I think I can really get into this homemade remedy
yours," she said breathlessly. She rose up on her toes a
met him halfway as he bent his head to kiss her.

Laughing softly, he scooped her up and carried her insi
the lean-to, setting her down on his sleeping bag on the c
"Oh, I *know* you're going to like it," he said, coming to re
beside her.

He gently smoothed her hair away from her face, and
she lay back, he paused, feeling as though he could bare
breathe. It was if someone had stolen his breath. She w
exquisite. A vision of dark beauty in the fading evening lig
Her hair, the color of midnight, spread out like a gatheri
cloud on his pillow, and her eyes, filled with question a
promise, stared up at him with more trust than he would ha
believed possible.

He slid her overalls and panties down over her slender hi
his fingers gliding over the smooth perfection of her limb
He flung her clothes aside and then moved slightly to pull c
his own. Teagan protested his unexpected desertion, and l
grinned teasingly, reaching down to put a finger over her lip
"Shh. Anticipation is everything."

"Savor this," she said, opening her lips and sucking h
finger into the warm wetness of her mouth. A shiver shot t
Zach's spine and he felt as though he might go over the edg
right them and there. But instead, he fumbled in the pock
of his pants, grabbing protection. He quickly shucked h
pants and tore open the round packet.

Teagan reached out and took the condom from his han
"Here, let me do that."

He watched in fascination as her slender fingers freed tl
condom and then slipped it over him, her touch lingerin
intimate and oh so erotic.

He bent his head and covered her lips with his own and she opened for him, her breath and tongue rising up to sweeten the length of his own tongue. As she raised her hips to meet him halfway and he sank into paradise, Zach thought about what he had missed all these years, and with a joy that was beyond comparison, he celebrated her return.

MEAGAN LAY SAFE in the circle of Zach's arms, the soft sound of his breath whispering against the outer edge of her ear. His legs lay intertwined with hers, and his chest was warm and hard against the length of her back.

One of his hands still cupped her right breast, the other lay under her neck, cradling her head. To the left, directly outside the lean-to, she could see a million stars wink down through the overhead canopy of leaves. A few yards away, the fire glowed a yellow-orange, an occasional crackle or snap of burning wood breaking the silence.

"That was just about perfect," she whispered.

He shifted slightly as if coming out of a light sleep, and nuzzled the back of her neck. "More than perfect. It was like coming home."

She smiled in the darkness, her skin feeling warm and tingly. He was right. It had been like coming home—a sense of such wonderful familiarity that it bordered on perfect joy. Somehow she'd forgotten how good it was. An intensity that filled her and chased away the strange hollowness that resided inside her. A hollowness that had hidden inside her for longer than she cared to remember.

His lips, hard and demanding, moved up the side of her neck to her ear. He sucked gently on the lobe of her ear and then whispered, "So, are you ready to tell me?"

"Tell you what?" she asked dreamily.

"Why you left?"

She stiffened beneath him and would have shifted away, but he didn't loosen his hold on her. Instead, his hands tightened around her, holding her even snugger against his hard

length. "Not this time, Tea. No running away. It's time
talk."

"Not now. Later. When the case over," she protested.

"We need to talk about it now." His hand slid down ov
her skin, tracing a line of heat from her breast to navel. H
touch was soft. Soothing. Comforting. "Just tell me. No an
ger. No recriminations. Just truth."

Something told Teagan that it was indeed time. It didn
matter if he understood or approved. He had been patien
gentle and she owed him the truth.

Taking comfort in the darkness covering the mountain an
the soft whisper of the night wind rustling through the su
rounding trees, she began. "When you left that day for clas
I met my father for lunch. He had called the day before. H
had some story about having to fly into the Plattsburgh Bas
for a meeting and wanting to see me."

She leaned her head back, nestling it against the streng
of his chest.

"I never suspected anything. I thought he just wanted
see me. I—I should have been suspicious. On guard. I kne
how much he disapproved of our relationship, and I'd tol
him during my last visit about how serious you and I wer
How much we cared for each other."

His lips touched the skin along her shoulder, nibbling, kiss
ing and laying down a trail of warmth and encouragement.

"We met at the Butcher Block." She reached down an
laid her hand over his. "He had been smart enough to leav
my stepmother, Sharon, at home. I actually thought we'd hav
a pleasant lunch. One without argument or guilt."

She lightly stroked his arm, loving the feel of his warm
skin beneath the tips of her fingers. "I should have know
better. We hadn't even gotten our salads before he was issuin
his ultimatums. He told me that if I didn't break off with yo
immediately, he'd cut my mother off." She swallowed hard
the familiar pain and resentment bursting forth, threatening t
choke her with the reality of her failed relationship with he

ather. "He said that he wouldn't send her any more money, and that he'd put an immediate stop to her private health insurance."

"How could he do that? Didn't they have some kind of divorce settlement?"

She nodded. "They *had* one. But shortly after she got the settlement, my mother went through the money in a matter of weeks. She was in one of her manic phases. She was destitute ess than a month after they divorced. It was the reason he got full custody of me." She took his hand and placed her own against it, palm to palm. She marveled at the striking difference in size and length. How beautiful his hands were. The long tapered fingers and the sprinkle of light wiry hair. Strong. Capable. That was Zach. But totally unversed in the ways of a crazy, dysfunctional family. What made her believe that he could ever comprehend the chaos that was her family?

He seemed to sense her fear and turned her to face him, his touch infinitely gentle and soothing. Every move, every touch, every glance was meant to assuage her fears. "What made him agree to continue to pay her after she went through all the money?"

She shrugged. "I like to think he had some compassion. But in reality, I think he did it to shut her up. To keep her from contesting the custody agreement. He agreed to pay her private medical insurance and a small monthly allowance and she would agree to keep her mouth shut."

"But she's disabled. Couldn't she get a government subsidy? Medicaid?"

Teagan sat up, the warm night air caressing her naked body. She regretted the loss of his arms around her, but she needed to see his face, to meet his eyes while she talked about the pain and shame that went with her parents' agreement.

"You don't understand, Zach. No one does. When you're mentally ill and on Medicaid, your care is minimal. With private insurance, her options weren't limitless, but they were a damn sight better. He made her choose, and then years later he did the same thing to me.''

''I'm sorry,'' he said softly.

She nodded. ''My father knew what he was doing. When he came to visit me seven years ago, my mother had just been admitted again. He knew I understood full well what dropping her insurance meant. I didn't have a job yet, and there was no way I could pay for private care. Of course he knew that there wasn't any possibility of me having the money to buy her a new policy.''

''So, he blackmailed you. Told you that if you broke it off with me, he'd continue to pay her insurance and monthly expenses.''

She nodded.

Zach reached out and cupped her foot, his strong fingers massaging. Caressing. She sighed, her contentment complete, her eyes closing. But he didn't allow her the chance to simply drift off, his questions unanswered. He leaned over her, laying down a line of hot kisses from the deep hollow of her neck to the tender tautness of her lower belly, flushing her with renewed need. Damn him. Just the touch of his perfect lips on her skin left her head swirling. How did he always know exactly what she wanted? What she needed?

She realized now that it had always been this way. Zach intuitively knowing what she needed and her taking it, lapping it up endlessly, almost mindlessly. Why hadn't she realized his ability to be there for her? To understand and sacrifice everything for her? Had she really been that selfish? That unprepared to accept the unbelievable gift he had been willing to offer her?

He lifted his head. ''Why couldn't you tell me all this? What made you believe that you couldn't trust me?''

Teagan shook her head, knowing deep inside that there was no way he could ever really comprehend. How could he? He came from an entirely different world. A place where family members cared and nurtured each other instead of scheming

o get what they perceived was their allotted portion of love
and commitment.

"Zach, you don't understand. He would have crushed you
ike a bug."

"But you didn't even give me a chance, Tea. You just
assumed that I wouldn't understand." He sat up and the
moonlight slid over his long lean body with a loving hand,
highlighting every muscle and hard ridge.

Teagan drew in a sharp breath and realized she wanted him
now more even than before. How could she have ever be-
ieved that walking away from him was the only workable
solution?

But then she knew why. There was no way that she could
have ever left her mother back then. Her father would have
destroyed her without a single thought. And on a deeper, even
more personal level, she knew that she could have never left
Zach open to her father's retaliation, either. She loved him
now as much as she had then.

Perhaps she had blocked that knowledge as a means to keep
herself sane. But deep in her heart, Teagan knew that her
sacrifice had been for the two people she loved most in the
world—Zach McCoy and her mother.

"I did what I thought I had to do," Teagan said softly.

"Then you were mistaken," he said, reaching out and pulling her to him. "If there's anything I've learned from my
parents, it's that loving means sharing the good with the bad.
You don't get to pick and choose."

Teagan leaned her head back, allowing her eyes to caress
his face. "When did you get so smart?"

He laughed; the sound was gentle and forgiving. But then
he stopped, and his face changed, filling with regret. He
reached out and cupped her face, his thumb lightly tracing the
line of her bottom lip. "Not so smart, Tea. I made the mistake
of not coming after you."

She sighed and her lips opened. He pulled her to him, holding her so tight that she could feel every hard muscle and

indentation. The blazing heat of his passion seeped deep down through her pores and warmed the edges of her wounded heart.

And as he pulled her down next to him, his lips settled over her with a fierceness that overwhelmed her with his need, and she knew without any doubt that he had forgiven her. He had accepted her reasons for leaving and forgiven her for all the hurt and pain suffered by the both of them.

Chapter Fourteen

Teagan snuggled deeper into the mattress and sighed with contentment. Her entire body hummed with contentment. She was actually comfortable. More comfortable than she'd felt in over a week.

Which, now that she thought about it, was strange. Feeling comfortable and content weren't things she was used to experiencing inside New Jerusalem.

She rolled over onto her back and stared up at the thick canopy of leaves overhead. Rays of sunlight filtered down through the lush green, warming her face. She slid her arms out from beneath the covers and stretched them overhead. The sound of jays calling to each other drifted in on a light breeze, and the sweet smell of fresh brewed coffee teased her nose.

She stopped midstretch. Leaves? Sunlight? Fresh brewed coffee?

She bolted upright, the covers sliding off her body and pooling at her lap. When she realized she was naked, she grabbed the covers with one hand and clutched them to her chest.

"No need to cover up for my benefit," Zach said.

She glanced in the direction of his voice to see him sitting on a log a few yards from her. His feet were stretched out in front of him and a cup of hot coffee sat between the palms

of his hands. The very hands that had made her body sing
last night.

He threw her a knowing look, and her cheeks blushed red
hot. He knew what she was thinking. He bent his head and
blew gently on the coffee.

His hair was dark and wet, plastered close to his head.
Errant strands curled over his ears and at the nape of his neck.
He was freshly shaven.

Obviously, he'd been busy while he'd let her sleep. He
must have used the specially jury-rigged shower she knew
he'd built years ago out behind the lean-to. She remembered
it from past visits. A large tub for collecting rainwater and
warmed by a uniquely installed solar panel spilled down
through a showerhead. Crude wooden walls enclosed the tiny
platform that served as the floor of the shower.

"What time is it?" she asked, running her fingers through
her tousled hair. She vaguely remembered them moving the
sleeping bag out of the lean-to and next to the campfire during
the night. It had been prompted by some romantic notion on
Zach's part about sleeping together under the stars. As silly
as it seemed, she couldn't help but smile in remembrance. He
hadn't changed much in the years. Still the romantic. Still the
best lover she'd ever had.

"It's seven-thirty."

Panic hit her hard and she glanced around for her clothes.
"You should have woken me up earlier. When we talked
about extending my curfew last night, I didn't mean the entire
night."

"You needed sleep. If you're going back in there, you need
your strength intact. A few hours longer than you originally
thought is fine."

Teagan shot him a frown and pulled her knees up to her
chest beneath the sleeping bag. "You make it sound so simple. But Daniel Mercy isn't a fool. He isn't going to be happy
when I come waltzing back into the camp after spending an

entire night away from the compound. In your company, no less.''

Zach took a sip of coffee. ''Let him be suspicious—hell, from what I've seen, the guy lives in a constant state of paranoia. He doesn't feel whole unless he's stressing about something. The important thing is that we've accomplished what we set out to do—pushing him off balance.''

She glanced around looking for her clothes. They were a good distance away, laying neatly folded on the edge of the lean-to. She was fairly certain she hadn't paused last night to fold them. Zach had been a busy man.

There wasn't much privacy when it came to getting dressed at his lean-to. There were no doors to close and unless she wanted to run for the woods, she was left with Zach watching her every move.

She glanced back at him. His smile widened, and she knew he'd guessed exactly what she was thinking. Well, dressing inside a sleeping bag wasn't impossible. It could be done.

''Would you mind getting my clothes for me?''

''They're closer to you than to me,'' he said pleasantly. He took another sip of coffee and regarded her over the rim of his cup. There was no mistaking the dare in his eyes.

Never one to beg or to ignore a dare, Teagan unzipped the sleeping bag and stood up. Without a backward glance, she strolled across the pine-needle carpet to her clothes.

She wasn't sure, but she thought she heard him take a sharp intake of breath when she stood up. She certainly hoped that was the case because the cheeky so-and-so deserved any feeling of discomfort he was now experiencing due to the sudden flow of blood to certain areas of his anatomy.

When she reached her clothes, she bent down and gracefully scooped them up, throwing them over one shoulder. As she turned back toward him, she didn't make any attempt to cover up.

The warmth of the sun kissed her skin, but it was nothing compared to the heat radiating from Zach's stare. He made no attempt to disguise his renewed desire, his gaze sweeping over her with outright want and need.

She allowed her own gaze to sweep over him with the same boldness. There was a noticeable tightening in his jeans, and the sight of it made her smile. She swept her eyes back up to his face and smiled insolently.

"Feeling a bit warm, Zach?"

His gaze smoldered, turning her just as warm. "Deliciously so."

She laughed and flipped her hair back off her shoulder. "I was going to ask to use the shower, but if you're feeling the need for a cold shower, feel free."

He grinned, but never shifted his position. He wasn't the least chagrined by the need she created in him. "Only if you're planning on joining me."

Teagan shook her head and her laughter died as quickly as it had appeared. "As much as I'd like to, I think it's time for us to get focused again."

Zach's grin disappeared and he nodded grimly. "You're probably right. You finish dressing and I'll get things squared away out here."

Teagan walked around the back of the lean-to and opened the crude wooden door to the shower. She let the door swing shut behind her as she stepped up onto the wooden platform, her mind already whirling with thoughts of what she could expect once she walked back through the gates of Reverend Daniel Mercy's sanctuary.

A SHORT TIME LATER, Zach pulled onto the road leading to the New Jerusalem compound. The gate stood locked as usual, but he could see the sentry in the watchtower moving over to get a better look.

The early-morning sun hit the barrel of the rifle slung over the man's shoulder and sent a shaft of reflective light dancing off into space. A cold chill washed up the center of Zach's spine. He was backed into a corner and he didn't like it.

He was obligated to send the woman of his heart back into the nest of vipers. It didn't matter that they had talked their plans out, discussed every aspect of what might happen by crossing Mercy. All that mattered was that he loved Teagan and he was sending her to her possible death at the hands of an egotistical maniac bent on destruction.

"I'm coming in with you," he said as he jammed his foot on the brakes and brought the truck to an abrupt halt several inches from the front gate. "I can't let you go in there alone."

They sat in silence for several minutes, the seat of the old vehicle vibrating beneath the rough beat of the idling engine.

Teagan reached over and gently laid her hand over his. Her fingers curled around his, passing her warmth into his cold flesh. "We've already discussed this. It's important that you drive off without coming in. You know it'll push his anxiety off the charts. It's the best way to get a reaction out of him."

"It's *how* he might react that has me worried," he ground out from between clenched teeth.

Her index finger gently stroked the curve of his hand. His heart ached.

"You're not alone with that worry," she said. "But you and I both know that no one is safe right now. Not you, not me, and certainly not the people sitting inside that compound, waiting for Reverend Mercy's judgment day."

He nodded. "I realize that. But you're the one who becomes the sitting duck once you walk back through those gates." He sighed. "Wait. I have something for you." He leaned forward and opened the glove compartment of the truck, fishing out the pen flashlight and tiny lock-picking device. "Here. Take these, you might need them."

She hefted the lock-pick and grinned at him. "Who would have thought a lawman would be carrying something like this? For shame, Sheriff." She shoved them both into her pocket. "Thanks. I'm sure I'll put them to good use."

"Be careful, Tea."

"I'll be okay. Trust me." She gave his hand a final squeeze

before sliding over to the door and pushing it open. "Remember, wait for me at the back gate, tonight around 2:00 a.m. Hopefully, I'll have found his stash of weapons by then. But even if I haven't, I'll bring Becca Chandler out. At least we can get her out, and her father won't have any reason to broadcast Reverend Mercy's sermon. No TV show means we've essentially shut Daniel Mercy down."

Zach turned to glare in the general direction of the front gate. "I still don't like it. How do you know Mercy hasn't already figured out that you're the traitor he's been ranting about all this time?"

She got out of the truck and then turned back toward him. He could see the anxiety in her eyes, but the determined tilt to her chin told him that she wasn't backing down.

"He's going to be too busy with his plans for tomorrow to worry about me."

The gate swung open.

Mercy stood framed in the center, Cyrus and Eddie close behind him. The good reverend was dressed all in black. He stood with his weight shifted onto one hip, his arms folded across his chest. A pair of dark sunglasses shielded his eyes, the lenses staring blankly out at them.

Zach knew that behind the dark lenses, the man's eyes were focused directly on him. He could feel the smoldering heat of Mercy's rage burning a line of fire down the center of the driveway directly to him. He didn't like it when people failed to do what he expected.

"He doesn't look happy to see us," he said out of one corner of his mouth.

"Guess we succeeded in getting to him." She paused for a minute and then said, "Zach?"

He turned to look at her.

The clear coolness of her green eyes cut across the length of the truck cab. "You need to trust me on this. I know how to handle him."

"I know you do." His fingers tightened on the wheel, and

he fought the urge to yank her back into the safety of the truck. "But he's also an unpredictable lunatic with a stash of automatic weapons and a load of Titadine dynamite."

"And that's why you and I need to stop him. Right?"

He nodded, his hand still gripping the steering wheel for fear he would follow through on his overwhelming desire to drag her back into the cab.

She closed the passenger side door and walked toward Mercy. The heels of her sandals kicked up tiny puffs of dust. Zach watched her square the set of her slender shoulders, preparing for the onslaught they both knew she faced at the hands of the cult leader. She looked very insignificant next to the dark figure framed in the open gate.

"Be safe, Tea. I'll be back soon," Zach whispered. He shoved the truck into reverse, backed around and then jammed it into drive. Stepping on the gas, he roared out of the driveway, a thick cloud of dust lifting up to obscure his final glimpse of Teagan.

MERCY NEVER MOVED from his spot. He waited for her to approach. The dark lenses of his sunglasses seemed to stare at her accusedly, but she kept her expression blank. Unafraid.

She stopped a few feet in front of him.

"Where have you been?" he demanded.

"With the sheriff."

His lips tightened. "You know the rules of the community, Teagan. You know how I feel about unmarried women consorting with men—it is sinful. A poor example for our young people."

"I'm well aware of how you feel, Father. I sometimes wonder, however, about the hypocrisy of your rules."

"How dare you speak to the Father in such a manner," Cyrus growled menacingly, stepping forward with a hand raised to strike her.

Mercy lifted his own hand to deflect the blow. "Enough, Cyrus. I wish to hear what she has to say."

Teagan didn't look away. Now was not the time for her to be meek and subservient. She needed to push him just a little bit further. He was already teetering on the edge.

She shrugged, holding her palms up. "I don't feel a need to defend myself, Father. You were the one who told me to befriend Sheriff McCoy. I only did as you asked."

"He didn't ask you to submit yourself to him, woman," Cyrus said, spitting the words out like sharp stones meant to hurt her.

Teagan effected a look of confusion. "But that's exactly what Father asked me to do." She met the reverend's gaze. "And you should be glad I did because now the sheriff won't fight anything you plan to do—not even the Day of Unity."

Reverend Mercy slowly removed his sunglasses, his expression intense. "He wasn't angry that I used the sheriff's department as a cosponsor?"

Teagan shrugged. "Perhaps initially he wasn't pleased." She smiled. "But later he had no complaints."

A chilling grin stretched Reverend Mercy's lips. "Perhaps I spoke too soon, Sister Teagan. You appear to have done quite well."

Behind him, Cyrus snorted in disgust, but the reverend ignored him. He stepped forward and slipped an arm around Teagan's shoulders. "I have much to be pleased about. I think a small celebration is in order. Come back to my cottage and we'll toast your success." He pulled her close, and the hair on the back of Teagan's neck prickled in protest. As much as she wanted to throw him off the scent, she didn't want to do any celebrating with him.

She struggled to keep her body from recoiling in disgust. She had work to do and less than eighteen hours to get it done. If she planned on locating the guns and explosives before her rendezvous with Zach, she needed to move fast.

With a gentle twist of her shoulders, she slipped from his embrace. "As much as I appreciate your offer, Father, I think I need to spend some time praying for forgiveness."

He frowned, his eyes narrowing slightly as he studied her face. Her heart kicked up a few beats, but she kept her face guileless.

She could tell that he didn't like the fact that she'd refused his invitation, but he was torn. He appreciated her efforts to keep the sheriff in line, and in his eyes, her excuse about needing to seek forgiveness was plausible—after all, in his book, she *had* sinned. Even if it had been for the good of the community.

After a few moments, he nodded. "All right, I guess it would be selfish of me if I didn't allow you the opportunity to repent your sins. Go then."

Teagan walked toward the Temple, knowing that for the first time, she was entering the sanctuary alone. She could only hope that her recent favor in Reverend Mercy's eyes would translate into him not sending anyone after her.

As she opened the doors, she glanced back. The reverend and Cyrus were already walking across the yard toward his cottage. Relieved, she slipped through the door and entered the dimly lit Temple.

The candles lining the wall on either side of the room flickered in the breeze from the open door. Teagan allowed the door to close, enveloping her in the silence of the huge room. The chapel was completely empty.

She moved quickly to the front, but didn't venture past the platform. Instead, she knelt and bowed her head as if in deep prayer. She didn't trust Daniel Mercy. It was still possible that he'd send someone snooping around. She'd give him five minutes and then start searching.

The minutes crawled out endlessly until she could not kneel any longer. She stood up and walked the length of the platform, covering every inch of it looking for a trap door or opening of any kind.

Nothing.

The altar was next. She lifted the plain linen cloth that

covered the top and carefully checked beneath. Again nothing. Down near the floor, she could feel a cool draft.

She stepped around the altar and pushed aside the thick velvet drapes covering the wall beyond. Heavy steel stretched from one end of the room to the other.

Fumbling for the flashlight stashed in the pocket of her overalls, Teagan stepped behind the curtain. She ran her hand along the cold metal. It seemed seamless, one large sheet of heavy steel.

She worked her way down the length of it, moving quickly. Halfway to the other side, her fingers slid into a narrow groove. Excited, she ran her fingers along the indentation. It was a door built flush to the wall.

She stuck the end of the flashlight in her mouth and used her fingers to trace the entire length and width of the door. A small keyhole halfway down the door on the right was the only possible opening.

She dug into the pocket again and pulled out the pick. She grinned as she mentally thanked Zach for his foresight in giving her the tool. Directing the tiny beam of light on the lock, she knelt down and slid the pick into the lock. She turned the pick slowly.

Nothing. It wouldn't budge.

She pulled out another pick and inserted it into the lock. Suddenly, she froze. The door at the back of the Temple creaked opened.

Teagan snapped off the flashlight and crouched down. Hopefully the curtain was enough cover.

Footsteps echoed in the huge room, they moved slowly toward the front altar.

Frantic, Teagan turned the pick and the door clicked softly open. She slipped through and then closed the door after her, leaning against it and listening intensely.

The room was chilly, the feeling of dampness overwhelming. She shivered in the dark. Moving away from the door, she clicked her flashlight back on.

She was in the actual mining cave. Daniel Mercy was using it as a storeroom of sorts. Stacks of wooden crates lined one side of the cave. Teagan knew without even opening the boxes what she'd find. This was the good reverend's secret stash of weapons.

She moved over to several long tables covered with the same vests worn by the "Chosen Elite." They appeared bulkier than the ones worn by the guards.

Puzzled, she pulled one closer and opened one of the pockets. Her mouth went dry and the hair on the back of her neck stood on end. All the pockets, front and back, were filled with explosives. In the center of the table stood a box with detonators. Reverend Mercy was building his own army of suicide terrorists.

Her heart pounded as she backed away from the table.

"You just couldn't leave things alone, could you?" a voice asked.

Teagan whirled around to see Cyrus standing just inside the steel door. The look on his face told her that he had wanted this confrontation to happen for a very long time. She was exactly where he wanted her.

"I—I thought I heard something back here. I came to check it out," she said, backing away from him.

"You came to check out something behind a locked steel door?" His amusement was obvious. He wasn't going to buy any of her excuses.

Teagan lunged to get around him, but he pulled her up short, grabbing her hair and yanking. She flew backward against him, but as she hit him, she jammed her elbow into his ribs. She took a certain amount of satisfaction when he grunted with surprise.

But it didn't slow him down. He swung her around and flipped her onto the table. Her feet scrambled wildly on the polished surface.

Cyrus's hands closed over her throat and he stared down

into her eyes. The maniacal gleam in his dark eyes told Teagan that there wasn't going to be any mercy from this man.

His fingers dug into the flesh of her neck, crushing her windpipe with his strength and weight. She gagged and gasped for breath. Reaching up, she viciously chopped his forearms and swung herself forward, head butting him in the face. His hands loosened for a second and his eyes watered, but then before she could wiggle loose, he tightened down on her neck again.

Teagan's breath rasped in her throat and her lungs screamed for air. Her eyes blurred and her vision faded around the edges. She knew she wasn't far from passing out.

Her hand dug in her pocket, closing over the lock pick. Pulling back, she jammed one end into Cyrus's meaty thigh. He screamed and jumped back. She drew her legs up and then slammed them against his chest. He flew backward, hitting the stone wall. His head hit with a sickening thud.

A look of total surprise crossed his face as he slid down to sit on the floor and then he slumped over sideways. The smear of blood on the cave wall told her that Cyrus wouldn't be getting up again.

She sucked in cool air, cringing as it burned the back of her raw throat. She bent down and felt Cyrus's neck. No pulse.

Gabbing his collar, she dragged him over next to the wooden crates. She opened the first one and checked inside. Sure enough, just as she had suspected. It was filled with the stolen semiautomatic weapons.

It took her several minutes to move one stack of crates out of the way. She then tucked Cyrus neatly behind the crates and pushed them back into place. It wasn't the best solution, but it was all she had left right now. She could only hope that his body wouldn't be discovered until after she had gotten Becca out later that night.

Checking around quickly to make sure everything was back the way she had found it, Teagan backtracked, letting herself out through the steel door leading to the Temple. She carefully locked it behind her.

A few minutes later, she walked out onto the main courtyard, breathing in the morning heat. A sentry in the tower glanced down at her and her blood pounded in her ears. She shoved her hands in the pocket of her overalls to keep him from seeing them shake.

He seemed unimpressed. After a few moments, he turned and walked back to the other side of the tower. Teagan released her breath and wiped her sweaty palms on the sides of her pants. She headed for the bunkhouse. One test finished, more than a few to pass before the day was over.

Chapter Fifteen

Teagan rolled up onto her side and checked her watch by the faint light drifting out of the open bathroom door—2:00 a.m.

Time to move. She threw back the sheet covering her fully clothed body and then lay absolutely still, listening.

From the bunk overhead came the soft snore of her bunk mate. Teagan knew that a cannon could go off down the middle of the bunkhouse and Betty still wouldn't wake up. But the woman sleeping across from her was another matter entirely. Rose had moved into the bunk last night, a transfer from the other women's quarters.

Rose had complained of not getting along with one of the other women there. But Teagan suspected she'd been planted as a spy, someone to keep an eye on her. Paranoid perhaps, but Teagan couldn't help being suspicious.

Sliding her legs off the side of the bunk, she sat up. The light from the bathroom at the other end of the building threw a narrow slice of yellow on the hardwood floor. All the bunks were filled. No one was up wandering around.

She lowered herself to the floor and crouched next to the bed. After a few seconds, she stood. Across the narrow aisle, Rose muttered under her breath and then flopped over onto her back.

Teagan froze.

A few seconds passed, and Rose started to snore, adding

an oddly comforting echo to the tune already coming out of Betty's mouth.

Grabbing her pillow and rolling up the blanket from the end of her bed, Teagan jammed them under the sheet. She quickly shaped them into some semblance of a human shape.

The trick wouldn't fool anyone for long if they looked closely, but hopefully, she was buying herself some valuable time while it was still dark.

She was halfway down the aisle, headed for the door when a soft voice asked, "Whatcha doing?"

Teagan whirled around, her heart in her throat.

Kenny sat cross-legged at the end of his cot, an inquisitive expression on his elfish face.

She knelt down in front of him, her finger immediately going to her lips. Kenny nodded his head, a mischievous smile crossing his lips. If she read her little boys right, he was seeing his discovery of her as an impromptu adventure.

"I'm going out for a short walk," she whispered.

He leaned forward and whispered back, "Are you going to the treasure room? Can I go, too?"

Teagan shook her head. "Not this time, kiddo. But if you're good and go right back to sleep, I promise to let you ride Elijah next time I'm on barn duty."

Kenny stuck out his bottom lip for a total of two seconds before reaching out to shake her hand. "Okay, it's a deal."

As soon as she shook, Kenny scrambled back up to the head of the bed, slipped under the sheet and rolled up onto his side. He pressed his face into his pillow with studied concentration. Teagan gently squeezed his foot and then left. She hoped the little guy didn't decide to go back on his promise and wake up his mother with tales of Sister Teagan roaming around outside looking for the treasure room.

Once outside, she cut across the compound, keeping to the shadows of the different buildings. The air was still heavy with the earlier heat.

Pausing at the corner of the mess hall, she studied the watch tower. The two guards up in the tower were leaning against opposite pillars, talking in low tones. Neither seemed worried about anyone out walking about at this late hour. One of them raised a mug to his lips and sipped something.

Teagan raced to the back of the mess hall, cut across the back and spied Reverend Mercy's cottage. Using the shadows from the roof of the dining hall, she tried to decide the best way to get to the back of the cult leader's house.

If she ran straight from building to building, she'd be out in the open for ten or fifteen seconds. Daniel Mercy had been smart. The cottage was separate from all the cluster of other buildings. It gave him a true buffer zone all around his quarters.

Although the two guards seemed engaged in a comfortable chat and they didn't appear terribly concerned about watching for intruders, the risk for a clear run across the clearing seemed high.

She checked her watch again—2:10 a.m.

Zach would already be in position outside the back gate. She had to risk the clearing. She knew he wouldn't wait long before coming after her.

A light breeze, still warm and humid, heavy with the promise of rain, brushed her cheek. She watched as the guard with the mug offered it to the other man. They both laughed and the sound carried on the night breeze.

She sucked in a deep breath and pushed off the side of the building. Barely breathing, she raced across the clearing, her entire body tense, waiting for a shot from the tower.

When she hit the building's shadow, she tripped and fell forward. Grunting softly, she rolled with the fall, coming to a bone-crunching stop against the cement foundation. Barely breathing, Teagan tucked herself up against the side.

"What was that?" one of the guards asked.

She watched him move to the side of the watchtower. He leaned forward, searching the darkness.

"I didn't hear anything," the other guard said, his voice impatient, irritated that their conversation was interrupted.

"I thought I heard something."

"Probably a damn bear. This godforsaken place seems to have beasts roaming all over the place."

The guard near the railing straightened up and returned to his previous position. "Better not let the Father hear you refer to his paradise as godforsaken."

Teagan sat up and rubbed her left hip. It was going to have a big bruise. Staying low, she crept to the back of the cottage. She counted over three windows. Knowing a few of the women who cleaned the Reverend's cottage paid off when it came to knowing which window opened onto his bedroom.

Standing on tiptoes, she tried to see inside. Nothing. The drapes were drawn.

She pushed the window upward. Luck was with her. The lock wasn't latched. But then why would Reverend Mercy latch his window inside the safety of his own compound?

She boosted herself up and her sandals skidded on the side of the house, making a soft scraping sound. She parted the drapes and slithered through the open window. She landed on the floor with a soft thud.

She lay in the dark for several seconds, waiting for her heart to stop thumping wildly. Lifting her head, she glanced around. A double bed, a ladder-backed chair, a small nightstand and dresser were the only furniture in the room.

Becca Chandler was asleep on the bed, lying on her back with her silver piercings glittering in the faint light from the window.

Teagan shut the window and pulled the drapes closed again. Only a small sliver of moonlight filtered through the heavy material. The air in the bedroom was cool. Teagan smiled ruefully. Leave it to Reverend Mercy to air-condition his house while his loyal followers boiled in the midsummer heat.

Keeping low, she tiptoed across to the bed. She eased herself down onto the side of the mattress and gently placed her

hand over Becca's mouth. The girl's eyes snapped open, wi‐
ening with shock and surprise.

She immediately started to struggle, but Teagan presse
harder and motioned with a finger to her lips for her to b
quiet.

"I'm not going to hurt you," she whispered, leaning i
close.

"Can you be quiet?"

Becca nodded. Teagan lifted her hand but stayed ready
slap it back over the young woman's mouth if she cried ou
She didn't.

"What are you doing here?" she asked.

"I'm here to get you."

Reaching over to the bedside table, Teagan flicked on th
small lamp. When the light hit the young woman's eyes, sh
blinked and swayed slightly, as if she was having trouble fo
cusing. Teagan didn't doubt she was drugged. Her pupils wer
so large, they almost took up the whole of her iris.

"Get me? Get me for what?" Becca asked groggily. Sh
glanced around the room. "Has the Father called us to praye
again?"

"Yes. He's having a special service down by the lake, bu
only a few members have been invited to attend," Teaga
lied. She stood up and grabbed the pair of overalls slung ove
the chair. "Here, put these on."

Becca rubbed the side of her face and yawned. "Specia
service?" She flopped back down, burying her face in he
pillow. "I'm too tired. Tell the Father I'm too sleepy."

"Come on, Becca." Teagan coaxed her back up. "We nee
to go. The Father is waiting. You know how he gets when h
has to wait."

The mild threat worked. Becca popped up again and thi
time she attempted to swing her legs over the side of the bec
Instead, she toppled over backward, her head hitting the ma
tress with a bounce.

She giggled. "G-guess I'm still a little high."

"I can see that," Teagan said dryly. She slid the girl's legs over the side of the bed and reached over to pull her to a sitting position. Becca swayed slightly but caught herself before going over backward again.

Impatient, Teagan bent down, grabbed the overalls and moved them over the girl's bare feet.

"That tickles," Becca complained.

Teagan ignored her and pulled her to a standing position. The girl swayed against her, but Teagan steadied her with one hand as she yanked the pants over Becca's nightshirt. She slipped her arms through the shoulder straps. Becca allowed her to pull and tug at her, limp as a rag doll.

"Sit," Teagan ordered.

Becca complied. Teagan bent down again and retrieved a pair of sandals sticking out from under the bed. As she strapped them on Becca's feet, the girl yelped, "Ouch. Be careful of my pinkie toe. I stubbed it earlier."

Nervous, Teagan glanced over her shoulder, but the door was still closed. She could hear the muffled voices of Daniel Mercy and a few others talking and laughing. She needed to get the girl out without them hearing.

She grabbed Becca's arm. "Listen to me."

The teenager stared up at her blankly, and her body swayed. "What?" Her words were slurred, her voice thick. She seemed more disorientated than a few minutes ago.

Teagan grabbed her shoulders, holding her still. "We're going to play a game. The Father wants to see how quiet you can be getting to service. He wants us to sneak out there like we're soldiers of the faithful going on a mission."

Becca nodded her head drunkenly, almost toppling over again. Teagan caught her by both shoulders and held her steady.

"Do you understand, Becca? We have to be very quiet—

like two mice. If the guards hear us we'll lose the game, and the Father will be angry."

Becca frowned at the word *angry*.

"You don't want the Father to be angry, do you?"

Becca shook her head violently and fumbled to get her finger to her lips to signal she knew how to be quiet.

"Okay, good. Now stand up."

Becca grabbed Teagan's hand and pulled herself up. But her momentum was a little too fast and she stumbled forward. Teagan caught her before she pitched forward onto her face. Slipping an arm around the girl, she led her over to the window.

"We're going to go out the window, Becca. But we have to be very quiet." She propped Becca against the wall, and eased the window open. "If anyone hears us, we'll lose the game. Remember, the Father is waiting."

Teagan slid over the sill and dropped down onto the grass. She froze, waiting to see if anyone heard. But Becca was suddenly in a hurry. She stuck a leg out of the window and the rest of her body followed. A bundle of nerveless energy, she tumbled out and fell into a heap. She let out a loud grunt as she hit the ground.

Teagan dropped on top of Becca and covered her mouth. The spotlight from the tower swept along the yard a few feet from them. Teagan held her breath, sure that they'd be discovered. But the spotlight passed by, just missing them.

Beneath her hand, she felt Becca's body shaking. Concerned, she glanced down, the girl was giggling.

"This is fun," she said.

"It won't be if you're not quiet," Teagan warned. She stood and pulled Becca along with her.

Taking the girl's arm, Teagan pulled her along after her. They skirted the rear of the cottage and headed for the barn. Becca stumbled a few times but Teagan managed to keep her

pright. When they reached the wooden structure, she pulled
Becca down into a crouch beside her.

"My head hurts," Becca whined.

"We're almost there, Becca. Just keep quiet a few minutes
longer." Teagan moved to the end of the barn and checked.
It was all clear. The gate was open a crack and she could see
Zach waiting on the other side. He didn't speak, but his eyes
told her he wasn't happy about how long this rescue was
taking.

Grabbing Becca, she ran across the clearing and slipped
through the gate.

"What took you so long?" Zach asked, grabbing Becca as
she shot through the opening and kept her from falling on her
face. He crouched down next to her. He was dressed all in
black, a cap pulled over his head to dampen the gold bright-
ness of his hair.

"Becca here wasn't real cooperative," Teagan said grimly,
closing the gate and making sure the latch fell into place. She
crouched down, too. "Apparently she and the good reverend
were celebrating. I found her passed out on the bed."

"Did you find the weapons?"

Teagan nodded. "He's got them stashed in a special chamber behind the main Temple. But I had a problem."

He raised an eyebrow.

"Cyrus found me snooping around back there and jumped
me."

"I'm guessing that since you're here and he's not that you
took care of him."

She nodded again. "Brother Cyrus went to his Maker
sooner than he expected. I hid him behind some crates. I think
it will be a while before they find him."

"All right, let's get moving. I left my truck up at the lean-
to." He started to get up.

Teagan reached out and stopped him. She glanced at Becca,

but the girl's eyes were closed and she was massaging he head. "There's another problem."

"What?"

"Reverend Mercy had all the "Chosen Elite" vests lai out in the back chamber."

"And…?"

"And they were all stuffed with explosives and wired t go off with remote detonation."

Zach blinked. "He loaded the dynamite into the vests?"

She nodded and then leaned in closer, not wanting Becc to overhear. "That's the reason for the pockets in the fron and back. He's planning some kind of suicide mission."

"Damn!" Zach's hands tightened into fists, and he glance back toward the compound, her information registering a shock on his face. "We should have realized. He's plannin a mass suicide."

"He's planning on taking as many people as he can wit him. I'd guess he's set on doing it on national television."

Zach stood up and dragged Becca up with him. She stum bled against him and tried to pull away. But Zach simpl slipped an arm around her and held her tight to his side. "I we can get her to safety, Chandler won't televise anything And Mercy will lose his audience." He took off, headed fo the tree line.

Confused in the dark, Teagan stuck close to Zach's heels They had gone less than fifty yards when a shout went u from the tower.

The spotlight careened across the landscape, illuminatin the thick line of pines clustered around the edge of the lake The spotlight poked pockets of light into the thick darkness beyond.

"Keep down, but don't stop," Zach ordered. He dodge some shrubs, dragging Becca with him. As Teagan followed the powerful spotlight hit her from behind; she stumbled, fall

ng forward to her knees. With one hand, Zach reached behind
im and hauled her to her feet.

"Come on!" he urged.

"I'm coming." Her knees stung, but she ignored the pain,
ollowing him into the safety of the forest.

Several yards in, Zach crouched down and allowed Becca
o slide down to sit at his feet. "They're on to us," he said,
glancing back toward the compound. "We didn't get enough
of a head start."

Becca raised her own head and stared beerily about.
'Where are we?" She reached up and pulled a handful of
pine needles out of her tangled hair, staring at them with a
onfused look on her face. "Why are there pine needles in
my hair?"

Teagan ignored her. "We'll have to make do. If we stay
ahead of them, we'll be fine." She struggled to fill her lungs
with precious air. Beside her, Zach stiffened and swore softly
under his breath. She turned and her heart sank at the sight
of the back gate opening and a group of armed cultists exiting.
Several of them pushed beat-up dirt bikes.

Zach reached across and gently took her chin in his hand,
his eyes met hers, delving deep with their burning intensity.
'Listen to me, Tea. We need to split up—"

"No." She hit his hand and tried to pull away, but he held
her steady, not allowing her to back off.

"Listen, we don't have time for this. They're going to catch
us if we don't separate." He stood up, pulling her with him.
He dug into his pocket and took out a small compass. "Take
his and head southeast. It'll bring you out near the bottom of
Sunset Lake Road." He jerked Becca to her feet and handed
her over to Teagan. "Keep her moving and don't stop for
anything."

Teagan opened her mouth to protest again, but the high
whine of the dirt bikes' engines revving up traveled across

the field behind them. She clamped her mouth shut and nodded.

"Get her out and then come back for me." Zach leaned forward and pressed his lips to hers. She clutched him to her for a brief moment, savoring the feel of him in her arms.

"I promise I'll be back," she said.

He grinned, his teeth flashing white and pure in the darkness. "You better. Now get going."

Teagan ran, the compass tight in the palm of her hand and a strung-out Becca behind her, crying and whimpering in protest.

Chapter Sixteen

few hours later, Zach found himself captured, bound and
agged back to the compound. Mercy had his men install
m in a room at the back of the Temple. They secured his
nds to a metal ring drilled into the rock wall.

Shaking his head, Zach tried to clear it. He was seeing
uble. Mercy's men hadn't been too pleased with the wild-
ose chase he'd led them on. More than a few of them had
ken a shot at his jaw when they caught up with him. But
e pain was well worth it, knowing that Teagan had probably
tten out and delivered Becca Chandler safely into the hands
her father.

Across the room, the steel door opened and Mercy strolled
. The smug smile on his face set a twinge of concern shoot-
g through Zach. But it wasn't until the man stepped aside
at Zach's heart truly sank.

Four members of the "Chosen Elite" hauled Teagan into
e room. She didn't come in quietly. It was taking every
nce of muscle the four men had to wrestle her into the
om.

A quieter, much more frightened Becca followed close on
r heels. Apparently Teagan hadn't been any more successful
an he had been at eluding the "Chosen Elite."

Teagan stopped struggling and lifted her gaze to meet his.

He tried to say something, but his lips were too swollen. No[_]
ing came out.

He saw her jaw tighten when she realized how battered [_]
face was. He knew without seeing for himself that he look[_]
pretty bad. The guards had been none too gentle. Blood cak[_]
one side of his face, the side someone had slammed into [_]
side of one of the dirt bikes when they caught up with hi[_]
Zach was pretty sure he looked like he'd gone a few roun[_]
with the current heavyweight champion of the world.

The two guards dragged Teagan past him, and she tried[_]
touch him as she passed, but Mercy stopped her. "I would[_]
touch him if I were you."

Teagan pulled back and then shot a defiant look in Mercy[_]
direction. "Why? What did you do?"

Mercy grinned and reached into his pocket, pulling ou[_]
nail clipper. As he carefully clipped his nails, he explaine[_]
"Because Sheriff McCoy is now wired from his toes up [_]
his handsome ears." His face hardened. "If he moves jus[_]
little too far in either direction, twenty pounds of Titadi[_]
dynamite will blow him into tiny pieces." He held one ha[_]
out in front of him and carefully inspected his newly clipp[_]
nails. "There won't be enough left of him for the local co[_]
oner to identify." He met Teagan's gaze. "Is that cle[_]
enough for you?"

Teagan didn't answer, but when the guards pushed h[_]
down a short distance from him, she didn't fight them and h[_]
expression registered her shock. Zach watched as the guar[_]
used thick rope to tie her hands and feet. She didn't resi[_]
All the fight seemed to have melted out of her.

"Tea," he called to her through swollen lips.

She shook her head. "Shhh. Don't talk. Don't even move[_]

Off to the side, one of the guards dragged Becca over[_]
sit next to Teagan. She moved docilely until they started[_]
tie her up. Then she screamed and tried to break away. T[_]
guard pushed her roughly back against the wall. She whim[_]
pered softly but didn't try to fight him any more.

"Gently, Eric," Mercy cautioned. "We wouldn't want to harm our prize possession. After all, if it wasn't for Becca here, we wouldn't have national TV coverage."

"Please," Becca begged, "please don't hurt me. S-she tricked me. I—I didn't want to go with them. She forced me."

Mercy laughed and walked over to pat her cheek. Becca rubbed her cheek against his hand. "You're not angry with me, are you, Father?"

"Not in the least, Becca. Not in the least." He turned his attention to Teagan, his eyes the color of black diamonds, cold and flat. Crazed. "FBI or ATF?"

"ATF," she said through clenched teeth. "And you might as well give up because by now your compound is surrounded."

Zach knew that probably wasn't the case, but he didn't blame her for trying. Paine wouldn't take the risk of invading the surrounding woods until the deadline had passed and he hadn't heard from them. No doubt the ATF were close by, but no one was coming in to rescue them anytime soon.

"I wouldn't want it any other way," Mercy said cheerfully. He pointed toward the TV monitor sitting on a table across the room. "I didn't want either of you to feel left out of the celebration. So I had them bring in the TV so you can have a front-row seat for my final sermon."

The monitor showed the entire compound. At the moment, the gates were still closed, but Temple members were bustling about setting up chairs in preparation for the upcoming celebration. The first streaks of dawn were already coloring the sky. Time was rapidly clicking down.

"I'd so like to stick around to get your reaction to my final sermon, but I think it's much more important that I be with my flock as they rise upon the wave of glorious destruction to meet their Master."

Beside him, Teagan leaned forward. "Listen to what you're saying, Daniel. You don't have to do this—you don't have to

hurt all these people. If you give up now, no one will ge
hurt.''

But Mercy wasn't listening. He motioned to the guards to
accompany him and he left the same way he'd come in, clos
ing and locking the steel door behind him.

SEVERAL HOURS LATER, Mercy stood on the front porch o
his cottage and watched the townspeople surge through th
compound's gates. The people laughed and chatted as if on a
holiday outing. Several in the group walked with children, th
youngsters pulling on their hands and begging the adults to
hurry.

Mercy leaned against a post and savored the intense feelin;
of self-satisfaction that settled over him. Little did any of th
people realize that in less than two hours, they would be ac
companying him on a wondrous journey. A journey tha
would bring them face-to-face with their Maker and their fina
judgment.

His fingers caressed the rim of the glass in his hand. H
had won. Soon the world would speak his name with hushec
reverence. He and he alone had managed to find a way to
bring his Father a gift beyond comparison. And now, all th
religious men who had scorned and dismissed him as incon
sequential would learn that he had succeeded where they ha
failed.

Of course, just the fact that the gates of the compound wer
wide open made him uneasy. But Mercy knew that he coulc
not control everything and still obtain his goal. The Lord hac
told him that he needed as many people as possible to pas
through those gates, and he was listening and obeying. He
would give his God the warriors He asked for.

His gaze swept across the compound. The ''Chosen Elite'
had literally transformed the place, creating something warn
and inviting. Colorful Japanese lanterns were strung about to
give a festive air, and a large wooden platform, painted a
bright yellow, had been constructed in the middle of the yard

he children had spent several hours blowing up balloons and ing them to the backs of the chairs lined up in front of the latform.

Upon request, a few of the more musical members of the hurch had gotten their instruments and taken up positions on he platform. Lively music with a country-and-western flair rifted over the compound. Although no one had played music like that inside the walls of the compound before, musicians seem to understand that this was a special occasion. The ymns would come later.

Several of the townspeople had gotten into the spirit of hings and they danced in front of the stage. Off to the side, rge plank tables held an overabundance of food, more food han most of the Temple members had seen in months. But one of them stepped forward to touch a morsel. Instead, they id as they were told—moving in and out among the townseople, chatting and laughing, helping them to feel at ease.

More than a few church members watched with hollow yes as their guests filled plates with succulent pieces of barecue chicken and heaping scoops of potato and macaroni alad. But none of his parishioners dared to help themselves anything. They knew only too well that the "Chosen Elite" as watching them closely, taking names.

Around the outside perimeter of his guests, a troop of men n red T-shirts with the name *Hard Exposure* Crew printed cross the back, ran cables and set up camera equipment. The ollection of cameras, cables and sound equipment cluttering he courtyard seemed almost unmanageable. Mercy could nly hope they were ready in time for the show at 8:00 p.m.

He moved over to one of the white Adirondack chairs and at down, watching two men hoist an oversize lighting unit p a pole. Once the sun started to go down and the light began o fade, the television crew would turn on the artificial lights nd Mercy knew that their power would illuminate the entire ompound as if it were daylight. Not one person, sitting in

their comfortable living room and watching *Hard Exposu*
would miss the grand finale.

As he watched the men secure the light and move onto th
next one, Mercy fought against a flash of anxiety. He didn
like all these people running around inside the compoun
Any one of them could be an ATF or FBI agent. In fact, h
was sure quite a few of them were.

Irritated, he forced himself to sit back. It didn't matter
he had moles inside his compound. The good Lord didn't ca
who His warriors were. The agents would face their fin
judgment with the rest of them, and Mercy had no dou
they'd be found wanting.

It was time for him to stop worrying about the possib
infiltration of the camp and get his mind wrapped around h
upcoming sermon. This was to be his final performance, th
one his Father would judge him by. It had to be his best.

He lifted the tall glass of whiskey sitting beside him an
sipped, trying to soothe his jagged nerves. He had effective
taken care of ATF Special Agent Teagan Kennedy and Sheri
Zach McCoy. The "Chosen Elite" had all donned their vest
now filled with twenty-five pounds of explosives, metal an
rat poison. His sacrifice and gift to his almighty Father wa
almost complete.

"Chandler is on his way up."

Mercy turned to see Eddie standing in the doorway, a ce
phone clutched in his hand. "Is he alone?"

Eddie nodded. "Except for his chauffeur."

"Does it look like anyone is following him?"

"Not as far as our men are able to tell."

Mercy nodded wearily. They'd hardly see the FBI or AT
if they were tracking the car. Mercy wasn't a fool. He kne
that Chandler had talked to the Feds. His only ace in the ho
was the man's daughter. The newsman's little whining darlin
was Mercy's only leverage. But then soon it wouldn't matte
Soon he'd be in the center of the bomb blast for all the worl
to see, rising up to sit beside his Father for the final judgmen

TRUSSED UP like a Thanksgiving turkey and exhausted beyond belief, Teagan was fairly certain she dozed off for a short time as the hours clicked by. When she opened her eyes and tried to straighten out her legs, her muscles cramped. Air hissed between her teeth as she tried to work out the pain.

She shifted around on the cold, damp floor and glanced over at Zach. He was awake but still looking pretty ragged.

The swelling on the left side of his face had turned a deep, rich purple, and his left eye was swollen completely shut, the lid puffy and shiny. The odd markings on his cheek told her that the swelling came from the sole of someone's boot. She wondered if his cheekbone was broken.

"You look as bad as I feel," he croaked.

"Gee, thanks," she said softly. "Got any bright ideas?"

"The celebration has started," he said, nodding his chin in the direction of the TV monitor.

Teagan glanced at the monitor. The compound gates were wide-open and people flowed into the yard, met by Temple members. The crowds of people were startling. No doubt the townspeople's curiosity about the religious sect had brought about the good turnout.

Beside her, Zach sucked in air. Concerned, she turned to see him staring at the monitor, the lines of his face composed into an expression of horror.

She glanced back and forth between him and the TV monitor. "What's wrong?"

"Krista. Emily. My nieces." The words seemed to be torn from somewhere deep inside him, the sound raw and raspy. She had a feeling the sound had more to do with shock than actual pain of his injuries. "Their sitter wasn't suppose to come anywhere near this place."

Teagan studied the monitor, catching sight of two little girls with blond pigtails, pink ribbons and matching short sets. They held the hands of a young woman and walked through the front gates, their eyes wide with wonder and excitement.

"He can't do this," Zach said, anger filtering into the pain.

Teagan could see the rage building in him. His muscle tensed and he looked ready to tear his restraints off with hi bare teeth. "Stay still, Zach! Don't move. You don't kno how much it takes to set the explosives off."

He turned angrily in her direction. "We can't just sit her and watch! He's going to kill innocent men, women and chi dren out there. Think, damn it. Think!"

"You're no good to Krista and Emily dead, so sit still."

He seemed to hear her and settled back against the wal but she could feel the anger radiating off him. Her hand tightened into fists. There had to be a way out of this. He wa right; they couldn't just sit here while Mercy blew up th entire population of Bradley.

"Birdie," Zach whispered.

"What?" Teagan looked up. "What did you say?"

"Look! Birdie. She found us." He nodded toward the bac of the cave.

Glancing in the same direction as Zach, Teagan saw th bluetick hound trot out of the dark recesses of the cave int the light. Her paws and coat were badly smudged with di and grime, but she gave them one of her lopsided dog grin her tongue lolling out one side of her mouth. There was n hiding her pride in the fact that she'd tracked them down.

"How'd she get here?" Teagan asked in amazement. "Yo left her up at the lean-to."

One corner of Zach's mouth lifted; the other corner wa too swollen to even move. "She came in from above. There an old abandoned shaft leading to the cave near my camp.

He winced as he tried to shift to a more comfortable po sition. Teagan was sure he had a few broken ribs, but sh didn't dare touch him. They had no idea how sensitive th bomb was.

"The opening is small and if you don't know where it i you'd walk right by it. This whole mountain is filled wit shafts and tunnels."

"Lot of good a stupid dog is going to do us," Becca grun

led from her place against the wall. "If you two hadn't
crewed up we'd be out of here instead of waiting to get
lown up when that nut job hits the button."

Both Teagan and Zach ignored her, concentrating on the
dvance of the bluetick. She stopped to lick Teagan's face
efore moving over to give Zach a similar greeting. "Careful,
irl," he warned softly, holding as still as possible while hav-
ng his face messed with. "Tea, hold up your hands and see
she'll play tug with you. If we're lucky, she'll loosen the
ope enough for you to slip your hands out."

"Tug, Birdie, tug!" Teagan urged, holding her hands in
ront of the hound.

Birdie wheeled around and headed back to Teagan, a def-
nite bounce in her gait at the unexpected invitation to play
er favorite game. She grabbed the rope between Teagan's
ands and pulled, shaking her head to give it an extra hard
ank.

Teagan pulled back on the rope, and the hound growled,
igging her hind legs in and tugging back. The back-and-forth
truggle went on for several minutes. Teagan's wrists burned
rom the violent rub of the rope on her sensitive skin.

"How much more time?" she asked.

"Don't worry about the time, just concentrate on getting
oose," Zach said.

As he said the words, Teagan pulled one wrist free. The
econd hand followed a few seconds later. Birdie grabbed the
iscarded rope, shook it violently and growled. She shot Tea-
an a triumphant grin.

"Good girl," Teagan said, bending down to quickly untie
er ankles. Reaching over, she made quick work of Becca's
and restraints.

Leaving the girl to untie her own feet, she moved over
o Zach.

"Careful," he warned as she leaned over to check the wir-
ng of the bomb. "What do you think?" he said after several
econds.

"Bombs are not my area of expertise," Teagan said softly

"Oh, great, now you tell me. I might have requested another ATF agent if I'd known that sooner," he joked.

"I'm glad you're finding all of this amusing." She wasn't familiar with the wiring. She was fairly certain it wasn't complicated bomb, but she also didn't want to underestimate Daniel Mercy. She wouldn't put it past him to booby-trap the bomb.

"You need to leave it alone. There's nothing you can do Tea," Zach said.

"Be quiet. I can figure this out." She bit the inside of her cheek, trying to remember everything she'd ever learned in basic training. She wasn't willing to give up, even though she had no specialized training in defusing bombs. Her expertise lay in the area of firearms.

"You need to get out of here."

"I'm not leaving you." She knew that was what he was thinking, what he was going to say before the words even passed between his lips. But she wouldn't—no, *couldn't* listen. The thought was too painful. It was as if he was going to ask her to cut out her heart. They had to figure this out. Together.

"Tea," he said softly, his voice insistent. Commanding.

She ignored him, concentrating on the workings of the bomb.

"Tea," he said again more forcefully.

Finally, she lifted her eyes to meet his gaze. "I'm not leaving you this time," she said.

She closed her eyes for a minute, trying to keep the panic out of her voice. "I can get you out of this."

"We're not going to argue about this, Tea. You know what your job is. You need to get Becca out of here. If Chandler knows she's safe, he won't broadcast Mercy's sermon. And if Mercy's sermon isn't broadcast, he loses. And we win. There will be no mass explosion."

Tears welled up in her eyes, and she swiped them away

with the back of her hands. "Damn you. Don't you see that
can't leave you behind?"

But even as she said the words, she knew he was right.
There was no getting around it. She was going to have to
leave him.

No matter how long she stared at the inner workings of the
bomb, she wasn't going to know which wire to cut. And if
he cut the wrong wire and blew the three of them up, Mercy
got what he wanted. As much as she hated to admit it, she
knew what her duty was. She needed to get Becca out.

"Tea," he said softly again, and she looked up into the
endless beauty of his eyes, knowing he was right but hating
the fact that he was going to ask her to do it no matter how
much it hurt.

"You know this is the right thing to do," he said.

In spite of the waves of sorrow building within her, she
nodded.

He smiled and she had a flash that it might be the last time
she ever saw that smile. A smile she had walked away from
seven years ago. And now, at a time when she'd thought she
had earned the right to see it each and every morning, it was
being snatched away from her again.

She leaned forward and gently kissed him, a soft brush of
her lips against his. A kiss so sweet and sad that she felt as
though her heart—her very soul—was dropping down through
the center of her body and disappearing into a dark pit of total
nothingness. So this was what true love, true commitment felt
like. Why hadn't she realized this sooner?

"I love you," he whispered. Then his expression hardened.
"It's eight-fifteen."

He glanced up at the TV monitor. The party out on the
compound was in full swing. The sun was setting and a light
summer dusk was surrounding the outside edges of the party,
the people totally oblivious to what was planned. The television lights had snapped on a few minutes ago, bathing

everyone in a brilliant light. He could see Mercy making his way toward the podium.

He glanced back down at the timer on the bomb. "There's forty-five minutes left on the clock. I'm guessing that he'll start his sermon at the opening of the show. No one is going to get more than fifteen minutes of his rant before the fireworks begin." He allowed his head to drop back against the stone wall. "Don't even consider coming back for me once you're out. Save the people inside the compound."

She nodded but only because she wasn't going to take the time to argue with him.

"Tea, I'm not fooling around here. Stay out of the shaft."

She turned around and headed across the chamber toward Becca.

"Promise me," he called after her, the urgency in his voice echoing in the chamber.

She turned around, her gaze caressing his face for what she knew might be the very last time. "I can't promise you anything other than I love you, and we're going to get out of this somehow." She slapped her thigh. "Come on, Birdie, take us home."

The hound took a final look at her master, her deep brown eyes seeming to beg him to allow her to stay behind with him.

"Go, girl. Take Teagan home," he ordered.

The dog reluctantly rose and trotted after Teagan. As they entered the tunnel, she raced out ahead, taking the lead.

CLIMBING OUT of the narrow shaft, Teagan glanced around. For a moment she was disoriented. Confused. She could hear the music from the compound, something light and twangy, but she wasn't sure what direction it was coming from. The thick trees and high grass threw her.

She dug her flashlight out of her overalls and snapped it on. Its tiny beam cut through the thick vegetation. She moved in a full circle until the beam hit something metallic.

Zach's truck parked about fifty yards away next to his camp.

"Help me," Becca whined from behind.

Turning around, Teagan grabbed the girl's arm and hauled her up out of the tunnel. Becca stumbled out and fell to her knees. She used her sleeve to wipe a smudge of dirt off her cheek. She had cried most of the way through the tunnel, complaining and falling in the darkness. Teagan had done her best to help the girl while trying to ignore the endless wailing.

She kicked aside a few broken planks lying next to the tunnel opening. They explained how Birdie had gotten into the shaft in the first place. It was still a mystery to Teagan how the hound had known that Zach was at the other end of the shaft. But if there was one thing she had learned it was to never question the intellect or the powerful nose of a blue-tick hound.

"We need to get up to the camp. Zach left his cell phone in the truck."

Becca flopped down onto the grass and groaned. "I'm too tired. I can't walk another step."

"Okay, stay here. I'll get the cell phone."

She started up the slope toward the lean-to.

"Don't leave me here alone," Becca cried out.

Teagan ignored her. She'd done her job, gotten the girl out. Now she had only—she checked her watch—less than thirty minutes to figure out how to warn the people inside Mercy's compound and defuse the bomb connected to Zach.

She raced for the truck, pulling open the driver's side door and grabbing the cell phone off the seat. Her fingers flew over the buttons as she punched in the number of Paine's cell phone.

"Paine. Go ahead."

"It's Kennedy, sir."

"Where are you?" he snapped.

"I just got free, sir. Becca is here with me. Get the people

out of the compound. Daniel Mercy plans to blow the enti
compound up on national television. Get the people out!''

''Where're the explosives?''

''In the red vests worn by guards loyal to Daniel Merc
There's another bomb wired to Sheriff McCoy in a sm
room off the back of the Temple. I'm going to need he
defusing that one.''

''I'll get someone there as soon as possible, but I'm co
centrating on the civilians inside the compound first. Do wh
you can!''

Paine clicked off. Teagan stood next to Zach's truck, t
cell phone silent in her hand. She wasn't getting any hel
She had to defuse the bomb on her own.

She glanced at her watch. Less than twenty minutes left.

She climbed up onto the back of Zach's truck and yank
open the toolbox behind the cab. Every tool imaginable sat
neat little assigned spots. Frantic, she pawed through the
not even sure what she was looking for. A clock ticked aw
in her head.

She threw the top tray out of the box and beneath it s
spied what she was looking for. She grabbed a pair of wi
cutters and stuffed them in her pocket.

Leaping off the back end of the truck, she took off runni
for the shaft opening.

Becca, sprawled out on her back, stared up at her from h
spot on the grass. She hadn't moved an inch since she
climbed out of the tunnel. ''You're not going back in the
are you?'' she asked incredulously.

Teagan nodded. ''Someone will be by to get you soo
Don't wander off. There's a lean-to with food and water ju
over the rise. Help yourself.''

As Teagan started for the shaft, Birdie moved to stand ne
to her.

''Stay, Birdie,'' she commanded. ''Stay with Becca.''

The hound gave her a look that screamed betrayal. Som
how she knew that Teagan was headed back into the tunn

to get Zach. Teagan bent down and gently stroked the dog's head. "Be a good girl. I promise I'll bring him back to you."

She lowered herself back down into the shaft, her fingers grabbing and holding on to the rotting rungs of the ladder leading down into the tunnel. She hit the ground below running, the air whistling in and out of her chest. Every muscle in her body screamed in protest, but she ignored their cries, snapping on the flashlight. The yellow beam illuminated the dark tunnel.

She was barely aware of the rocks and debris in her way. She remembered falling several times, but she rolled with each fall and scrambled back to her feet before the pain of the fall ever reached her brain.

Gasping for breath, she reentered the main cave.

"I thought I told you not to come back," Zach greeted her.

"And you once told me that being in love with someone meant taking the good with the bad," she shot back, skidding to a stop in front of him. "I've decided that I'm sticking around for the bad part."

"I didn't want this, Tea."

"I know that." She knelt down in front of him and flipped open the flap on the bomb's inner workings. "But you don't have any choice in this. I'm not clearing out."

She pulled a pair of wire snippers out of her pocket. "Good thing you have a well-equipped toolbox on the back of that rust bucket of a truck of yours."

He laughed and winced from the pain in his ribs. "That bucket of rust has been hauling your butt around all week. You never complained until now."

"Well, I had to get your mind on to something else, didn't I?"

She gently slipped the needle-nose cutters under the yellow wire, careful not to touch either of the other wires.

"Why the yellow one?" Zach asked.

She grinned, her mouth stretching painfully under the tension, the fear. "What can I say, I'm a sucker for the color yellow."

"You mean you're not sure which one to cut?"

She locked eyes with him. "Come on, Zach McCoy, live dangerously with me."

Holding her breath, she glanced up Zach, using the intensity of her gaze to lock his eyes to hers. What better way to go than to drown in his pools of blue ice if she cut the wrong wire.

She tightened her fingers slightly, memorizing every inch of his face, the slight crinkle in the corner of his eyes, the smooth curl to his hair that sprayed across his forehead. She bit her bottom lip, trying to ignore the slam of her heart against her breastbone. She wondered if he heard her heart and knew her fear.

She held his gaze as she closed the blade of the cutter over the wire. The wire snapped in half.

Her body stiffened and she waited for the explosion.

Finally, Zach broke the silence. "Some rescuer you are. Your eyes were closed the entire time."

Teagan looked down at the timer on the bomb.

The clock read fifteen seconds.

The air trapped in her lungs released with a single whoosh and she collapsed next to him. "I did it. I actually did it."

Zach turned his head and grinned down at her. Her heart flooded with a warmth that reached deep inside her, and she realized for the hundredth time just how devastating and beautiful that smile was. The fact that she was here to see it made the smile all the more perfect.

"Bet you were thinking the whole time that I was going to snip the wrong wire, weren't you?" she quipped.

"Never had a moment of doubt that you'd get it right, Tea."

And in her heart, Teagan knew that he really hadn't doubted her. He had believed in her. Trusted her. Lived for her, and in the end, she had come through for him. A deliciou sense of wonderment washed over her and she leaned against his shoulder.

In the dampness of the cave, dirty, tired and overcome with emotion, they both glanced up at the monitor. Outside, the compound was a flurry of activity. Daniel Mercy was already in handcuffs and surrounded by a circle of ATF agents. For once in his life, he wasn't talking. His shoulders were slumped and even over the monitor, Teagan could see that some of his charisma had slipped away. His face was closed and distant, as if that special part of him had abandoned him in his moment of greatest need.

All around him streams of bewildered townspeople were being herded out of the front gate to safety. Cult members were just as confused and bewildered, but the ATF agents had separated them into groups off to the side. None of them would leave the compound until they had been searched for explosives and firearms.

A separate group of the "Chosen Elite" stood off to the side, surrounded by a heavy contingency of ATF agents. Their vests were gone, stripped off of them and defused. They were handcuffed, their manner subdued.

They watched as a tall ATF agent scooped Zach's two nieces up and carried them out the gate. "Looks like Krista and Emily are going to be just fine." As she spoke, her head slipped sideways to rest on his shoulder.

Every muscle, every nerve ending screamed in protest. She felt as though she could sleep for the next century.

"Uh, before you nod off, do you think you could get this contraption off me?" Zach asked, his amusement obvious.

Startled, Teagan sat up and rubbed her palms over her face. What was wrong with her? She had almost fallen asleep leaving him tied up and strapped to a bomb. "Sorry," she said, scrambling around to unstrap the bomb and untie him.

Within minutes, she had the bomb off him and the detonator removed. She slipped an arm around him and helped him to his feet. He sagged against her, his legs cramped from sitting so long in one place.

As they walked toward the steel door, someone started pounding on it.

"I guess that would be the calvary," he said dryly. "A tad late I'd say."

She reached up and took hold of his hand draped over her shoulder. She pressed her lips to the center of his palm and then smiled up at him. "Oh, I told them to hold off. Because this time, I wanted to be the one to rescue you."

He laughed and then winced slightly in pain. He bent his head and kissed her, a head-dizzying moment that seemed to last for an eternity, and in the distance, the pounding continued.

Teagan wasn't sure how he managed the kiss with his lips so swollen and his body so stiff, but she didn't question it. She simply returned the favor. And when they were done, she slipped an arm around him and helped him walk out into the light.

Epilogue

Following Mercy's arrest and the roundup of the other less peaceful members of his dismantled cult, Teagan spent the remainder of the day working to wrap up loose ends. But she struggled to keep herself focused. Thoughts of Zach and his condition constantly interfered, making her crazy.

Her calls to the hospital had been met with polite but impersonal updates—"Sheriff McCoy is resting comfortably." "If you need any additional information, you need to contact his immediate family." "All information is confidential."

By midmorning the next day, Teagan knew she couldn't wait any longer. She needed to see him. Needed to talk to him and touch him. She had to make sure he was okay.

Marching into Paine's temporary office, she handed him a typed, double-spaced, perfectly organized report and then promptly demanded a few hours of personal time. Paine didn't question her, but as she headed out the door, he called out, "Be sure to give Zach McCoy my fondest regards."

LESS THAN AN HOUR later, she stepped off the hospital elevator and shifted the gift basket she'd bought downstairs in the hospital gift shop to her other hand. She made her way down the polished hallway to the nurse's station.

An attractive brunette in blue scrubs glanced up from her spot behind a desk. "Yes, may I help you?"

"I'm looking for Zach McCoy's room." As she spoke, Teagan noticed Zach's sister, Helen, standing behind the nurse examining a chart. She resisted the urge to slink off rather than have to face the barracuda and nodded politely. She wondered if the good doctor would run her off the floor on a rail.

"Sheriff McCoy has had quite a few visitors today, miss," the nurse said. "And his doctor instructed me to make sure he gets some rest. Are you family?"

"No, I'm—"

"She's family, Trish," Helen said, snapping the chart closed and carefully meeting Teagan's eyes. Her smile was tight, revealing her tension, but it was also genuine.

"Oh, then you can go right in," Trish said cheerfully. "He's in room 322, directly across the hall."

"Thank you," Teagan said. Suddenly unsure, she nodded her appreciation to Helen, and then she turned to go into Zach's room.

"Teagan?"

She paused and turned around. Helen stepped out of the nurse's station.

"Sometimes I make mistakes about people," Helen said softly. "I just wanted to thank you for saving my brother's life."

Teagan smiled, warming to the sincere apology in Helen's voice. "There's no need to apologize. I was the one that made the mistake. But that was years ago, and I plan on making up for it in the years to come."

Helen's grin widened, lightening the tiny shadow of concern still lingering in her eyes. Her fierce protectiveness toward Zach wasn't lost on Teagan. She might not have ever had that before in her own family, but she respected it.

"You're going to have your hands full with him," Helen cautioned.

Teagan laughed. "Oh, I'm well aware of that, Dr. Wade. He tends to be a bit bossy at times, isn't he?"

Helen snorted. "Bossy? The man can be downright tyrannical and disrespectful. But we love him." She paused for a moment. "Please, call me Helen. I have a feeling we're going to see a lot of each other."

"I believe we will."

Helen's grin turned mischievous, looking suspiciously similar to one Teagan had seen more than once on her brother. "The trick to taming Zach is to feed him French toast with gobs of powdered sugar and real Vermont maple syrup. Do that and he's yours forever."

Teagan hefted the basket in her arms and pointed to the jug of pure Vermont maple syrup sitting in the center of a bouquet of daisies. "I came prepared."

Helen laughed. "Oh, I can see that he's met his match in you."

Teagan started for the door and then paused. "The girls… They're all right, aren't they?"

"They're fine. I brought them in earlier to torment their uncle." She shifted her weight and rubbed her upper arms as if unsure how to put what she wanted to say. "I don't know how to thank you enough. Zach tells me that you were the one that got the call out that led to their rescue—everyone's rescue. I—" She shook her head. "Not just me, but my whole family owes you a great debt."

Teagan shook her head. "You don't owe me anything, Helen. Having Zach is all the reward I'll ever need."

Helen nodded, and in her expression, Teagan saw total acceptance.

"Hey, what's going on out there?" Zach called from inside the room. "You're not holding up my guests, are you, Helen?"

Helen laughed and waved Teagan into the room.

Zach lay on the bed near the window, light from between the blinds drifting down to dance across the burnished gold of his hair. The bruises on his face stood out in startling contrast to the white of the bedsheets, but they did nothing to quiet the song of contentment that sang in her heart.

He smiled a slightly lopsided grin of welcome. The swelling around his eye and cheek hadn't gone down much since yesterday, but she'd received word through the grapevine that nothing was broken. His stay in the hospital was strictly a precaution taken by his physician due to his concussion.

"Boy, am I glad to see you," he said. "You have any pull with the doctors? If I don't get out of here soon, I'm going to go slowly insane."

"Sorry, bud, but I'm in total agreement with the docs."

His face turned serious. "Your people did a good job. My deputy told me that they were able to round everyone up— Mercy and his henchmen all in jail, and the firearms and explosives are safely tucked away again."

She nodded.

"Everyone else okay?"

She moved over to sit on the bed next to him. "Everyone made it out. Becca's home safe and sound with her daddy. Most of the cult members are being treated, debriefed and then released. Kenny, his sister and his mom will be on their way back to California any day now. I guess they have some family members waiting for them out there, ready to give them a new start."

He reached out and cupped her chin. "Then why all the anguish in those eyes of yours?"

She swallowed hard. "I had to call Miguel's wife last night." A tear slipped from between her lashes and rolled down her cheek. She used the back of her hand to impatiently brush it aside. "She was pretty broken up. In shock. I have to go and see her, try to explain what happened."

He reached out and wrapped his hand around hers. He squeezed and held on, and she basked in the surge of strength and reassurance he seemed to pass on to her with that simple act of tenderness.

"You can't explain away the hurt, Tea. All you can do is

savor the memories, good and bad, and go on with life. Miguel's wife won't need a lot of details. Just give her the good stuff, the memories of a fallen hero. Those are what she'll cherish.''

She nodded. ''You're right.'' She reached up and lightly skimmed the tips of her fingers along the swollen crest of his cheek. ''Hurt much?''

''Not anymore.'' He grinned and wrapped his arms around her, pulling her close for a kiss.

She laughed and gently brushed her lips over his. ''Careful, I don't think I've ever kissed anyone with a fat lip before.''

''Get used to it, woman. I plan on doing a lot of this over the next couple of days.''

''Gee, only a couple of days? I was hoping for a longer commitment than that.''

He pulled back, his eyes searching hers. ''Are you serious?''

She kissed him again, longer this time and then lifted her head. ''What do you think?''

He dropped his head back against the pillow as if stunned and grinned. ''I think I'm in heaven.'' He lifted his head again. ''If I'm not mistaken, I just got proposed to.''

She laughed and climbed into bed next to him, fitting her length to his and throwing one arm across his broad chest. Beneath the thin sheet, she could feel his warmth and the beat of his heart. ''I got tired of waiting for you to ask.''

''Hey, I was a little busy there for a while. But I would have gotten around to it. I wasn't about to let you get away this time.''

She rested her head on his shoulder. ''I'm glad. Think they'll arrest us for indecent behavior in the hospital?'' she asked.

His arm slid under her and pulled her closer still. ''Nah, I happen to be on very good terms with the local sheriff.'' He reached over and stroked her hair, his fingers threading themselves through the thick strands and sliding around to the back of her neck. Goose bumps pebbled her body.

She lifted her head to look at him. "Oh, really? Do you think he could pull some strings and get me a job around here? I've taken a real liking to the town of Bradley."

He laughed, something deep and wonderful and magnificently reassuring, and Teagan knew she'd found where she belonged.

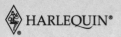

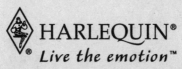

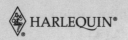

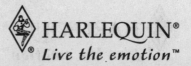

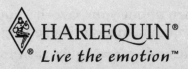

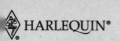

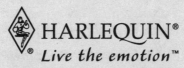

National Bestselling Author

brenda novak

COLD
FEET

Despite the cloud of suspicion that followed her father to his grave, Madison Lieberman maintained his innocence...*until* crime writer Caleb Trovato forces her to confront the past once again

"Readers will quickly be drawn into this well-written, multi-faceted story that is an engrossing, compelling read."
—*Library Journal*

Available February 2004.

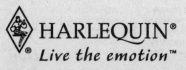

HARLEQUIN®
Live the emotion™

Visit us at www.eHarlequin.com

PHC

If you enjoyed what you just read,
then we've got an offer you can't resist!

Take 2 bestselling love stories FREE!

Plus get a FREE surprise gift!

Clip this page and mail it to Harlequin Reader Service

IN U.S.A.
3010 Walden Ave.
P.O. Box 1867
Buffalo, N.Y. 14240-1867

IN CANADA
P.O. Box 609
Fort Erie, Ontario
L2A 5X3

YES! Please send me 2 free Harlequin Intrigue® novels and my free surprise gift. After receiving them, if I don't wish to receive anymore, I can return the shipping statement marked cancel. If I don't cancel, I will receive 6 brand-new novels each month, before they're available in stores! In the U.S.A., bill me at the bargain price of $3.99 plus 25¢ shipping and handling per book and applicable sales tax, if any*. In Canada, bill me at the bargain price of $4.74 plus 25¢ shipping and handling per book and applicable taxes**. That's the complete price and a savings of at least 10% off the cover prices—what a great deal! I understand that accepting the 2 free books and gift places me under no obligation ever to buy any books. I can always return a shipment and cancel at any time. Even if I never buy another book from Harlequin, the 2 free books and gift are mine to keep forever.

182 HDN DU9K
382 HDN DU9L

Name	(PLEASE PRINT)
Address	Apt.#
City	State/Prov. Zip/Postal Code

* Terms and prices subject to change without notice. Sales tax applicable in N.Y.
** Canadian residents will be charged applicable provincial taxes and GST.
    All orders subject to approval. Offer limited to one per household and not valid to
    current Harlequin Intrigue® subscribers.
    ® are registered trademarks of Harlequin Enterprises Limited.

INT03

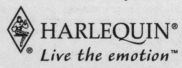